Treason Trail

Cape Fear Legacy, Volume 3

Kit Hawthorne

Published by Kit Hawthorne, 2024.

This is a work of fiction. Similarities to real people, places, or events are entirely coincidental.

TREASON TRAIL

First edition. June 18, 2024.

Copyright © 2024 Kit Hawthorne.

ISBN: 979-8224848959

Written by Kit Hawthorne.

*To those who have known the sting of treachery, and learned to love
and trust again.*

Chapter One

October 1782.

Nessa Shaw stood on the bare bluff, the twilight afterglow warming her shoulders like a memory of sunshine. Across the Ashley River, a bank of storm clouds was slowly massing in the eastern sky, threatening rain.

But she turned her back to the clouds and headed down the tree-lined trail. After the day she'd had, she desperately needed a stolen hour to herself in the peaceful, sweet-scented woods. She had to escape the noise and stench of the camp, and remind herself who she was and what she was doing here.

If all went well, she might even find a handful of late greens or muscadine grapes to give color and nourishment to a dreary supper of army rations, or some herbs to replenish the hospital's depleted stores. She carried a basket at the crook of her arm and a knife in her pocket just in case.

Leafy branches closed over her head, casting an inky shade on the trail. Live oaks, mostly, thick with the dark-green leaves that they kept year-round, while hickories and sassafras added splashes of yellow and orange. She'd be back to harvest some sassafras in a couple of months, after cold weather made the sap sink to the roots. Sassafras tea was good for strengthening and it reduced inflammation. And once winter hit, there'd be coughs and sore throats aplenty, in addition to all the cases of malaria already filling the General Hospital.

She quickened her pace, trying to drive out the image of men's bodies, racked with fits of uncontrollable shaking one moment, and soaked with sweat the next, jerked back and forth between fever and ague. The sickness wore them out, wasting their flesh away with terrifying rapidity. Nessa did what she could for them, even if it was no more than keeping them company in their final moments.

You'll be all better soon. I'm going to look after you. That was what she always said to them. She did look after them, to the very best of her ability, but most of the time they didn't get better. But what else could she do? Tell them that in all likelihood they would continue to weaken and die a slow and painful death? Nay. Where there was life, there was hope. And Nessa would always, always choose to offer hope.

She must hold on for just a little longer. Then the war would end, and life could finally go back to how it used to be.

But they'd been saying that ever since the first shots were fired far away in Lexington and Concord. The most confident among the Patriots had said that the fighting would soon be over, that the Crown would relent and stop trampling the rights guaranteed to the American colonists under the British Constitution. And yet here they were, seven years later, still waiting, still holding on, still crying out to God for justice. The American victory at Yorktown was supposed to be the end, but it was only the beginning of the end, and maybe not even that. Who could tell what was happening far away across the Atlantic at the peace accords in Paris? The American and British delegates might have reached a settlement at last, or they might be no closer to an agreement than when they'd first gathered there. And in the meantime, Nessa's countrymen were dying in skirmishes with the British over food and horses, or wasting away from disease in the crowded camps. It was all so pointless. Nessa considered herself a reasonably patient person, but her endurance was strained to the breaking point.

The shadows deepened as she made her way along the familiar trail, trying to pound out her troubles beneath her hurrying feet. While she walked, she continually scanned the foliage for anything edible or medicinal.

And finally, she found something. With a glad cry, she knelt and caressed some dark-green leaves, glossy and heart-shaped, and mottled with silver. Her sister Catalyn could have told the plant's Latin name, but Nessa knew it only as arrowleaf ginger—good for digestive trouble, colds, and fever, and as a wash or poultice for wounds.

It was too early for harvest. She'd have to wait until the foliage had died back before gently taking some of the rhizomes. But the leggy valerian growing nearby, with its long, pointed, compound leaves, was ready now. Valerian root made a potent sedative—foul in taste, but effective.

Nessa set her basket down beside her. As she reached into her pocket for her knife, her elbow bumped the basket, sending it rolling down a shallow slope to the center of the trail. She crawled over to reach for it—

And froze.

Lying on the packed ground, just visible around a bend in the trail, was a human hand.

A long hand, a shapely hand, almost certainly male, with strong, slender fingers. The square nails were broken and rimmed with crescents of dirt.

Nessa pressed her own hands to her mouth. Her heart raced sickeningly as waves of revulsion and dread washed over her.

Presumably the hand was attached to an arm, and to the rest of a man, though from this angle it was impossible to be sure. Nessa steeled herself, then leaned around the bend to see more.

It was indeed an entire man, lying face down in the track, arms stretched over his head.

Well, she'd seen death before, more times than she could count. No reason to start flinching from it now. Still on her hands and knees, she crept over to the man's side.

He was dressed in a linen shirt and knee-length drawers, and nothing more. That was hardly unusual. Many of the soldiers of the Continental Army at Ashley Hill were meagerly clothed. But those men weren't covered in dirt and leaf litter as this man was. They got grimy enough from work details or going too long without a wash, but not like this.

She could see no wound to his back or limbs, but his hair was caked with dried blood. She laid a tentative hand to his neck and was surprised to find the flesh warm and pliant, with a faint pulse.

He was alive.

A curtain of matted hair hid his face. She lifted it to reveal a high cheekbone, a short, straight nose, and a beard of several days' growth. His skin was tanned a deep golden brown.

Should she move him? Or go for help? She glanced around her, as if some responsible person would suddenly materialize and tell her what to do, and immediately despised herself for it. Wasn't she always fuming about the lack of skill among some of the surgeons, and telling herself that she knew at least as much as they did? Here was her chance to prove it.

With difficulty, she flipped the man onto his back. He let out a groan, and his eyes opened—blue-grey eyes, startlingly pale in the tanned face. A sharp, lucid gaze met hers, and his lips parted as though he would speak.

Then his eyes rolled back in his head, and the breath went out of him with a sigh.

The front of his shirt was as dirty as the back, but not bloodstained. As far as she could tell, his only injury was to his head. He didn't look quite like dying yet, but she had to get him out of here.

But where to? The General Hospital was on the other side of camp, and crowded with malarial men. For now, she would concentrate on taking him to the camp itself.

And how was she to do that? He was a tall man, broad through the shoulders and strongly built. Even with her to support him, she doubted he could walk the whole way—assuming she could wake him and get him on his feet.

She laid a hand against his cheek. "Can you hear me?" she asked. "We must get you moved. Can you stand?"

He didn't reply, but he must have heard and understood, because his legs slowly bent at the knees, and his head and shoulders lifted from the ground in an apparent effort to sit up. Then he collapsed again with a groan.

A growl of thunder sounded to the east, and a shiver of wind passed through the trees.

"Listen to me," Nessa said in a loud, clear voice. "There's a storm coming. We have to get you under cover before the rain starts. Just a few feet, and then you can rest while I go for help. Do you understand?"

She had been nursing sick and injured men for months now, many of them sunk into unconsciousness for days at a time, and she had learned that they often did understand more than seemed possible, and remembered what they'd heard after they recovered. This man drew a deep breath, then raised himself to his elbows. Nessa slid her arm beneath his, and together they managed to move him off the trail and under the shelter of a massive live oak tree. The trunk had a groove in it that cradled the man's back, keeping him in a sitting position, with his long legs stretched out before him. He was panting with effort and pain.

"Very good," said Nessa, in the soothing tone she always used with the sick. "Now you wait here, and I'll be back before you know it."

She cupped his cheek in her hand, willing him to hold on, to keep breathing, to mend.

Then his hand gripped hers with surprising strength, and his eyes opened again.

"Help me," he said, his voice rough.

"I will," she replied. "But I can't move you on my own. I've got to get someone to—"

He shook his head impatiently, then winced against the pain. "Nay, not that. There's something—something I must do." His eyes clouded, and she could see him struggling to stay conscious. "Help me," he repeated.

"I will," she said again. "Whatever you need."

Her assurance must have satisfied him. His eyes shut, and his hand dropped away from hers.

It felt wrong, horribly wrong, to leave him hurt and alone with darkness falling and a storm on the way. But Nessa was a good strong runner. She fairly flew up the path as the thunder rolled overhead, and reached her brother's tent in the sutler's row ahead of the first drops of rain. Her hair was slipping out of its knot, and she was panting like a racehorse, but she'd made excellent time.

Rory was sitting at the small folding table that served him as a desk, lighting a candle. He took in the sight of his sister and asked, "What's wrong?"

"I found a hurt man on a trail in the woods," she gasped out. "I need you to help me move him."

Rory was already on his feet. He was tall for fifteen, with a frame that promised great size and strength at maturity, but still lightly muscled. "One of the soldiers from the camp?"

"Maybe. I didn't recognize him, but 'tisn't as if I know every one of them personally."

A tin lantern stood near the tent flap. Nessa picked it up and held it while Rory used his desk candle to light the candle inside the lantern. Then they were off.

The lantern light cast grotesque shadows in the darkening woods. By the time they reached the bend in the trail where Nessa had first found the stranger, fat drops of rain were pelting their shoulders.

For a moment Nessa couldn't see the injured man. Then lightning flashed—and there he was, propped against the hollow trunk of the old oak, exactly where she'd left him.

His arms hung slack at his sides, and his chin rested on his chest. Nessa knelt beside him, filled with dread. What if he'd died all alone in the dark, not knowing if she would ever return? She held the lantern to his face. His eyelids fluttered as if he was dreaming.

Rory was already crouching at the man's other side. "What happened to him?" he asked.

"A blow to the head. Do you think the two of us can get him to your tent? The hospital's too far away."

Rory took the lantern from her, looped its handle over his arm, and nodded. "We can do it."

The man opened his eyes and looked blearily at Nessa. One corner of his mouth edged up in a smile. "You came back," he said.

"Aye," she said, encouraged by how lucid he sounded. "And I've brought help. We're going to take you to shelter."

Nessa grabbed his arm and draped it over her shoulders. Rory did the same on his side. The two of them exchanged a quick nod and hoisted the man to his feet. Supporting him between them, they made their way back to the camp along the trail. He wasn't altogether dead weight, and getting him to Rory's tent wasn't as hard as Nessa had feared it would be, but still it was hard enough. Her limbs were shaking by the time they eased him through the flaps at the front end of the tent.

The rain came down in earnest then, slamming into the tightly woven linen canvas overhead, as if it had been waiting for them to reach shelter first.

A yellowish halo surrounded the candle in its brass candlestick, casting a dim light that was reflected by the tent's pale walls. The scent of smoke and burning tallow filled the small space. Rory carefully set the lantern on the floor.

As usual, Rory's bed—a straw-tick mattress lying on the ground against one of the slanted walls—was covered with a litter of books and scraps of paper. With one arm, Nessa swept them away and pulled back the blanket. Together, she and Rory laid the man down, the straw fill crackling beneath his weight.

Rory picked up the candle from the desk and brought it over, angling the reflector to shed light on the man's face. "I don't recognize him, either. I wonder how he came to be alone in the woods with a broken head. A skirmish with the enemy, perhaps? But he has no weapon on him. Or a brawl with another Patriot soldier?"

"It couldn't have been much of a brawl," said Nessa. "There's no mark on his face, and his knuckles aren't scraped. Perhaps he was waylaid by some of those bandits from Georgia, robbed and stripped and left for dead. 'Twould explain the lack of clothing."

"If any explanation is needed," Rory said drily. "Plenty of soldiers in the camp aren't as well-clad as this fellow. But that track isn't exactly a highway for travelers. And how would the bandits get past the sentries on the other side of the forest?"

Nessa thought about that. "He might have been attacked outside the woods, and then managed to get away. But it would be a long way to crawl, and he'd have to get past the sentries himself."

"He looks as if he may well have crawled on his belly a mile or so, and rolled around in the leaf litter for good measure," Rory said critically. "He's filthy."

Nessa gazed down at the man's face. It was a good face, with its broad brow and square chin. The light beard edging his jaw was a pale gold, lighter than the tangled hair. His mouth had flattened into a severe line, and the cords of his neck were drawn tight with exertion and pain. He was breathing hard.

"Who are you?" she asked softly. "Where did you come from? What happened to you?"

The man didn't answer. Gradually the tension eased from his face, and his breath slowed until she knew he was sleeping.

She wished she could open his mind like a book and read his story.

Chapter Two

He was lying on his back in cool water, the sun hot on his chest and face, arms stretched out at his sides, eyes shut, fingers stirring faintly in the wavelets. Pondweed tickled his feet. A faint breeze whispered through the trees, and birds sang fierce territorial songs.

Then something took firm hold of his head and pushed him down, plunging him deep beneath the surface. He exhaled in a shocked gush of bubbles, and water filled his mouth and nose. His eyes were open now. He saw his own hair writhing above his face, and the sun shining through the clear water in a blurry ball of pale light. His fists flailed through the water, trying to make contact with the body of his attacker, but the arm holding him underwater was long, and his own arms spun uselessly, like windmill blades. So he grabbed the wrist in both hands and tried to wrest it away—vainly, because he had nothing solid to brace himself against. His heart pounded as if it would burst, and his lungs screamed for air.

Suddenly the scene changed. He was in a dim, close room with a ceiling that sloped sharply down on both sides from a center ridgeline. His mind immediately identified it as an army tent of the sort commonly assigned to cavalry soldiers, low-ranking officers, and clerks. The pond, the unknown attacker—nothing but a dream. He was safe now. He drew in deep, grateful breaths of air, his heart still racing as if he had truly surfaced from underwater only moments before.

The scene changed again, but subtly this time. Everything looked the same, every detail of the room remained as substantial and real as ever, but a heavy weight settled on his chest, as if some enormous thing were crouching on top of him—a thing with malice and will, slowly pressing his life out. He couldn't see it, but he could feel its hatred. It wanted him dead.

He knew perfectly well that he was dreaming, but knowing it made no difference. The presence held all the power here in his dream-world. It would kill him before he could wake up.

If he could only cry out, or move so much as a little finger, he would be free. The invisible presence would vanish away like smoke. But he couldn't do either. He thrashed his body wildly, and yelled with all the breath in his lungs, but he knew in his heart that he was lying perfectly motionless, with only a thin thread of sound escaping his lips.

Some thick covering dropped down over him, like a blanket or a shroud. Woolen fibers scratched his skin. He felt his own breath hot against his face. Soft clods thumped onto his body. He could smell their damp earthy scent and hear the scrape of a shovel.

He had always had a deep horror of being unable to breathe. Fear clawed inside his chest like a frantic animal, but he couldn't move a muscle to free himself. He was going to die here in the pitiless ground, cut off from light and air forever.

And suddenly it was all over. A girl was leaning over him, looking down at him, with a face so lovely it didn't seem possible.

"There, now," she said in a calm, low, soothing voice. "Don't be frightened. You're safe, and I'm with you."

He was in the tent again, or else he'd been in the tent all along—but there was no evil phantom trying to press the life out of him, only this sweet-faced girl with her thick sheaf of red-brown hair tied back loosely at the nape of her neck. He stared up at her. If he was still dreaming, then the dream had taken a very different turn indeed.

"Are you real?" he asked. His own voice sounded cracked and dry.

She smiled. "I think I am."

As she laid a cool hand against his forehead, a curving tendril of russet hair slid free and brushed his cheek, and he knew that he was well and truly awake now. He was alive, and the girl *was* real—the realest thing he'd ever seen.

"*Cogito, ergo sum,*" he said.

It was a clumsy attempt at a joke, but the girl's smile deepened. "*Res cogitans, ergo sum,*" she said, completing the phrase.

He smiled back and felt his lips crack. They were parched, and his throat was painfully dry. As if she'd read his thoughts, the girl picked up a cup and held it to his mouth, sliding an arm behind his shoulders to ease him upright. A sharp pain shot through his head. What had happened to him? Where was he? Questions swirled through his mind, along with a vague uneasiness about some forgotten task left undone.

He drank greedily, and would have drunk more, but the girl took the cup away after only a few sips.

"That's enough for the time being," she said. "Now rest."

He shut his eyes and fell into the soft, exquisite comfort of dreamless sleep.

Chapter Three

Nessa sat on a wooden stool beside Rory's straw tick with her pile of mending at her feet, patching shirts by candlelight and keeping an eye on the sleeping stranger. He was stripped to the waist, with a linen sheet covering him—and clean, or as clean as she had been able to make him. After being laid on the bed, he'd sunk back into unconsciousness, and she'd gone to work removing his filthy shirt—no easy task, for the stranger was a big man. She'd even considered cutting it away, but shirts were too precious to waste. Eventually she and Rory between them had contrived to get it off him. In the process, much of the dirt formerly on the shirt had been transferred to Rory's bed.

Once the shirt had been removed, Rory left to fetch water, and Nessa began taking a filled basin and a soft cloth to her patient's face and body.

What was underneath the shirt was surprising on more than one count. The man had plenty of good healthy flesh on his well-muscled chest and arms, markedly different from the lean, stringy look of most of the men in camp. And that flesh had been relatively clean compared to his clothing and his exposed limbs. This was a man who until very recently had been washing himself regularly.

All the skin that had been bare when she'd found him—face, hands, forearms, feet, and lower legs—had been covered with scratches and scrapes. She'd washed them as best she could. Then she'd taken the shirt outside the tent and shaken out the worst of the dirt. The shirt showed a few rends that had been neatly mended. Though not new, it was in better condition, and of better quality, than most of the shirts currently in her pile.

Next, she'd made a preliminary examination of the injured head. She couldn't tell much through the blood-matted hair, but she'd found an egg-sized swelling on the crown of his head, slightly to the left.

She'd gone to work rinsing the dried blood out of his hair, removing twigs and debris and freeing it from the worse of its tangles. This had been a long process, requiring many changes of water, and Rory had emptied the basin and refilled the pitcher repeatedly for her, going out willingly into the rain. The man had plenty of thick golden-brown hair, not long enough to be tied back, but longer than the current fashion for men, around chin length.

With his hair reasonably clean, Nessa had felt the wound again. She'd found little broken skin, considering the amount of blood, but then head wounds always did bleed a lot. Most of the damage had plainly been done under the surface.

And this, she hoped, would heal. Probing his skull, she'd detected no spots where the bone gave way beneath her fingers—a good sign.

After treating the broken skin with an herbal wound wash, she'd slid a clean cloth between his head and the folded blanket serving as his pillow and picked up the first shirt on her mending pile.

The tent flap opened, and Rory came inside with yet another filled pitcher of water. Seeing Nessa busy with her sewing, he said, "All finished with the washing, then?"

"For now," Nessa replied.

Rory set the pitcher on the wooden stand. His tent was modestly furnished, but comfortable enough, with a bed and a desk, two stools, and room for a small washstand. It was bigger than Nessa's simple triangle tent, and had actual walls, not just the two sides of the roof sloping down directly to the floor. They were low walls, only a couple of feet high, but they provided the extra space and headroom Rory needed as a clerk who worked in his tent.

"How's Himself?" Rory asked as he ran a linen towel over his own rain-soaked limbs.

"Himself?" Nessa repeated.

Rory grinned. "I heard an officer from Ireland refer to General Greene that way. 'Tis a term for an important personage, I think. We don't know this fellow's name, so it seems appropriate enough."

Very appropriate indeed, Nessa thought, and not only because of the unknown name. Whatever his origin, the mysterious stranger was already an important personage in her eyes.

"Himself has been resting quietly for the most part," she said. "But he did have a bad dream while you were gone."

She told her brother how the man had lain frozen, eyes wide open, breathing hard and making a thin strangled cry, until she'd woken him.

"He looked as if he were being ridden by a hag," she said. "Some wicked spirit crouching on his chest, paralyzing him."

Rory made a scoffing sound as he drew up another stool beside her. "You cannot mean that, sister. We live in a great era of reason and philosophy, free from the superstitions of the past. The man had some imbalance in his brain that temporarily incapacitated him and caused him to hallucinate. That is all."

Nessa rolled her eyes. She knew how clever her little brother was, and she was proud of him for earning a clerk's post in the Continental Army at his age. But he could be maddeningly arrogant at times.

"Nay, 'tis not all," Nessa said. "There are more things in this world than can be explained by rationalism, Rory."

"Come, Nessa. You cannot honestly believe there was an invisible witch or demon in this tent, sitting on that man's chest."

"Probably not," Nessa conceded. "But he was afraid of something—desperately afraid. And whatever it was, amounted to more than an imbalance of humors in his body or a disordering of his brain."

Rory rested his lanky forearms on his knees. "Did he say what it was, after you woke him?"

"Nay. But he did quote Descartes."

Cogito, ergo sum—I think, therefore I am. A surprising thing for a man with a broken head, just awakened from a terrifying dream, to say. But addled as he clearly had been, that was what he had said. And he'd been surprised in turn to hear Nessa reply with *Res cogitans, ergo sum*—I am a thinking thing, therefore I am. She'd seen the astonishment on his face, along with unmistakable pleasure, before he'd dropped back into the deep well of unconsciousness.

"Did he indeed?" Rory asked, sounding pleased. "Well! 'Twould appear that Himself is a philosopher."

"Aye, and a man of some education," said Nessa. "He spoke like a gentleman. I wonder who he is, and what happened to him."

"We ought to be able to deduce some of that for ourselves," Rory said. "Let's marshal our facts. What do we know about him? You found him alone, unarmed, and half-naked. Which could mean either that he's an ill-clad Continental soldier, or that he was robbed. A footpad could have lain in wait for him and knocked him on the head."

"Or," said Nessa, "his assailant might have attacked him out of malice, or for some other purpose, and taken his things to make it look like a robbery."

Rory looked startled. "Do you really think so?"

"'Tis possible," Nessa said. She didn't like to think of one Patriot striking down another in cold blood, but tempers in the camp were growing more frayed by the day.

"His wound is high on the crown of his head, and he's a tall man," she went on. "So either his assailant attacked him from above—say, from a tree—"

"Or else Himself was sitting at his ease, suspecting nothing, and the assailant struck him from behind," Rory finished. "A footpad might manage that, but so might a trusted companion."

"'Twould take a big, powerful man to strip off Himself's outer clothing," said Nessa. "You and I could barely contrive to get his shirt off. But as you said, he might have been wearing nothing more than shirt and drawers to begin with. Many of the soldiers in camp scarcely have enough clothing for decency." She frowned. "But even the barefoot soldiers generally find some rags to bind about their feet. Himself's feet are none too clean, but the soles aren't hardened enough for him to have been going about unshod for long. And his face and hands are tanned, but not his legs, so he's been wearing trousers or breeches until recently."

There was a time when Nessa would have blushed to speak so frankly of a man's bare limbs, but after several months as a camp follower, she had seen too much of the male form to be troubled with excessive modesty.

"There's another possibility that we haven't mentioned yet," said Rory.

"I know," said Nessa. "He might not be one of ours."

"Exactly."

They both studied the man in silence a moment. Then Nessa said, "We'll deal with that later. Whether he's Patriot or Tory, British or hired Hessian, I must look after him. He's hurt and helpless, and he's my responsibility."

"*Our* responsibility," Rory corrected her. "Well, I imagine we'll know soon enough. And if he does turn out to be an enemy, perhaps he'll be someone of value in a prisoner exchange."

Nessa didn't answer. She didn't want Himself to be an enemy, or to be sent away. She went on staring, willing Himself to open his eyes and tell them precisely who he was and how he'd come to be knocked on the head and left for dead. But Himself slept on.

"Should we take him to the hospital?" Rory asked.

"Not tonight, in all this rain. Tomorrow, perhaps. There isn't anything the surgeons could do for him that I haven't already done."

"Aye, and I daresay you've done a great deal better than many of them would. What about sleep for the two of us? How shall we manage that?"

Nessa felt a pang of conscience. "Oh, I've given him your bed, haven't I?"

Rory waved this off. "What else could you have done? Anyway, 'tis no trouble. I'll be awake a while yet, copying dispatches."

"And I have my mending to do. I'm too stirred up for sleep, anyhow, and I don't want to leave Himself alone. But the night's far from over, and you're a growing boy, Rory. You need your rest."

She regretted the tactless words as soon as they were spoken. Rory didn't like being coddled or reminded of his tender years. He was eager, almost desperate, to prove himself a man among men.

"I often stay up until the end of Second Watch, finishing paperwork," he said stoutly. "I get by very well on a few hours of sleep a night."

"Why don't we take it in turns?" asked Nessa. "We'll both work for now, and the first one to start nodding off can go to my tent to catch an hour or two of sleep. 'Tis so close by that we won't have far to go to wake each other and make the switch."

"Nay, we'll bring your mattress in here," said Rory. "I'm not leaving you alone with a strange man."

Nessa refused to let herself be nettled by his masterful tone. She knew the reason for it. He had failed once—at least, he saw it as a failure—to protect his female kin from enemy raiders who'd come to their family's farm to plunder and destroy. She was tempted to remind him that the raiders had left without making good on the worst of their threats, and that there was nothing more that he, an unarmed boy of fourteen, could have done against half a dozen British and Tory soldiers. But she knew from experience that it would do no good.

The rain had let up enough for them to move her straw tick from her tent without getting it too wet. They laid it alongside the wall opposite Rory's bed, with the desk wedged firmly in the middle. Rory set the candle on the corner of his desk, where the two of them could share its light, and they both went to work.

The shirts in Nessa's mending pile had more darning and patchwork in them than original fabric, but those who owned them were grateful for even that much covering. Some of the men were going about in little more than loincloths, which had actually not been too bad in the summer months in South Carolina. But with winter on its way, it would take more than threadbare linen to clothe the soldiers of the Continental Army.

Candlelight flashed in silver gleams on Nessa's needle as she pushed it in and out of the pile of fabric on her lap. The stranger slept peacefully, his breathing slow and regular. Nessa kept stealing glances at him, and not merely to monitor his condition. He was well worth looking at, with his strong chin, chiseled cheekbones, and finely arched eyebrows. The candlelight gave a bronze sheen to his skin and picked out glimmers of pale gold in his beard. Was he a gentleman? Not necessarily. Men didn't have to own land to read books and improve their minds, and plenty of men who did own land were ignorant fools. But Himself's hands, though dirty, were not the hands of a laborer. Was he a shopkeeper? Lawyer? Apothecary? Did he run a printing press? He might be a surveyor, or a silversmith, or own a tavern. There was no way to tell.

Rory was the first to start nodding off, as Nessa had known he would be. Out of the corner of her eye she saw his head slowly dip down before jerking upright. Once, twice, three times.

"Go to bed, Rory," she said after the fourth time. "You can barely keep your eyes open."

"I'm awake," he said shortly. "And I must finish these dispatches."

"You'll have to do them over if you make a mistake or spill your ink. Lie down on the straw tick. If Himself wakes up and starts talking, you'll hear him soon enough."

In the end, Rory did lie down, but only after arming Nessa with an old sword he'd acquired during his militia service last year, and tucking a pistol under the rolled-up coat he was using as a pillow, where he could quickly reach it. Once he lay down, he was asleep within moments, as Nessa could tell from his breathing.

It was only a few minutes later that Himself opened his eyes. He stared up at the tent's ceiling for several seconds. Nessa watched him, her needle pushed halfway through a seam, waiting to see if he would stay awake or drop off to sleep again without speaking.

His gaze met hers. He started to sit up but immediately fell back to the mattress.

"Lie still," she told him. "You've had a bad knock to the head."

He put a hand to his head and gingerly felt his wound.

"What happened to me?" he asked, his voice sounding clearer and stronger than when he'd last spoken.

"I was hoping you could tell me that," Nessa replied. "You don't remember how you were hurt?"

He shut his eyes. Slowly he shook his head. "I—nay, I don't remember anything about it."

"That's all right," she said soothingly. "'Tis often that way with head injuries. You might never recall exactly how you came by your wound—but if we work together, perhaps we can get a rough idea of what happened to you. First things first. What's your name?"

A silence passed. He opened his eyes again and fixed them on her.

"I don't remember that either," he said.

HE SAT UP QUICKLY. A sharp pain shot through his head, and the linen sheet slid down over his bare skin. His mind registered the fact that he was stripped to the waist, but that didn't matter, and neither did the pain. Nothing mattered except the all-important question of who he was.

"I don't remember," he said. "I don't remember anything about anything. Not my name, or where I come from, or anything at all. What's wrong with me? Why don't I remember?"

The red-haired girl quickly knelt beside him and took his hands. Her own hands were slender and strong, and he held tight to them, as if she were the only solid thing left in the world.

"There's no reason to be alarmed," she said. "Loss of personal memory after a head injury isn't uncommon either. You'll probably get it back within a few days."

She was comforting him as if he were a small frightened child—which was exactly how he was behaving. *Pull yourself together,* a stern voice inside his head admonished him. Instead, he heard himself asking, "What if I don't? What if I never get it back?"

"Don't worry about that now. Let's see what we can figure out about you. What *do* you remember?"

He searched his memory. It was like riffling through the pages of a blank book, empty except for one thing.

"You," he said. "You were there when I woke up in the woods, and again when I woke up here."

She smiled encouragingly, as if he'd solved a tricky arithmetic problem. "So I was. That's good! You made a new memory. Can you remember coming here from the woods?"

He cast a cursory glance around the tent with its steeply pitched roof. A wooden desk was wedged firmly against his mattress, holding a tallow candle that gave off a hazy yellow light.

"Vaguely," he said. "But I don't know where here is. What is this place, Miss...?"

"Shaw. Nessa Shaw."

"Nessa Shaw," he said to himself, impressing it on his memory. "Nessa Shaw. Where are we, Miss Shaw?"

Before she could answer, there was a brief commotion on the other side of the desk, and suddenly a boy was pointing a pistol at him.

"Unhand my sister," he said.

He was a gangly youth, with long, lanky limbs and an untidy mop of hair, but deadly earnest, and holding the pistol with the assurance of one who knew how to use it.

Without pausing to think, the man turned loose of Nessa Shaw and reached under the rolled-up blanket that had been serving as his pillow. But there was no weapon to be found there, and he wasn't sure why he'd thought there would be.

"Put the pistol down, Rory," Nessa said with weary exasperation. "I'm in no danger."

"He was clutching you," said the boy, still pointing the pistol.

"He was disoriented. He had a blow to the head, remember?"

Slowly, the boy lowered his weapon. "You should have woken me," he told his sister.

There was reproach in his voice, and something else, like wounded pride, or shame that he hadn't woken instantly on his own.

"Well, you're awake now," Miss Shaw said crisply. "Everyone's awake, and there's no reason for any of us to shoot each other."

She turned to the man. "Do you recognize Rory?"

"Nay," he said. "Should I?"

"He helped me bring you here after I found you in the woods. You were in and out of consciousness then."

A ghost of a memory drifted through the man's mind—of lurching unsteadily through the darkness, his bare feet half stumbling, half dragging along the rough ground, his arms draped over two pairs of shoulders in the classic posture of a drunkard being hauled home by two long-suffering friends. That could have been no easy task for this slender pair.

The man gave Rory a slight bow. "I'm very much obliged to you, sir, and sorry to give you cause for alarm just now. Please believe that I meant no harm or insult to your sister. I have nothing but the highest respect for her, and I'm grateful to you both for your kind assistance."

The words had come from some deep well within himself. Somehow he knew the proper way to speak to a fledgling youth with ruffled feathers.

Some of the tension eased out of Rory's face, and he nodded back, one gentleman to another.

Now that the crisis was over, a wave of nausea washed over the man, and he lay back with a groan. His head pounded, and he could feel his own pulse throbbing fast and hard in his temples and behind his eyes.

Miss Shaw bent over him. A little furrow appeared in the middle of her wide, creamy forehead, and her full, red, beautifully shaped lips fell open a bit. This was a strong face, a fearless face, and achingly pretty.

"All this excitement isn't good for you," she said. "Sleep is what you need most. You'll probably have your memory back when you wake up."

"Have his memory back?" Rory echoed.

"Himself doesn't remember his name," Miss Shaw told him.

"Himself?" said the man.

Miss Shaw smiled down at him and smoothed the hair from his brow. "That's what we've been calling you, since we didn't know your name. I suppose we'll have to go on doing it for a while. But not for long," she added quickly. "I'm sure you'll soon have your memory back in full."

He liked the feel of her hands on his face, soothing the pain in his head, and the sight of her bending over him that way, gazing down at him with that tender smile.

Rory came around to the other side of the desk and perched on a stool beside the bed, his long legs bent sharply at the knees. All his previous hostility was gone. His expression was eager and curious, as if Himself were a puzzle to solve.

"Clearly you remember some things," Rory said. "How to talk and walk. What a pistol is for. And Nessa said you quoted Descartes earlier."

"That's right," Himself said slowly. "I did."

"Classical pronunciation, or ecclesiastical?"

"Classical," Nessa and Himself said at the same time.

"That's another clue," said Rory. "You're probably not Catholic."

Himself thought about that. He didn't think he was Catholic—he didn't *feel* Catholic—but was that because he really *wasn't* Catholic, or because of what Rory had just said? He couldn't be sure. There was a compartment in his mind for René Descartes—mathematician, natural philosopher, metaphysician—but none for his own identity. How was that possible?

He lay still a minute or so with his eyes shut, breathing deeply. The pounding in his head slowly subsided to a dull ache.

When he opened his eyes, Nessa and Rory were still there, watching him.

"Where was I found?" he asked. "Was I alone?"

"I found you on a trail in the woods," Nessa answered. "Alone, dressed only in your linen, with a wound to the back of your head."

"Dressed only in my linen," Himself repeated. "Where was the rest of my clothing?"

"I saw none," said Nessa. "Of course, I didn't make a thorough search. It was dark, and I wanted to get you to shelter before the storm hit."

"We thought you'd probably been robbed," said Rory. "Either that, or you'd had nothing but your linen to wear to begin with. Plenty of soldiers in camp are clothed in little more than rags."

"What camp?" asked Himself. "Where are we?"

"At Continental Army headquarters at Ashley Hill," Rory replied.

Himself let that sink in. "South Carolina?" he said softly. "What am I doing in South Carolina?"

"Is there some reason you shouldn't be in South Carolina?" asked Rory.

Himself searched his memory but found no answer. "Nay, not that I recall," he said at last. "For all I know, I might have lived all my life in South Carolina."

"But it wasn't what you expected," said Miss Shaw. "Perhaps that's significant. Your mind still knows who you are and where you belong, but the pathway to that knowledge is blocked. It may be that we can get there through a back door, by putting together what you do know, and filling in the gaps. Ere long, something will trigger your memory, and all will be restored."

"Do you truly think so?" he asked.

"I've seen it happen in my work at the hospital."

He wanted to hear more about her work at the hospital, and where she came from, and a thousand other things. He wanted to know all about her. But he said only, "I'm willing to try."

"Excellent!" said Rory. "Let's see...Can you tell me what year it is?"

The man pondered for a moment. "Seventeen eighty...one?"

"Close," said Miss Shaw. "This is 1782. Do you know the month?"

"How can he be expected to remember the month when he doesn't know the year?" Rory scoffed.

"There's no harm in asking," Nessa retorted.

"I don't know the month," the man said.

"Today is October the ninth," said Nessa.

"The tenth," corrected Rory. "'Tis well after midnight." He asked the man, "What's the most recent thing you remember about the war?"

"Yorktown." The word was out almost before the man knew he was going to say it. He stopped, thought again, and felt his way forward, slowly at first.

"A siege," he said. "A French fleet under the Comte de Grasse, guarding the entrance to the Chesapeake, keeping the Royal Navy from reaching Cornwallis in the town with reinforcements and supplies."

He paused. They nodded their encouragement.

"The French fleet beat the Royal Navy," he went on. "Beat them soundly. And then—Washington and Rochambeau...The French engineers laid a line of trenches. The British tried to stop them with artillery fire, but they hadn't enough ordnance left. But the Allies had mortars, howitzers, twenty-four-pounders...General Washington himself touched off the first cannon on the American side. We shelled them for a week. Punched holes in their defenses. There was some hand-to-hand fighting...but not for long. We had them beaten. They flew a white flag and asked for parley. And then...they actually had the gall to ask for honorable terms of surrender. Ha! After the disgraceful way their side treated General Lincoln and his men after defeating the Patriots at Charlestown! We didn't give it to them, of course. They and their Hessian allies were marched out with flags furled and cased, and rightly so."

He was speaking with confidence now, a fierce joy rising in him as he remembered more and more of the glorious victory. "Cornwallis didn't even attend the surrender ceremony. He sent a deputy in his place—General O'Hara. Cornwallis claimed to be ill, but no one was fooled. O'Hara tried to hand over Cornwallis's sword to the Comte de Rochambeau. No doubt 'twas less onerous to surrender to a French nobleman than to an American general of common birth. But Rochambeau refused the sword, deferring to Washington. And Washington...Washington deferred to Lincoln! What a handsome and generous act on Washington's part! A finer gentleman never lived."

He had thoroughly warmed to his subject. The final words tumbled out in a torrent, and he flashed a triumphant gaze at his listeners.

The two of them exchanged glances, and Miss Shaw said, "Spoken like a true Patriot."

That was all she said, but Himself caught her meaning at once. The fierce joy vanished, replaced by a kind of shocked relief, as if he'd suddenly been pulled back from a precipice that he hadn't known was there. What if he hadn't been a Patriot? What if he'd been a Tory?

The very thought made him sick.

"I am," he said. "I am a Patriot."

He heard something like fear in his voice. He was desperate for them to believe him, and just as desperate for it to be true. But of course it was true. Of course he was a Patriot. How horrible it would be to get his memory back only to learn that he was on the wrong side of this war that had consumed everyone's lives for the past seven years! But surely he would only feel that way if he *were* a Patriot. He couldn't *not* be a Patriot. The thing was impossible.

He started to sit up again, but Miss Shaw gently pushed him back down, her smooth hands cool against his bare shoulders.

"That's enough for one night," she said. "You need your rest. Go to sleep."

He didn't think he'd be able to sleep again, not with all the questions swarming through his aching head. Questions about his own identity, for the most part, along with an uneasy sense of some task he had to perform, something he'd left undone.

But it felt good to stretch out on the crackling straw tick as Miss Shaw drew the sheet up to his chin, and to see her sweet face smiling down at him.

The last words he heard before sleep took him were, "You'll be all better soon. I'm going to look after you."

Chapter Four

The rain stopped around dawn, abruptly enough to wake Nessa from the deep sleep she'd fallen into on the straw tick Rory had brought from her tent. The first thing she saw when she opened her eyes was the sleeping face of the injured stranger. One bare arm was stretched toward her, its rounded muscles showing through the golden-brown skin. The other was curled in front of him with the loose fist tucked close to his body, giving him an achingly vulnerable look.

She lay there a moment, watching his chest slowly expand and contract, and studying his face—the firm mouth, the sturdy chin, the wide brow. There was a bit of wave in the hair that lay on his cheek. She longed to smooth it back, to gently ease its tangles free with her fingers, to rest her palm against his skin.

Rory's feet, clad in worn shoes passed down from their eldest brother, were planted firmly on the floor beneath his desk, not far from Nessa's face. The scent of burning tallow, and the soft scratching of his quill, told her that he was still at work. His much-mended stockings needed to be darned again.

Nessa pushed herself upright and stretched, easing the stiffness out of her limbs and back. The stack of blank foolscap on Rory's desk had shrunk considerably, and the stack of finished documents had grown proportionally, since she'd seen them last.

Without looking up from his work, Rory said, "Himself's been sleeping peacefully for hours now. No more bad dreams, as far as I can tell."

"Good," said Nessa. On her hands and knees, she crept past Rory's desk to Himself's side and felt for the pulse in his throat. It was stronger than before, and his skin was warm but not feverish. He didn't wake at her touch.

"We could move him now that the rain has stopped," Rory said, but doubtfully. "Get him to the General Hospital."

"Nay," said Nessa without taking her eyes from Himself's face. "What he needs now is rest, and plenty of it. He can get that just as well here as in the hospital—better, in fact."

All true, but not the whole truth. Himself was *her* patient. She'd been the one who'd found him, and she wasn't ready to give him up. He was a puzzle, a mystery—one that she wanted to solve.

She heard Rory lay down his quill and push back his stool. "I thought you'd say that. Very well, we'll keep him here. You're scheduled for the morning shift at the hospital today, aren't you? I can stay with him while you're away. I have more than enough paperwork to fill a morning. I do have a meeting to attend at noon, though."

"I'll come back in time to relieve you. I can have my dinner break here." She hesitated. "I'm sorry you have to give up your privacy. You have so little space as it is."

Rory waved off her concerns. "You'll hear no complaints from me. A semi-private tent is luxury enough compared to the accommodations I had with the militia."

He didn't often speak of the months he'd spent serving with the Wilmington militia last year. The men had lived rough, in the woods and swamps surrounding the Northeast Cape Fear River, while a British force occupied the town. Rory had been only fourteen then, but he hadn't been the only boy serving, or even the youngest.

"I'll see to your breakfast before I go," Nessa said.

She returned to her own tent to wash herself and fix her hair. Her gown was rumpled from having been slept in, but she couldn't exactly have stripped down to her shift for the night. She stood beneath the ridgepole, the only place in the tent where she didn't have to crouch, and smoothed the wrinkles as best she could. The space seemed comparatively roomy with the straw tick gone, but it was still cramped enough, lacking even sufficient room for her to hold her arms straight out without skimming the tent's sloping sides.

With her appearance tidied as much as possible, she went outside to make breakfast—some salt pork from a barrel, boiled with rice to make greasy rice. She wished she had some purple hull peas or collard greens to serve with it.

But she didn't, and there was no sense in repining for what she didn't have. So she loaded a tray with food, tinware, and chicory coffee, and took it to Rory's tent.

Nudging the flap open, she saw Himself lying awake on his back and staring up at the sloping ceiling. Rory hurried over to pull the flap back for her, and Himself pushed up on one elbow and watched her come in. Under the scrutiny of those grey-blue eyes, she felt a faint flush rising in her cheeks.

"Good morning," he said, speaking clearly and with gentlemanlike gravity.

"Good morning," Nessa replied. "How is your head?"

"It aches, but not as much as before. When I lie perfectly still, it hardly troubles me at all."

Nessa held the tray while Rory shifted the papers on his desk to make room for it. Glancing at Himself, she asked, "Did you sleep well?"

"Very well, I thank you. Do I smell coffee?"

He sounded doubtful, as well he might.

"Chicory root, mostly," said Rory, "and a few other bitter herbs. There isn't much coffee to be had, so we must stretch it as best we can."

There wasn't much of anything to be had. Each soldier was allowed one-and-a-quarter pounds of beef a day, and one-and-a-quarter pounds of rice—or a pound of wheat flour, when it was available, which it usually wasn't. Sometimes cornmeal was substituted instead. And when there was no beef, they could usually fill in with salt pork, but not always.

As a camp follower, Nessa received the same ration as a common soldier. For the time being, she and Rory would have to share their rations with Himself. But when Nessa offered Himself some greasy rice, he shook his head.

"I'm not hungry. And I doubt I could keep anything down just yet."

"Then you're wise not to try," Nessa said. "Your appetite will return when your stomach is ready to accept food. In the meantime, go on sipping water. And I'll make you an herbal infusion before I go. Peppermint and plantain—good for a sour stomach."

"Go?" he repeated. "Where are you going?"

"To work at the General Hospital."

The disappointment on his face was unmistakable, and it warmed her heart.

"I'll be back at noon," she assured him. "And Rory will stay with you. Do you remember Rory?"

Himself's gaze drifted to Rory taking his first sip of his morning approximation of coffee. "Rory is your younger brother," he said. "He pointed a pistol at me last night."

Nessa smiled. "Correct. And who am I? Do you remember my name?"

"You are Nessa Shaw," he said without a moment's hesitation. "You found me in the woods and brought me here."

Was she imagining the tenderness in his voice, the affection in his eyes? Even if they were real, it was hardly remarkable for a man to be favorably disposed to someone who had possibly saved his life.

"And where is here?" she prompted him.

"The Continental Army's camp at Ashley Hill, South Carolina."

"Excellent! And who are you?"

He opened his mouth, then shut it, his expression clouding.

"I don't know," he said. He sounded almost ashamed, as if he'd failed an examination.

"Never mind," said Nessa. "Your memory will come back in good time, just like your appetite. Get as much sleep as you can. That's the best thing for you now."

"Very well. I shall endeavor to knit up the raveled sleeve of care."

Nessa laughed at the Shakespearean reference, and at his earnest determination. "Well, don't endeavor too hard, or you'll drive sleep right away. Just relax and let sleep come to you. Don't try too hard to remember, either. You'll only confuse yourself."

He bowed his head. "As you wish, madam."

There wasn't time for further talk. Nessa quickly ate her breakfast, then went back to her own tent, where she kept her private stores of dried herbs in clay jars, along with a chipped ceramic teapot that she'd brought from the Shaw family home in North Carolina. The sight of the teapot sent a pang of homesickness through her. She missed her family, the house she'd grown up in, the dogs and horses, the chickens and cattle, and the longleaf pine trees. She missed wide open spaces and the freedom to move about a room without constantly crouching and stepping over things. She had never realized just how good and comfortable a home she had until she'd left it.

A dusty herbal scent hung over the clay jars, like a memory of summer. Nessa opened the teapot and spooned in some plantain, followed by some peppermint. Then she took the pot outside and filled it with boiling water from the kettle over the campfire. A clean, soothing fragrance rose up with the steam, and she took a deep breath of it. Pleasant scents were rare and precious in an army encampment.

When she took the filled pot to Rory's tent, Himself took a deep breath too, and his eyes brightened. "That smells good," he said.

"Aye, and 'tis good for you," said Nessa. "Let it steep a few minutes more before pouring. Don't drink too fast. Sip it slowly. Give it time to absorb. Take some sips of water, too. And sleep as much as you can. Sleep is the best thing for you now."

She was repeating things she'd already said, stretching out the time until her departure. But there were suffering men at the General Hospital as well, waiting for her to comfort and care for them.

"I'm off, then," she said.

Himself dipped his head. "Thank you for all you've done for me, madam. Until the noon hour, *adieu*."

The army's camp was just south of Middleton Place, a large, gracious plantation belonging to Arthur Middleton, who'd served in the Continental Congress and signed the Declaration of Independence. The army's previous encampment had been at Bacon's Bridge, a low-lying swampy area. They had relocated to the high bluff of Ashley Hill three months earlier, in July, hoping the site would prove more healthful for the soldiers. Perhaps it was more healthful, but a mere change of air was not sufficient to cure the men who were already suffering from malaria before the move.

Nessa and Rory lived in the sutler's row, the portion of the camp reserved for camp followers: laundresses, cooks, nurses, surgeons, teamsters, tradesmen, and all the others who acted in supporting roles. Smoke rose from the campfires where breakfasts were underway. Most of the meals consisted of salt pork prepared in various ways—roasted over open fires, fried in pans, or boiled for greasy rice—but Nessa also saw cornbread cakes being cooked.

She crossed into the main camp where the soldiers dwelled. The tents were laid out in a grid pattern, with the paths between them worn to hard-packed tracks. General Greene did his best to maintain a clean, orderly camp, but with so many men living so close together, there was only so much to be done. It pained Nessa to see the piles of ash, the slop buckets, the ground denuded of vegetation. How long would it take the land to recover, and erase the scars from the army's presence? More to the point, how long would it be before the army actually departed from the camp? The Continental forces couldn't go while the British remained in Charlestown, and as of yet there had been no date fixed for the British to depart. There were procedures to follow, orders to be given and received, plans to be made and remade—all based on the assumption of the war's being officially declared at an end, which might have happened weeks ago, or might not happen for months to come, if at all. When Nessa thought about the miles of ocean stretching between the enemy's headquarters in America and the British authorities on the other side of the Atlantic, miles that must be crossed back and forth and back again before any decisive action could be taken, something like despair rose up inside her.

But she pushed it back down. Despair was a sin, born of lack of faith in God. She must turn away from it, and do her appointed work with patience and diligence, and trust that God would make all things right in his time.

As she entered the General Hospital, she sent up a silent prayer of thanksgiving for the blessing of work. Vexatious though it might be, and futile as it often seemed, it was hers to do, and she did it well. She had always been a busy, active sort of person, and she shuddered to imagine what life in the latter stages of the war would be like without meaningful tasks to occupy her mind and hands.

The great majority of hospitalized men were suffering from malaria. Jesuit's bark was the only treatment that had ever proven effective against the disease, but it was in short supply. There wasn't much more to do for the sick men besides giving them plenty of fluids to drink to replace those lost in fever and perspiration, and changing their sweat-soaked bed linens. Left to their own recuperative powers, and palliative care from Nessa and other nurses, they might get better, and they might not.

The first patient she visited today was already sitting up in bed with his breakfast tray on his knees.

"Why, Sergeant Philips!" she said. "How very well you look this morning!"

Sergeant Philips was a Pennsylvania man who had been sick with malaria since before the camp had been moved to Ashley Hill. Malaria tended to hit the northern soldiers harder than those from the South, who'd been exposed to it for most of their lives and grown toughened to it.

Sergeant Philips beamed at her over his bowl of rice. "I feel fitter than I have in months, miss. I haven't had a shaking fit nor a bit of fever in over a day now, and I'm hungry enough to eat a cavalry horse."

She gave him a stern look. "Careful, Sergeant. That's the kind of talk that could end in a court martial. You know as well as I do that horses of any sort are far too short in supply to put into stew pots. If I hear of any going missing, I might have to turn you in."

He held up his hands in mock surrender and laughed. "Very well, miss, I'll make do with rice and salt pork and leave the horses alone. I daresay they'd be too lean and stringy to make for good eating, anyway."

"That's better. Now, finish your breakfast, and then we'll see about a nice wash and a change of linen for you."

"Aye, miss, that's exactly what I'd like. I can't tell you how happy I am to put that wretched illness behind me once and for all."

She didn't mention the possibility of relapse. It happened sometimes, especially to those whose bouts had been particularly severe. They'd appear to make a complete recovery, only to fall into more fits of fever and ague days, weeks, or even years later. Perhaps Sergeant Philips had never heard that, or perhaps he was choosing to ignore the possibility. Either way, there was no good purpose to be served in sapping his courage now.

He finished his breakfast, and she gave him his wash, working briskly and cheerfully. It was important to keep these things on a businesslike footing. For her, it was merely a task to be done, like all aspects of nursing. She washed and fed and cared for dozens of men each day. But to them, far from home and starved for female companionship, it often meant something more.

When it was over, and the sergeant was clean and refreshed and clad in a fresh shirt, he leaned back on his pillow with a sigh. "Thank you, miss. I feel like a new man."

"I'm happy to hear it, Sergeant Philips."

He glanced shyly at her. "Edward," he said.

"I beg your pardon?"

"Edward. That's my Christian name. Folks back home call me Ned. I come from a big family—brothers and sisters, uncles and aunts, and more cousins than I can count. We've been in Philadelphia for three generations, ever since the city was founded. My father owns a cooperage there. I learned the trade from him, but I also apprenticed to my uncle at his chandlery."

Barrel-building and rope-making—companion trades, suitable for businesses owned and run by members of an extended family. There was likely a tinsmith uncle as well, and some cousins employed at shipyards. The sergeant was dropping hints as to his desirability as a potential husband. He probably thought he was being subtle, poor man. But after several months spent nursing soldiers, Nessa had learned to detect incoming marriage proposals, and head them off before they landed.

"It must be a great comfort to you, having a large family and a good livelihood to go home to," she said, sidestepping his invitation to call him Edward or even Ned. "Keep building up your strength, and I hope you'll be back in Philadelphia before many weeks have passed. Now I'll take away these soiled linens and leave you to rest."

She was gone before he could reply.

Throughout her morning's work, as she bathed, fed, and medicated other men, her thoughts kept drifting back to Himself. Was he resting comfortably? Had he had any more nightmares? Had he recovered his memory yet? Most importantly, who was he, and where had he come from?

At last noon came. Nessa left the hospital, but instead of going straight to Rory's tent, she stopped at the office of the Quartermaster Department, in charge of provisions and dispersing. If Himself was going to go on sleeping in Rory's tent, she would need a new mattress for her own tent. She and Rory couldn't keep taking turns snatching a few hours' sleep on one bed.

Procuring a new straw tick was easy enough. A far greater challenge was getting something to put in it. Forage for horses was scarce, and the

Commissary Department was reluctant to turn loose of the precious hay that could be used to fill the bellies of the lean horses of the Continental Army. Anyone requesting fresh mattress stuffing must demonstrate legitimate need.

All of which was perfectly reasonable. But if Nessa told the suspicious requisitions clerk about the unconscious man she'd found in the woods, the clerk would say that Himself ought to be admitted to the hospital, where his bedding would be procured through proper channels. And perhaps he would be right.

And yet something stopped her, something more than her desire to keep her handsome patient to herself. Somehow she felt—nay, she knew—that telling anyone about Himself was the wrong thing to do, at least for now. She couldn't explain it, but her intuitions were generally correct, and she'd learned to trust them.

She was still wrangling with the clerk when a voice behind her asked, "What seems to be the trouble here?"

It was a quiet, level voice with a suggestion of power—a voice she recognized, and was glad to hear. She turned to see a tall man, broad through the shoulders but with a wasted look to his flesh, as if he had once carried a great deal more muscle—not unlike those cavalry horses whose fodder the commissary clerk was guarding so jealously. He wore a dark-blue uniform coat—shabby and threadbare, but neatly mended and spotlessly clean—and wore a signet ring on his right hand. His close-cropped hair was almost black, like the straight brows above deep-set, hooded eyes of steely grey.

Nessa dropped a curtsey. "Major Elliot! How do you do, sir? I am very glad to see you."

"Miss Shaw," said the major, with the dip of the head that sufficed as a bow for him. "Are you in need of supplies? Perhaps I may be of assistance."

"I certainly hope so," said Nessa. "I'm trying to get fresh fill for my straw tick, but—well—"

The major turned his gaze on the clerk, who drew himself up and cleared his throat.

"Major Elliot, sir. Of course I'd be happy to oblige the young lady if I could. But you know how scarce hay is right now, and with the army horses little more than skin and bones."

"What about all the straw from the rice harvest at Middleton Place?" asked the major. "Surely some of it is cured by now and ready to use as bedding. And rice straw is no good for animal fodder, so 'twould not be taking food from the horses' mouths, so to speak."

"Aye, we've got a decent amount of rice straw," the clerk said cautiously. "But we're holding it back for the officers."

"You'll give some of it to Miss Shaw—and not a few paltry handfuls. I want her straw tick to be plump and soft, and I will follow up to make sure that my orders are obeyed."

"Aye, Major," said the clerk. "The straw will be delivered by the end of the day."

"Excellent," said the major.

He offered Nessa his arm and led her out of the queue.

"This is very good of you, Major Elliot," said Nessa. "I cannot thank you enough."

"Please do not mention it, Miss Shaw. It is nothing at all compared to the kindness you've shown to me."

His gratitude touched her. She only wished that her kindness, as he called it, had been of greater material use to him.

Major Andrew Elliot came from a prominent Charlestown family of merchants and landowners. His chief property was Magnolia Grove, a plantation within half a day's drive of the camp at Ashley Hill. Prior to the outbreak of fighting in the South, he had served in both the Provincial Congress and the General Assembly of South Carolina. Later, he'd been commissioned as a major over an artillery regiment in the South Carolina Continentals. All who knew him agreed that he had comported himself with honor and gallantry.

But his career as a field commander had ended when an exploding howitzer had driven shrapnel deep into his shoulder, neck, and chest. That had been at the Battle of Guilford Courthouse, over a year earlier. Nessa didn't know what sort of care he had received at the time, but it must have been merely palliative, because no surgeon in his right mind would ever have supposed that anyone could survive so grievous a wound. Other men had surely needed attention as well, and resources had to be rationed.

Major Elliot did not die. He lingered a day, and another day, and then a week. Eventually his wound healed, after a fashion. A fragile layer of scar tissue, laced by thick, rope-like welts, now covered what must initially have been an enormous area of raw flesh. Nessa couldn't even begin to imagine how many agonizing weeks it had taken for the edges of the wound to come together. The massive system of scars ran from the right side of his neck, just beneath the jaw, down his right arm past the elbow joint, and down his right side to the bottom of his ribcage.

All of which meant that Major Elliot would never again snug a musket's stock against his shoulder, or live an active, outdoor life on Magnolia Grove. Even a sedentary life held risks for him. Because the scar covered joints, it was in constant danger of reopening—and it had done so on more than one occasion.

The last time the major's wound had suppurated, Nessa—known to possess a strong stomach—had been chosen to assist the attending physician. The wound had stunk, indicating infection deep beneath the surface. After Nessa had cleaned the wound, the physician had applied copious amounts of mercury ointment, which he claimed would speed healing by encouraging the production of laudable pus. Nessa had had her doubts about this treatment course, but the choice had not been hers to make.

Having sustained so grievous an injury in the service of his country, the major might have retired from the army with honor. His days of combat were plainly over, and no one could expect him to give more than he already had. Instead, he'd moved to the Quartermaster Department, which certainly had an urgent need for able, intelligent officers—especially now, when there was never enough of anything to go around. It was a vexing and thankless task, but a vital one, and everyone admired him for doing it.

Nessa could see the thin, shiny, pinkish-white scar tissue extending from the top of his shirt collar to his jaw. His hair was going grey at the temples, and deep lines marked his face, though he was still a young man, only thirty-two. She wished she could tell him how sorry she was for all he'd suffered, and that she held him in the highest regard for continuing to serve his country. But what words could possibly suffice?

"Have you been to Magnolia Grove lately?" she asked.

"Not since late in the summer. I cannot be there as often as I would wish. My steward, Scipio, oversees the running of the farm when he is not at the camp with me. He rejoined me here just the other day."

"And how was the harvest?"

"Middling. War is hard on farmers. I haven't been able to properly look after the place for years. After the British leave, that will change." He held up his right hand. "Do you see this signet ring? It has been in my father's family for over a hundred years, since they first departed England for the New World. Every master of Magnolia Grove has worn it. I was eleven years old when it came to me. It was too big for my finger then, but I kept it with me always."

It fit rather loosely now, but Nessa did not point this out.

They reached her tent. She released his arm—it was his left arm, the uninjured one—and dropped another curtsey.

"Thank you again, Major Elliot."

"You're most welcome, Miss Shaw. Please give my best to your brother."

He dipped his head very slightly and was gone.

THE WATER WAS EVERYWHERE—ABOVE him, below him, filling his ears and mouth, his eyes and nose. He clawed at the hand holding him down, but it was as immovable as iron. Frustration gave way to terror. He groped around for something to use as a weapon, but his hands met nothing but pondweed and rotten wood from fallen tree branches. His struggle to free himself only depleted the life in him that much faster, clouding his mind, weakening his limbs. His lungs screamed for air. He couldn't hold out any longer. He had to take a breath, or die.

He sat up with a start.

He was sitting on a straw tick in an army tent, soaked in sweat, shaking all over, and sucking in great gasping breaths of precious air.

The next instant, Nessa Shaw was at his side.

"Another bad dream?"

He nodded. But it had felt like more than a bad dream. It had felt like a memory.

Was it, though? It didn't seem likely that someone had tried to drown him, then dragged his unconscious body to a wooded trail and left it there. Besides, this was October, and the dream had had the distinctive feel of a summer's day—warm water, glaring sunshine, riotous birdsong. Perhaps it was only a garden-variety bad dream, like being naked in a crowded room, or unable to run while being chased—but if so, it was a remarkably lifelike dream.

The two of them were alone in the tent. Judging from the diffuse light shining through the canvas roof, it was somewhere around midday.

"How do you feel?" she asked.

He took an inventory of his body. Head—still throbbing, but less than last night. Limbs—aching and weak. Stomach—empty and hungry.

"Better," he said. "But I still don't remember who I am or why I'm here."

She laid a gentle hand on his upper back. "You must be patient. I know 'tis frustrating, but you are making progress. Let the memories come, and don't push yourself."

"But I can't afford to wait. There's something I must do, something important. I don't know what it is—but I know that I must do it quickly."

"Something to do with the war?"

"I think so. If 'tis not done soon, something terrible may happen. It might be happening now—all because my stupid brain refuses to cooperate."

He hunched forward, rested his elbows on his bent knees, clasped his hands to his head, and gave it a shake.

"Stop that," Miss Shaw said sternly. "You won't get your memory back by sheer force of will. Healing takes time. If you'd been shot in the shoulder, you wouldn't be angry at yourself for being unable to move your arm. And if you forced yourself to do it anyway, you'd be setting back your recovery, and perhaps doing permanent damage. An injury to your head is no different."

He sighed. "I know you're right. But this thing I have to do—what if someone is waiting for me to do it, at this very moment? What if people are depending on me, and I'm failing them?"

"If 'tis as important as all that, then you must do your best to get your memory back—properly. And that means resting, and taking things slowly."

She rubbed his back softly, as if he were a frightened child. He lifted his head and looked into her sweet face.

"I suppose I don't have a choice in the matter," he said.

"You always have a choice. Be sure to make the right one."

She glanced at the tin cup she'd left at his bedside, empty now. "I see you drank all the plantain and peppermint brew."

"I did. I liked it."

"Good. I'm sorry the raveled sleeve of care still has some knitting up to do."

"Actually...I do feel better now. My head isn't throbbing so much, and I'm hungry."

He sniffed hopefully. There was a promising food-like aroma in the air, and a covered pan stood on Rory's desk as before. Nessa dished up a bowlful and handed it to him. It was plain rice with no meat—a dish fit only for invalids.

"I wish I had some broth to give you, but this is the best I can do," she said. "Don't eat too fast."

The rice was fluffy and hot—bland, but good. He wanted to wolf it down, but he forced himself to take small spoonfuls and chew slowly. Even so, he reached the end of it far too soon.

He set the empty bowl back on the desk. "Has Rory gone to his meeting?" he asked.

"Aye, and I've finished my morning shift at the hospital. I'm free until evening. And if you're feeling up to it, perhaps we can do some gentle probing into that memory of yours. Well, not probing exactly. I thought we could talk in a general way about the war and other things, and see if anything gets shaken loose. What do you think?"

He thought it was the most perfect way he could possibly spend his afternoon, and not merely for the sake of his memory. He wanted to know more about this beautiful, vivid creature.

But he said only, "If you believe 'twill help, I'll be happy to try."

"Good! Now, when we talked earlier, I asked you the last thing you remembered about the war, and you said Yorktown. You gave a good account of the siege, the battle, and the victory. Do you remember what happened next?"

"Aye. British Parliament passed a resolution to negotiate peace with the United States. I assume our representatives are still hammering out terms with the British in Paris?"

"As far as we know," said Nessa with a sigh.

He nodded grimly. One of the most frustrating aspects of the war was the long time it took for news to travel across the Atlantic.

"What else do you remember from the latter days of the war?" she asked.

He shut his eyes and let the memories come. "Cowpens—a brilliant victory. Guilford Courthouse—a tactical defeat, but barely, and more costly to the enemy than to us. The Articles of Confederation..." He opened his eyes. "Ratified?"

"Aye, finally, and put into effect. Can you remember the last state to ratify?"

"Maryland."

"That's right! Look how well you're doing."

He felt absurdly pleased by her praise, as though he had pulled off some prodigious mental feat. He pondered again. This time, the memory that drifted up was not a happy one.

"Benedict Arnold," he said. "He led a force to Richmond, and burned it."

"Aye, he did," Nessa said softly.

A silence fell. General Arnold's betrayal had been a sickening blow to the young nation.

"There was something else," he said. "Something about Richmond...Bloody Ban! He took some cavalry there to capture the legislature and Governor Jefferson. Did they get away in time?"

"Aye. Some of the legislators were captured later, but most of them got away, and so did the governor."

He let out a breath. "Now you tell me something," he said. "What has been happening here, in South Carolina? Have the British left Charlestown yet?"

"Nay, more's the pity, though we think and hope they will soon. Peace is so near, almost within our grasp. But with the enemy bottled up in the city, and our own force so close by, and both sides worn out from war and running short of necessities, we can hardly avoid further bloodshed. 'Twas in August that General Leslie announced his intention of withdrawing from Charlestown. Naturally the withdrawal couldn't be accomplished all at once, and in the meantime, General Leslie must feed his troops and his horses. He actually offered to purchase provisions instead of foraging from the countryside. 'Twould have been a good thing for the inhabitants, who would at least receive payment for the food and supplies that would be taken from them in any event, with or without recompense. But South Carolina's civil authority made General Greene refuse General Leslie's offer. They said General Leslie would use the opportunity to buy ammunition and take it to the West Indies in order to fight against our French allies. So Leslie had to continue provisioning his men by force—and naturally General Greene is obliged to oppose him. All of which has only prolonged hostilities between our army and the British garrison and led to a lot of pointless injuries and deaths. We lost Colonel Laurens in a skirmish with a foraging party only two months ago, in August—a sad end for so valiant an officer."

She stopped and peered at him. He was staring straight ahead at the tent wall, his mind lit up by the certainty that had just blazed into being.

"What is it?" she asked. "Have you remembered something?"

He nodded mutely.

"About Colonel Laurens?" she prompted him.

"Nay. About August."

"Something else that happened then?"

"Nay. 'Tis my name, my Christian name."

He met her gaze again and tapped himself on the chest. "August," he said. "That's who I am."

Understanding and joy dawned on her face. "How marvelous! Do you remember your surname?"

His own happiness clouded a little. "Nay."

"That's all right," she said quickly. "'Twill come soon enough. August! It suits you."

It *suited* him? What did that mean?

"How so?" he asked.

She shrugged. "There's a sort of dignity about you, a nobility."

Was this true? Was he noble and dignified? "I'll have to take your word for it," he said.

August. It was only a name, and not a full one, but it was his, and it made a world of difference.

He ran a hand over his jaw and felt the long stubble there—more than stubble, a light beard.

"Would it be all right—might I have a wash and a shave?" he asked. "Perhaps a change of linen?"

"I can provide a clean shirt, and there's water in Rory's pitcher," she said. "But you'll have to wait on the shave. Rory doesn't own a razor—and I've had enough trouble with the Quartermaster Department already today, when I requisitioned a new bed."

A new bed? That sounded as if he would be staying in his present accommodations for a while rather than moving to the hospital. The idea appealed to him.

She searched through the pile of linen that was stacked near the desk and found a plain shirt and pair of drawers. "These look as if they'd fit you. Generous in the sleeve, and roomy enough, I think. You're more filled out than most of the men in camp."

August looked down at himself, at the bare chest running down to a flat abdomen ridged with muscle, the long hard thighs in their linen drawers. This was his body, but it might as well belong to a stranger. Apparently this August person, whatever else might be true of him, had been dining rather better than the soldiers of the Continental Army in the South.

And Nessa had seen enough of his body to have an opinion as to its fitness—a favorable opinion, judging from her words. The thought was an agreeable one.

The pitcher stood inside a chipped basin on a plain wooden washstand. Underneath was a round metal tub. A towel hung from a bar on the washstand's side, along with a smaller cloth. Nessa looped them both over her arm and picked up basin, pitcher, and soap.

It took August a moment to realize that she meant to bathe him personally. Without meaning to, he drew back a little and raised the sheet that had fallen to his waist.

"I can do it myself," he said.

The words sounded childish in his own ears, like those of a small child asserting independence.

Nessa smiled at him and brought the bath things to his bedside. "I've been nursing sick and wounded men for several months, August. You needn't worry about offending my feminine delicacy."

The sound of his name spoken by her voice sent a strange thrill through him. And the idea of his being only another body to her, something to be washed and dried as matter-of-factly as a soup tureen, did nothing to ease his discomfort.

"Besides," she went on, pouring water from the pitcher into the basin, "I already washed you earlier, when Rory and I first brought you here."

A rush of heat flooded his face and he knew that he was blushing like a girl. "I don't remember that," he said.

"You weren't conscious then."

Before he could protest further, she dipped the cloth in the basin and raised it to his face.

The water was refreshingly cool, but not cold. She started with the skin around his eyes, then moved on to his cheeks and forehead. He didn't know where to look at first, with her right in front of him, but he finally settled his gaze on her face. It was either that or cut his eyes to the side, which would be silly. Her own gaze was intent, but also somehow distant—she was focused on the task, not on him. The whole situation was horribly uncomfortable, and at the same time exquisitely pleasant. If nothing else, it gave him an excuse to drink in the sight of her—those brown eyes, that wide mouth, that creamy skin. Her face was beautifully proportioned, with strength and sweetness in equal measure, and he could stare at it all he wanted.

She moved on to his neck, his chest. His skin tingled all over, and not from the cool water. Could she feel his heart hammering against his ribs? She rinsed the cloth, raised it, and slowly lowered it back to the basin. She was looking him in the eye now. Her mouth fell open just a bit, revealing the tips of two perfect white teeth above the curve of a full, red lower lip. August longed to touch that lip with his fingertips, to skim his hand along that silky-smooth cheek and down the graceful line of her neck, to bend his face to hers and—

Abruptly, Nessa stood, leaving the cloth at the basin's edge. "I believe you were right after all," she said. "You are quite strong enough to bathe yourself. I'll wait outside the tent, and you can call to me if you need me."

She was gone almost before he could form a coherent reply.

He drew a deep breath and let it out. Then he picked up the cloth and began to wash himself.

Sounds came in through the tent's canvas walls, sounds of a busy army camp—footsteps, men's voices, the clatter of cooking implements. Were the sounds familiar, or did he only imagine that they were? He focused on them, trying to blot out the thought of the auburn-haired girl outside the tent. She was a beautiful girl, a remarkable girl, but he mustn't allow himself to be distracted by her. He had to remember who he was and what he was supposed to do.

There was no room in his life for anything else.

Chapter Five

Nessa paced back and forth outside the tent, her cheeks burning with shame despite the cool October breeze. Never before had she reacted that way to a patient. She had prided herself on always maintaining the necessary professional distance. True, sometimes the men had fallen for her anyway, and she had done her best to let them down gently. But this was the first time her own heart had been touched. Never in her life had she felt anything like this—for any man, patient or otherwise.

She couldn't give in to it. She must not—she would not. August was a handsome, intelligent, attractive man, but he was her patient, her responsibility. It would be wrong—unethical—to allow romantic feelings to enter into a caregiving relationship.

The way he'd looked into her eyes, and glanced down at her mouth—she'd never been kissed before, but she knew he'd been on the verge of kissing her. What would it have felt like? His lips against hers, his hands on her face, in her hair—her own hands at the nape of his neck, drawing him closer—

Stop it, she told herself. Giving in to this longing would be a terrible mistake, and a disservice to August. An injured man with no memory, no history, no family or friend to belong to—of course he would crave closeness to another human being, but he was in no position to be forming romantic connections. Why—the thought stopped her in her tracks—he could be married for all either of them knew. He could be some woman's husband, and father to her children.

Nessa laid a hand to her chest and felt it thumping, as if she'd been yanked back from a precipice she hadn't known was there. If August *had* kissed her—if she hadn't come to her senses in time—she couldn't bear to think of it.

"What are you doing?"

She jumped, feeling as guilty as a burglar caught in the act, and saw Rory, back from his meeting, with his satchel slung over one shoulder and a curious look in his eye.

Trying to keep her voice level and casual, she said, "August is having a wash. I'm giving him his privacy."

"Who's August?" Rory asked.

"Himself. He remembered his Christian name."

"What excellent news! But is he steady enough to bathe himself? I'd have thought he needed help."

He probably did need help. He was probably struggling and exhausted right now, on the other side of this canvas wall. What if his recovery was set back, all because Nessa couldn't control her feelings? What sort of nurse was she?

Rory, not tormented by such thoughts, simply opened the tent flap and walked through.

"You can come in," Rory said over his shoulder. "He's decent."

Nessa took a deep breath and tried to marshal her wits. This was a fresh start. She would pretend the near-kiss had never happened, and most likely August would too, and they would both forget all about it soon enough.

She went inside the tent to see August not drooping with fatigue, but dressed and sitting on a stool, his face composed.

"Here I am," he said. "Clothed and in my right mind."

Nessa smiled at the biblical reference.

"How do you feel?" she asked. "Are you lightheaded at all?"

"Nay. I feel...not precisely fit as a fiddle, but as fit as a slightly out-of-tune lute with none of its strings missing."

Rory had gone to his desk and taken some papers out of his satchel. "Well, there's nothing wrong with the part of your brain that stores idioms and quotations," he said. "Whatever else you may be, 'tis clear you're a scholar."

"You appear to be something of a scholar yourself, Master Rory," August replied. "Are you a clerk, or a private secretary?"

"Clerk. I'd like to be someone's private secretary if I could."

"You seem rather young for either position."

Rory lifted his chin. "I'm fifteen—older than John Quincy Adams was when he acted as his father's secretary in Paris, and not much younger than he is now that he's secretary to Francis Dana in Russia."

While they spoke, Nessa piled together August's discarded linen and hung up the damp towel he had used. Then she went to work stripping the bed. The sheets were littered with the dirt that had covered August when he'd first been laid there.

"True," said August. "I'm told that young Adams has a remarkable facility for languages. Have you studied languages, Master Rory?"

He'd touched on a sensitive topic, but Rory answered equably enough.

"Not as much as I'd like. There was a preparatory school that my brothers attended before the war, but it shut down before I was old enough to go. I have their old Latin grammar book, and a French grammar that I picked up from a bookseller a few years ago. I do what I can with them."

"An autodidact! Impressive."

Rory shrugged. "I'm proficient in Latin, and I read and write French well enough, but I know my pronunciation is not what it should be."

"Aye, the war has interrupted the education of many a promising young man," said August. "But 'tis very much to your credit that you've kept yours up as well as you have, and I'm sure your diligence will be rewarded with an abundance of future opportunities. As Pasteur said, *La chance favorise l'esprit préparé.*"

Nessa turned and looked at him. "You speak French," she said. It was no more than she'd expected, but she was glad to have confirmation. The more she learned about August, and the more he learned about himself, the closer they were to finding out his identity.

"Aye, I suppose I do," he replied.

Nessa had freed the edges of the bottom sheet from beneath the straw tick. Now she gathered the four corners together, shaking the dirt toward the center, and forming a bundle with August's old linen inside.

"You realize the tent has a dirt floor," Rory said, watching her.

"It has a *straw* floor," Nessa retorted. "One that I intend to keep as clean as possible. In a rough-living situation like this, 'tis more important than ever to uphold standards."

She set the bundle aside, picked up a folded sheet from the stack of finished mending, and spread it over the straw tick. It was patched and threadbare, but clean. She tucked its edges under the straw tick as neatly as she could and followed it with a top sheet, which she drew up smoothly and tucked under at the foot before turning it back halfway.

"Back to bed," she said to August in the brisk, cheerful, no-nonsense tone she used with her patients.

August got the balky look that she had often seen on the faces of convalescent men growing weary of their restraints. But before he could speak, she said, "No arguments."

"Aye, Madam," August said meekly. He sat on the mattress but did not lie down.

"Is she not a tyrant?" asked Rory affectionately. "She rules me with an iron hand. I can hardly call my soul my own."

"She is a strong-minded lady," said August. "Are there other brothers and sisters in your family?"

"Two brothers and two sisters," said Rory. "Six siblings in all. I'm the youngest of all, and Nessa is the middle girl."

"Tell me about the others," August said.

Rory ran through them all in order of age—the eldest sister, Catalyn, married with two young sons; the eldest brother, Fergus, married with a baby on the way; the middle brother, Liam, a former midshipman in the Continental Navy, now a sailor on a merchant vessel somewhere on the Atlantic; and the youngest sister, Morna, the only one left at home, keeping house for their widowed father.

"And where is home?" August asked.

"A farm a few miles from Wilmington."

"Wilmington. The one in North Carolina, I presume? Not the one in Delaware."

"That's right," said Rory. "Look at that! You remembered the existence of Delaware."

He had remembered more than that, thought Nessa. The things he was aware of, and took for granted—details about John Quincy Adams and about Francis Dana's mission to Russia, the quote from Blaise Pascal in its original language—all suggested a man not only well educated, but well informed.

Nessa had mostly kept out of the way in the conversation. She suspected August would recover his memory far better in the context of relaxed talk than he would by trying to force himself to remember. And there was an agreeable give-and-take between him and her brother, a similarity of mind that was not only revelatory, but enjoyable to listen to. Just for a moment, she found herself wondering how August would get on with the rest of the family, but she quickly put a stop to that line of thinking. It was one thing for August and Rory to be friends, but she must confine herself to acting as his nurse—and if he went on recovering at this rate, she wouldn't be doing that for much longer. He would get his memory back and be gone.

Rory turned to her. "How was the hospital today, sister? Did anyone ask you to marry him?"

Nessa bent a bit more deeply over her work to hide the flush she could feel stealing into her cheeks. Trying for a light tone, she said, "Someone started to, but I managed to fend him off at the last minute."

Out of the corner of her eye she saw August glancing back and forth between them. "Is this a common occurrence?" he asked. "Do you often receive marriage proposals at the hospital?"

"Sometimes more than one in a day," Rory said frankly, before Nessa could answer. "An occupational hazard of nursing work, apparently. A few spoonfuls of broth and a little smoothing of the fevered brow are enough to make some men fancy themselves in love—and to flatter themselves that she returns the feeling. A proposal of marriage soon follows."

Often it was a proposition of a very different sort, but Rory didn't need to be made aware of that. Any insult to his sister's honor would have him hoofing it to the hospital with vengeance in his heart. But he found her accumulation of marriage offers merely amusing. Nessa wished desperately that he would stop talking. The tent suddenly seemed stiflingly warm and close, and she could feel August's gaze on her.

But August only said, "Small blame to them. Your sister is a beautiful and charming lady. And I suppose it is natural enough to harbor a certain affection for one's nurse."

"How was your meeting, Rory?" Nessa asked. "Any word on when the British will leave the city?"

Rory accepted the change of subject without question. "Nothing definite. At times the general expects them to go any day now, and at others he despairs of their ever going at all. Even if they do go, it might be only to consolidate their forces in the West Indies, against the French. And with France defeated, they'd turn back here, and renew their efforts against us."

Nessa had heard it all before. It was a sobering possibility, and the only thing the Patriot forces could do about it was to present a strong front to convince the enemy that further aggressions against them would be futile. They must show no hint of weakness for the enemy to exploit. There were weaknesses enough, if the British knew about them. Holed up in Charlestown, they likely had no idea how small a force was camped at Ashley Hill—and a force weakened by sickness, at that.

"How horrible it would be," she said softly, "after so many years, to come so far, to sacrifice so much, to see victory and liberty just within reach, only to have them snatched away at the last moment, and go back to being a vassal state in the British Empire."

"Aye," Rory said soberly. "The enemy would relish a chance to humble the pride of France, and to take the stuffing out of the Patriots. Imprisonment, fines, confiscations, hangings—"

"And not merely from the British," said Nessa. "From Tories, too."

August nodded. "A British victory at any stage is something no Patriot could stomach. But at this stage, 'twould be a nightmare."

The mention of nightmares reminded Nessa of August's own sleep disturbances. Perhaps she should give him something to help him sleep. Not laudanum, but a mild sleeping potion—chamomile, hops, valerian...

She made an exasperated sound.

"What's wrong?" asked Rory.

"I left my herb basket and knife in the woods," Nessa replied. "I only just remembered. I found some valerian there last night, knelt down to harvest some...and saw August, lying there on the trail. After that I forgot all about my knife and basket—and they were rained on! They're probably ruined by now."

"Perhaps not," said Rory. "That's a sturdy oak splint basket, and the knife hasn't had time for much rust to form."

"Aye, you're right. I'll go now and fetch them," said Nessa, feeling both glad and sorry for an excuse to leave August's presence.

"Go back to that lonely trail all by yourself?" Rory said in an outraged tone. "You'll do no such thing."

"What do you mean? I've walked that trail alone dozens of times."

"Aye, but that was before we knew there were brigands or murderers about. You saw what they did to August. And you, a defenseless girl? Nay, I cannot allow it."

"Don't be ridiculous, Rory. I'm perfectly capable of looking after myself. Besides, 'tis full daylight now."

"Nay, I must insist, Nessa. Stay here with August. I'll fetch your knife and basket back."

"You may insist all you like. You cannot stop me from going."

Nessa was a bit ashamed of her tart tone, especially since there was sense in what Rory had said. But she resented being bossed so masterfully by a brother six years younger than herself, who wasn't even old enough to shave—and she didn't want to be left alone with August again.

Then Rory's hauteur vanished, and he said, "Nessa, what would I do if something happened to you? What would I say to Father?"

Nessa's irritation drained away, but she wasn't finished arguing yet. "I still have to get the valerian," she said. "You don't know what it looks like or how to harvest it properly."

August spoke up. "The solution is obvious. Both of you must go."

They turned to him.

"But then...who would stay with you?" Nessa asked.

"I'll stay by myself, of course. I'm not an invalid or a child. I'm perfectly capable of spending an hour or two unattended."

He certainly looked well enough—a bit wan still, but clear-eyed and sturdy, and in no visible danger of imminent collapse. In fact, he looked far too well for Nessa to trust herself to be alone with him again.

She gave Rory a forced smile. "He's right, brother. Let's go."

THE PROSPECT OF BRIGANDS and murderers didn't make Nessa enjoy the walk in the woods any less. It was good to be out in the crisp fall afternoon, especially after a morning spent in the hospital. All the colors seemed particularly vivid, as if rinsed clean by last night's rain. The trail was still damp, but pebbly enough to give good footing.

"'Tis a shame about the rain," said Rory. "If not for the storm, we might have been able to find traces of what happened to August, but I'm sure they've all been washed away."

They found the basket and knife not far from where Nessa had left them. The knife had the beginnings of a few rust spots, but nothing a good scouring wouldn't take care of. The basket was stuck in some mud and thoroughly wet—rather worse for wear, but not a total loss.

The rain and dew had dried from the valerian plant. Nessa dug around its base to loosen the soil, then carefully eased some of the larger roots from the soil and cut them cleanly with her knife, leaving plenty of smaller roots. She brushed the soil off the harvested roots, wrapped them in a clean kerchief, and put them in her pocket, since the basket was too wet to carry them. Then she worked the remaining roots back into place and tamped the soil over them.

She stood and gazed up at the bright-orange leaves of the sassafras trees overhead, wishing they could tell her what they'd witnessed here yesterday.

Rory was standing just beyond the curve in the trail where August had been found. He was staring not at the trail itself but at a brushy area beside it.

"What is it?" Nessa asked.

Rory pointed. "What do you make of that?" he asked, pointing to a sort of low tunnel through the brush, marked by flattened grasses, broken twigs, and ripped vines. The brush was disturbed only for a foot or two above the ground.

Nessa studied it. "It looks like a kind of animal track. A badger might have made it."

"Two badgers walking abreast, maybe," said Rory. "Or possibly a feral hog. The track is too low for a man to make. Unless..."

"Unless the man were crawling," Nessa finished.

They stared at each other. Rory put his hand to the pistol at his belt as if to reassure himself that it was still there, and Nessa shifted her grip on her herb knife. For a moment she feared that Rory would tell her to go back to camp, but then he gave her a quick nod and glanced in the direction of the low track—the track that had surely been made by August, creeping away on his belly from whoever it was that had battered his head and stolen his memory.

Nessa's mouth went dry, but she nodded back. She didn't actually believe that August's assailant was here at this very minute, waiting to attack them. But the echo of violence seemed to hang over the place.

Stepping carefully, they followed the low tunneling track away from the main trail, stopping occasionally to cut their way through tough, clinging vines. Nessa kilted her skirt and petticoats above her knees. She could move freely enough, but the underbrush snagged her stockings. She imagined August dragging himself through here hand over hand, hurt and confused, the thorns clawing at his flesh. Then she imagined him being struck from behind, his back turned trustingly to his attacker, and dropping to the ground without a cry. A burst of hot anger rose in her. Striking a man from behind was a despicable and unmanly act. Whoever had done it was either a common cutthroat, or a treacherous coward without a shred of honor, and she could hardly say which was worse.

The track led to a narrow opening in a thick stand of sassafras. Nessa and Rory reached the opening, flanking the track, and peered through.

Between the closely spaced trunks was an old clearing that was being slowly retaken by the woods. Near the center of the clearing stood a stone chimney, rising up from the ruins of a timber building.

Nessa and Rory halted at the exact same moment, taking in the structure and its surroundings, looking for signs of a human presence. If anyone *was* there, that person surely would have heard their approach and had time to take cover.

Rory gestured to Nessa to stay put, then crept forward, his pistol in his hand. The sight of that slender, boyish figure, going willingly into possible danger, made her throat swell. Rory might be irritating at times in his protective zeal, but there was no denying his bravery.

Stepping as lightly as a deer, he explored the area, thoroughly checking every conceivable hiding place, before finally telling her, "All right, I think 'tis safe."

Nessa didn't even roll her eyes as she joined him.

From this side, she could see how the second-growth sassafras trees had sprung up all around the fallen cabin in a rough ring, with the older trees at the outer edge, fading to saplings nearer the center.

"I never heard of an old homestead here," said Rory. "Did you?"

"Nay. It looks as if 'twas abandoned decades ago. 'Tisn't far from the trail, perhaps a hundred feet, but you would have to know it was here to find it. Perhaps August made camp here. It seems a strange spot to make camp, though, with army headquarters so close by, not to mention Middleton Place."

"Aye, for a man on legitimate Patriot business. But for an enemy spy, 'twould be ideal."

Nessa's jaw dropped as she turned to face her brother. "Rory! How can you say that? How can you even think it?"

"I don't like the idea any more than you do, sister. But we cannot dismiss the possibility out of hand. We've known the man, if it can even be called knowing, for less than a full day, and he's given no satisfactory account of himself."

"Because he's lost his memory! But you heard the way he spoke about Yorktown, about Washington. August is as much a Patriot as you or I."

Before Rory could reply, a loud *clank* coming from the cabin made them both jump. A cloud of dust, or possibly ash, was rising from the hearth.

The two of them advanced cautiously. Once they reached the cabin's footprint, it was clear what had caused the disturbance. The old chimney crane—an iron arm set on a swivel in the stonework, used for hanging pots over the fire—was lying on the hearthstones. The old masonry had given way, sending the entire mechanism—swivel, beam, hook, counterweights, and all—crashing to the ground.

Nessa crouched down before the old hearth. It was large, a good five feet in width. The cloud of ash was still drifting in the air—fresh ash, from a recent fire. The bottom layer was thoroughly charred, like big coals, and when Nessa held a hand to them, she found them still faintly warm, though the topmost pieces were barely blackened. Last night's rain must have dampened the fire without fully putting it out.

There were other things in the hearth besides firewood. She picked up an iron poker and nudged out a few items. A strip of leather, burned around the edges, such as might have come from the inner lining of a hat. Some scorched fragments of wool. A brass shoe buckle, dark with tarnish. Several brass buttons with a chased copper design, now edged in a greenish patina.

"Nessa."

She'd been so intent on what she was doing that she hadn't realized Rory wasn't with her anymore. Now she saw him standing in a relatively open space near the edge of the clearing, back in the direction of the trail, looking over his shoulder at her. His eyes were wide in his white face.

The ground beside him was recently disturbed, as if by a plow or a wallowing hog, leaving a patch of raw earth about six feet in length.

Her body understood before her mind did. A chill spread from her chest to her extremities.

"Is that..." she began.

"A grave," Rory finished. "Shallow...and empty."

Chapter Six

August's current living space was smaller than one of the barracks tents, where enlisted men slept shoulder to shoulder in a long row, sharing a single blanket. Rory's tent was arranged with separate areas for sleep, work, and personal storage. The addition of August as a tent-mate had complicated matters, with a second straw tick now running parallel to the first along the opposite wall, and the desk crowded between the two beds.

A small looking-glass lay propped against the washing basin in the tent's far corner, where it reflected the linen ceiling. It kept drawing August's gaze. Examining his own reflection seemed an obvious expedient to restoring his memory, but something stopped him from trying it.

The space felt empty without Nessa and Rory. August almost wished he hadn't sent them away. But they both had responsibilities to attend to, and it wasn't right that they should be constantly tethered to him, especially now that he was feeling—not well exactly, but nearly so. His head hardly ached at all anymore, though he didn't have his memory back yet. And he was still plagued by a sort of mental itch, as if there were something important that he must do.

He cast his gaze around the tent, and it landed on the row of books running along the back of Rory's desk.

That was what he needed—a book in his hand. Something to occupy his mind other than his own murky past. Something that made sense.

The desktop was clear of its usual layer of papers. Before leaving for the trail with his sister, Rory had gathered all the dispatches, letters, and notices and packed them in his satchel. August hadn't taken offense. He understood and approved Rory's caution in keeping potentially sensitive military paperwork away from a stranger with no bona fides. To do otherwise would have been unconscionably careless.

He took a seat at Rory's desk and scanned the titles of the volumes there.

A worn copy of Paine's pamphlet *Common Sense*, which had plainly been read and thumbed through many times. Von Steuben's *Regulations for the Order and Discipline of the Troops of the United States*—or the Blue Book, as it was commonly called. A Bible with creases in its spine. William Duane's *A Military Dictionary*. *Poor Richard's Almanack*. One of Vauban's works on siegecraft and fortification. The comic novel, *Tristram Shandy*, by Laurence Sterne.

August didn't make a conscious choice. He reached for the Vauban and opened it. There was some writing on the flyleaf.

To my dear Brother-in-law Rory, on the occasion of his fifteenth Birthday. May the Knowledge you collect in that capacious Brain serve you well, and may it one day be put to a more congenial use than the making of War.

It was signed *Melina Bryant Shaw*.

This must be the wife of the eldest brother, Fergus. Strange how August remembered the names and occupations of all the Shaw siblings when he hadn't the slightest recollection of his own family. Did he have brothers or sisters? Were his mother and father living? Had he said farewell to them before setting out from...wherever it was that he'd set out from? Were they expecting a letter from him? Anxiously awaiting his return?

The questions swarmed around his head like a cloud of gnats, begetting more questions, none of which had any answer.

August flipped through the book's pages until he reached the beginning of the text. His mind registered that this was an English translation, and a helpful voice in his head informed him that the work had originally been published in French, late in the last century.

As he read, his mind began weaving French phrases and sentences through the English text. Did that mean he had studied the book in French at some point in his forgotten past? Did he have a copy of his own, with a personal message written on the flyleaf from some friend or relation whose name and face he couldn't recall?

He shut his eyes. Instantly he saw the image of a map of a many-sided fortress, its parts labeled with numerals whose explanations were given in two neat columns below. He opened his eyes and searched the book. He had only to turn a few pages before he found the map, labeled in English rather than French, but otherwise exactly as he had envisioned it. Glacis, demilunes, bastions, redoubt—the words felt as soothingly familiar as a child's lullaby.

He read on, always with the sensation of being shadowed by half-memories from a phantom life. The helpful voice had another say, reminding him that although Vauban's book was a classic, there were other, more recent works on the same subject with more pertinent and up-to-date information. The names of their authors came to him without effort—Muller, Entick, Watson, Rohr.

As he turned a page, a small sheet of paper came loose and fluttered to the desktop. August picked it up. It was crowded with letters, all of them block capitals, one after another with no spaces between, spelling no words that he could recognize.

He slowly rose to his feet, still holding the paper. Was it a game? A word puzzle of some sort? Or an encoded message? It seemed unlikely that a piece of genuine spycraft would be entrusted to a fifteen-year-old clerk, no matter how clever, much less left stuffed inside a book. Perhaps it was a letter from a friend, a harmless personal message for Rory to decode.

August studied the arrangement of letters, searching for a pattern. Was it a simple Caesar cipher, with all the letters in the plaintext shifted down a set number of places in the alphabet? Or a keyword cipher, with the letters of a given word or phrase substituting for those at the beginning of the alphabet, and the remaining letters following in the usual order? If so, the cipher could be broken easily enough through frequency analysis. Of course, it was possible that the encryptor had done something clever to disguise or eliminate in his message the most commonly used letters in the English language, but that wouldn't stop a determined code-breaker, though it might slow him down. Theoretically, any cipher was solvable, given enough time, effort, and skill.

Difficultates mentem roborant, sicut labor corpus. The quotation floated to the surface of his mind, along with the translation—Difficulties strengthen the mind, as labor does the body.

Well, then. He would work on this little puzzle in hopes that the mental exercise would help bring his memory back. If nothing else, it would give him something to do.

The next thing he knew, he was hearing the distant drum signal for the troops to parade. He looked up and saw that the sunlight filtering through the canvas tent had shifted and dimmed. He'd grown so absorbed in the cipher that he hadn't noticed how much time was passing. Nessa and Rory would surely return soon.

Suddenly he realized how he would appear to them if they were to come into the tent right now—sitting at a desk that was not his, with an open book before him that hadn't been lent to him, reading a message that, whatever its origin and purpose, had never been intended for him. A flush of shame rose hot in his face. He replaced the paper in the book, set the book in its place, and hurried back to his bed.

He had scarcely stretched himself out on the straw tick when the tent flap opened, and Nessa and Rory came in.

He sat up, trying to look as though he'd been innocently resting for the past hour.

Then he saw their faces.

"What is it?" he asked. "What's wrong?"

They exchanged troubled glances. A pit formed in his stomach. They had learned something, something about him, and he wasn't sure he wanted to know what it was.

Nessa reached into her pocket and took out several tarnished brass buttons, some bits of claret-colored wool, and a scrap of buff-colored linen containing a point and a buttonhole that marked it as belonging to the front panel of a waistcoat. Rory opened his satchel and pulled out a coat of black wool, very dirty. The two of them laid the things on the ground before August.

"Are these yours?" Nessa asked.

August picked up the fabric scraps. They didn't appear to have come from a military uniform, but the coat was an army greatcoat. The buttons were of good quality, with a sunburst design in chased copper.

"I don't know," he said at last. "Where did you find them?"

"Not far from the trail where I first came upon you," Nessa said. "Someone had tried to burn them—as you see—but the fire must have gone out before they could be completely destroyed."

She and Rory exchanged another glance.

"What is it?" asked August. "What are you not telling me?"

It was Rory who answered this time. "We found a hole in the ground—a shallow grave with nothing in it. You weren't just left for dead, August. You were buried alive."

August stared at Rory's earnest young face in speechless horror.

Then a wave of remembrance washed over him, nearly knocking him back. He had to brace his hands on the mattress to remain upright.

"August?" Nessa's voice seemed to be coming from a long distance. "What's wrong? Are you remembering something?"

For a moment it appeared that his body had forgotten how to breathe. Then he sucked in a lungful of air and said, "I felt them draping something over me and then covering me with dirt. I heard the scraping of the shovel. I thought it was a dream."

He shuddered convulsively at the memory of the thick fabric against his mouth and nose. Bad enough to be knocked on the head, but to be tossed into unhallowed ground like a dead dog—

"How am I still alive?" he asked. "How did I ever get free?"

"We think we know," said Nessa. "At least, we have a good guess."

"Tell me," said August.

Rory swallowed. "The placement of your wound suggests that you were struck from above and behind. After you—went down—he must have stripped you to your linen. Then he dug a hasty grave and dragged you into it. He spread your greatcoat over you and shoveled the soil back in. The greatcoat would have kept the dirt from filling your mouth and nose. It probably saved your life."

August couldn't speak. He was overwhelmed by a sense of outrage and violation. It was his body that had been bludgeoned, stripped, and tossed away like refuse, his life that had been counted as worthless. Who had done this horrible thing to him, and why?

"Clearly, you weren't robbed," Nessa said. "A thief would have taken your possessions, not tried to destroy them. Whoever attacked you wanted to dispose not only of—of your body, but also of anything that could identify you. The greatcoat is army issue, such as any soldier might wear, but the other clothing is more personal and particular. So he built a fire in the chimney of a tumbledown cabin and laid your things on the flames."

"Why didn't he finish burning them?" August asked.

"He must have been in a hurry," said Rory. "It couldn't have been very long before you regained consciousness enough to crawl out of the grave and drag yourself to where Nessa found you. By that time, he must have been gone."

"And then the storm came, and dampened the fire," said Nessa. "It did come up suddenly, without much warning. Your attacker must have been back in the camp before the first clouds massed up."

"Back in the camp?" August repeated.

"Well, he had to go somewhere," said Rory. "It might have been Charlestown, or Middleton Place, or another plantation in the area. But the camp seems most likely. There are sentries at the far edge of those woods. Why should your attacker bother getting past them to meet you if he didn't mean to stay here? I realize that's taking for granted a certain amount of planning on his part. But all in all, it seems prudent to assume—at least for now—that whoever meant you harm is still here in the camp, and thinks you're dead. If he sees you alive and well, he'll want to finish the job."

"And you don't know who he is," said Nessa. "He could be anyone. So until you get your memory back, we must keep your presence here—your very existence—a secret."

August didn't answer. He didn't like the idea of staying here in this tiny tent while the man who'd tried to kill him walked about at liberty. Part of him wanted to go out this minute, and find that man, and make him pay. But how could he find someone he didn't know? Seeing the man might trigger his memory—but it might not, in which case the miscreant would have the advantage of him. Nessa and Rory were right. His best course of action, at least for the time being, was to stay here and concentrate on getting his memory back.

Speaking of which—

August got to his feet, walked over to Rory's washstand, picked up the mirror, and looked himself squarely in the face.

It was a good face, objectively considered, one that he supposed might be called handsome, with blue-grey eyes, a well-shaped nose, and a sturdy jaw edged with a heavy stubble. Its age might be anywhere from twenty-five to thirty-five. The hair that hung in unkempt, overly long strands was a shade darker than the golden beard.

He waited for a flash of recognition, but none came. He might as well have been looking at a stranger.

"Anything?" asked Nessa's voice behind him.

He shook his head and ran a hand over his light beard. The gesture felt embarrassingly intimate, as if he were touching the face of someone he'd just met.

"I need a shave," he said.

"I can try to get you a razor," said Nessa, but she sounded doubtful. "In the meantime, how about a haircut?"

August only nodded, unable to summon the energy to speak. All the shock and horror had gone out of him, leaving him drained and blank.

"I must go," said Rory. "General Greene wants my help with some documents about the army's reorganization."

After he'd left, Nessa seated August on a stool and started gently working the tangles out of his hair, starting near the ends. He was still holding the looking-glass in his hands, staring at his own face. There was a scar on his chin. He wondered where and when he'd gotten it.

It was pleasant having Nessa's hands in his hair—almost too relaxing, in fact. He saw his own eyelids thicken and his gaze turn glassy and doglike.

He angled the glass upward and caught her reflection. She had that same rapt, tranquil expression as when she'd washed his face for him.

"Do you cut Rory's hair?" he asked.

"When he lets me. He hasn't much patience for personal grooming."

August didn't answer. He felt as if he should say something along the lines of, *Neither had I, at his age,* but of course he didn't have the slightest idea what he'd been like as a boy of fifteen. And yet there was an undeniable kinship between Rory and himself, a likeness of mind and spirit.

"The war has certainly changed the fashion in men's hair," Nessa said. "For soldiers, at least. I think 'tis a change for the better. Short hair is easier to keep clean, and cleanliness is a preserver of health. My eldest brother, Fergus, still wears his hair long, but he has always loved the old ways best."

"Tell me more about your family," said August.

Nessa picked up a comb. "What do you wish to hear?"

"Anything. Everything. I want to know that there are decent, honest, upright, God-fearing people in the world, who don't knock other people on the head, bury them without ceremony, and burn their belongings."

Her reflection met his gaze, and she gave him a warm smile. "I think I can oblige."

She told him how her father and mother had met, decades ago in Antrim County, Ireland. Her father belonged to a family of Lowland Scots who had gone to Ulster Plantation for better opportunities and to escape religious persecution. Her mother's people were French Huguenots who had relocated to the same place for the same reasons. After marrying, they sailed for North Carolina and bought land in Wilmington, where they started a farm and turpentine orchard. Six children followed. Nessa had been only seven, and Rory one, when their mother had died of malaria.

"The whole family was ill at once," she said. "I don't remember it very clearly. Back and forth between fever and chills, day after day and night after night—'twas like a bad dream. And when I woke up...my mother was gone."

He listened without question or comment, letting her words wash over him. Occasionally they set off brief flashes of what might have been memories. The mention of her mother's death called up a dull ache of grief, as if he, too, had lost someone close to him, though he could not say whom or how or when. The story of her parents' voyage across the Atlantic transported him to the rocking deck of a single-mast, fore-and-aft-rigged boat, with salt spray on his face and his eyes squinting against the hard glare of sunlight on the waves.

As her shears snipped through his hair, she told him about her sister Catalyn's marriage to Tavish, a former shipwright's apprentice who now oversaw the family's cattle, and about the distant cousin who had come to stay with the family after the fall of Charlestown and ended up marrying Nessa's brother Fergus. This was the Melina who had given the Vauban book to Rory. She told about the military service—mostly militia—of her father, brothers, and brother-in-law. Some of them had fought at Moore's Creek Bridge, a decisive Patriot victory that had driven the British out of North Carolina, and kept them out, for four years. Fergus had been present for the disastrous Patriot defeat at Camden, and Liam, the middle brother, had run away to sea and served on a privateer.

All the war events Nessa touched on—battles, sieges, campaigns—agreed with August's own recollections. At times her words seemed to jog his memory, and he would think, *That's right—'twas 1780 when Charlestown fell* or *Aye, I heard there was a bagpiper at Moore's Creek Bridge.* There were no surprises, only reminders.

"And how did you and Rory come to be part of the Continental Army?" he asked.

She thought about that. "I suppose you could say it started when the British invaded Wilmington last year. Rory was thirteen. Father was away, serving his rotation with the militia, when we got the news that the British were headed our way. Fergus and Tavish went to join Father. Liam was still at sea. That left Rory as the only man at home."

"A heavy responsibility," said August.

"Aye, but there was nothing else to be done. If the men had stayed, they'd have been killed, and we'd have been worse off than ever. For a time, all was well, or well enough. The militia occupied the region around Northeast Cape Fear, harassing the enemy, keeping them from spreading into the rest of the state. Those of us at home looked after the farm and did our best to put food on the table. And then a British raiding party came."

August glanced sharply at Nessa's reflection. She had her attention focused on her work and did not meet his gaze.

"They slaughtered our oxen and hens, carried off our food stores, and burned some outbuildings," Nessa went on steadily. "We had hidden our mare and some of the food, so 'twasn't as bad as it might have been."

He swallowed hard. "Did they..." he began.

"They started to," said Nessa. "Rory tried to fight them off. 'Twas the bravest, most foolhardy thing I've ever seen—a gangly unarmed boy hurling himself headlong against half a dozen seasoned soldiers. 'Tis a wonder he wasn't killed. He did get some nasty cuts on his arms. He still has the scars."

He waited, still watching her reflection.

"There was an American among the raiders, a Tory," she said at last. "He threatened the lieutenant who was leading the raid—said he'd see him brought up on a court martial if he didn't get his men under control. So the raiders went away."

August quietly let out his breath. He could see it all—the red-coated soldiers, reveling in the destruction they wrought; Nessa and the other women, sick with fear and loathing; and Rory, just as powerless as they against an armed force, but determined to defend his kin anyway.

"Not long afterward, we received word that Father had been taken prisoner at a battle at Rockfish Creek," said Nessa. "He was held in a prison ship in Wilmington Port. 'Twas horrible to think of him wasting away, surrounded by sickness and foul air. 'Twas a horrible time all around for those of us at home, never knowing if our men were dead or alive, desperate for news and yet afraid to hear it. And then Rory went away to join Fergus and Tavish in Lillington's militia."

"He left you and your sisters alone?" August said. "After what happened?"

Nessa shrugged. "From his point of view, he'd already failed to protect us. I think he felt that the best way to ensure our safety was to drive the British out of our state. At least the militia could put a musket in his hands, and maybe even powder and lead to go with it."

August couldn't argue with that.

"It didn't take long for him to acquire the reputation of a great scholar," Nessa continued. "You've seen how he is—clever and mouthy. He started a letter-writing service for men who couldn't write. They'd dictate, and he'd set it all down, tidying up the grammar and adding verbal flourishes as he saw fit. His clients paid him with food rations and swallows of rum. Eventually they stopped dictating and simply told him to make it interesting. That went on until November. By then, General Greene had taken charge of the Continental Army in the South. After we received word of the victory at Yorktown, the Patriot militia regrouped and drove the British out of Wilmington. Fergus went to South Carolina to join General Greene's forces, Father was released from the prison ship, and Tavish and Rory returned to the farm. By Hogmanay, all the men were back home—even Liam, who showed up on our doorstep on New Year's Eve."

"That must have been a happy holiday," said August.

"The happiest I've ever known," Nessa said softly. "I thought the war was over. I never dreamed it would drag on for another ten months. Well, in the early spring, a major in the Fourth North Carolina Continental Regiment was preparing to join General Greene at his new headquarters in South Carolina. He'd been recently promoted from captain and was worried about the paperwork he'd have to do as a major, so he decided to hire a clerk. He recalled hearing about a bright boy in Lillington's militia who wrote letters for soldiers, and made inquiries. Ere long, Rory was on his way to South Carolina with the regiment."

"And you went with him," said August.

"Well, someone had to look after him, and make sure he remembered to eat, sleep, and change his linen. We've both been here ever since. Rory performed admirably for the major, keeping records of meetings, issuing orders, and writing letters. He has a rare gift for taking raw verbiage, perceiving the essence of the message, and converting it into clear, concise, intelligible language. By the time the major retired due to illness, General Greene had lost some of his own staff and was happy to take Rory on. The poor general has his own mountains of paperwork to deal with, and he's taken a friendly interest in Rory's education. He says 'tis a pleasure to feed such a curious, retentive mind. He hasn't seen his own young son in several years, you know, or his daughters. I've gotten to know him as well, when I've treated him for some of his health problems—asthma, malaria, inflammation of the eyes. He has been very good to us both."

August smiled. "The general sounds like a most amiable and honorable gentleman."

"Aye, he is that. We're deeply grateful to him. I believe Rory's time at camp would have been rather bleak and lonely but for him. Rory has always been a sociable boy, but it hasn't been easy for him to make friends here. He's the youngest by far of the clerks and aides, and somehow the others don't seem interested in befriending him. Some of the newest recruits aren't much older than he is, but they look askance at him too."

"He's an outsider in both groups," said August.

"Exactly," Nessa replied.

She laid down the shears and brushed some clumps of hair from August's shoulders. "As far as I can tell, he has only one real friend, a Charlestown boy called Harry Beach whose father and brothers all fought in the South Carolina Continentals—fought and died, to a man. Harry and Rory both have a fighting legacy to uphold, and they're both farm boys, so they have that in common, and Harry doesn't seem to hold Rory's status as a clerk against him. I think they mostly talk about horses and guns."

"One such friend could make all the difference in the world," said August. "'Tis natural, I suppose, when we are separated from our own family and friends, to seek out new friends and surrogate kin—as I have good reason to know. You and your brother have certainly shown great kindness to me, Miss Shaw, and I am very much in your debt. As things currently stand, you are my oldest—nay, my only friends."

He could have said more, much more, about her beauty and sweetness, and how she had captivated him from the start. But he had said enough for a man who had known her for less than a day, if it could even be called knowing when he hadn't even a full name to offer.

"I'm happy to do it," she said. "We both are—Rory and I. But you mustn't suppose that you are all alone except for us. Somewhere in the world, there must be people waiting to hear from you, praying for your safe return. Parents, brothers, sisters...wife."

There was a peculiar heft to the last word, though it was spoken in the same even tone as the rest. August saw the blood drain from his face in the looking-glass. Somehow, in all his wondering about his origins and identity, it had never occurred to him that he might be a married man.

Nessa's reflection caught his gaze. "What is it?" she asked. "Have you remembered something?"

He stood, turned toward her, and looked into her melting-soft brown eyes. "I never thought..." He swallowed. "Could it be? Is it possible that I have a *wife*? That I vowed to love and cherish and be faithful to some woman—and then forgot her name, her face, her very existence?"

Nessa sighed. "Certainly 'tis possible. You can't remember your father or mother. You might easily have forgotten a wife and child as well. It doesn't mean that they don't exist, or that you don't love them."

"A wife and child," he echoed. "That's right. I could have children. I could be someone's father."

Even as he raked his memory, part of him was insisting that he couldn't be married—he simply couldn't. He had forgotten *information*, true—but there were things he knew about himself, things that went deeper than dates and places and names, things of the heart. Surely his marriage, if he had one, would be in that latter category, with Latin quotations, and his sense of familiarity with the army, and his certainty that he was a Patriot. He might forget the name of the woman he loved, he might even forget her face, but he would remember that he loved—and his love for her would be a defense on his heart, guarding him from falling in love with another. If it were not so, then what sort of man was he?

The tent flap opened, and Rory stuck his head and shoulders through.

"Nessa, come quickly," he said. "You're needed at the command center. One of the officers is ill."

Chapter Seven

"But why send for me?" Nessa asked as she hurried along at Rory's side, clutching the satchel she'd hastily stuffed with all the medicaments she thought she might need—no easy task, considering she didn't know whom she was to treat, or for what malady. "Why not one of the surgeons or physicians?"

"I cannot tell you," Rory replied. "I only know what I was told—that one of the officers was taken suddenly ill, and that he had requested you specifically."

"Which officer?"

"I don't know that either."

Nessa pushed down her irritation. It did seem that Rory might have bestirred himself to request a bit more information before running off to fetch her. She could have prepared better if she knew what she had to deal with. And she didn't like leaving August so abruptly, when he was so distraught—though perhaps it was just as well. She hadn't seemed to be doing much good in that particular crisis.

She could still see the change that had come over his face—or, at least, the reflection of it in the looking-glass—when she'd suggested, ever so casually, that he might have a wife back in that lost life of his. The dawning realization, quickly turning to horror—had that been on her account? Was it possible that he felt for her the same stirrings of emotion for her that she felt for him?

Perhaps she was reading too much into it. Naturally it would be a shock for any man to come up against the possibility of a wife and family whom he'd completely forgotten. It didn't necessarily follow that August had any particular feelings for her, beyond friendship and gratitude.

And perhaps it had been tactless for her to bring the subject up at all. But she had needed for her own sake to say the words aloud, to put a hedge of protection between herself and a man who might very well be another woman's husband. And as difficult as the conversation had been, she could not properly wish herself to have done otherwise. There was no genuine kindness in allowing someone to believe a pleasing fiction, at least in so grave a matter.

The trouble was that they didn't know what the truth was in this case—and for the time being, they had no way of learning it. They could only wait, and see what transpired. She only hoped it would transpire quickly.

Somewhere in the world, there might be a woman to whom August had pledged his heart and hand. Any day, any moment now, his memory could be restored. It would all come back to him, the love and devotion of that attachment, and Nessa would shrink to her proper place as a rescuer and caregiver to whom he felt nothing more than kindly interest. Indeed, as she reminded herself again, she had no real reason to suppose that he felt anything more than that for her now. They had known each other, after all, for less than a day.

Until his memory did return, she must not do or allow anything that either of them could later look back on with regret.

And if, after he remembered, he learned that he was *not* married—what then?

She shook her head hard. She couldn't think of that now, couldn't let herself to brood over something so wholly outside her control. There was plenty of work left to be done that was most likely going to require all her mental powers and more, starting with her current errand.

General Greene's command center stood high on Ashley Hill, its location setting it apart somewhat from the noise and bad smells of the camp below. It comprised several tents. The two largest were the sleeping marquee, which contained the general's bedchamber, baggage chamber, and private office, and the dining marquee, for hosting councils of war and formal meals. Smaller tents were used for storage and as offices for those staff officers and aides-de-camp whom the general chose to keep nearby.

The sleeping marquee was oval in shape, with guylines fanning out from the perimeter, stabilizing the structure and keeping the canvas taut. A scalloped valance ran along the ridgepole of the hipped roof, which was flanked by turned wooden finials that topped the upright poles at either end. The dining marquee was like it, but larger. Each tent had a member of the general's life guard standing at its entrance.

A young aide-de-camp had evidently been posted as a lookout to watch for Nessa's arrival; Nessa believed he was called Captain Baker. He pounced upon her and herded her toward the sleeping marquee, leaving Rory behind.

"Thank goodness you've come, Miss Shaw. I don't know what we'd have done if you couldn't be found, for he's insisting he'll not have the care of any of the physicians or surgeons. 'Twas a stroke of good fortune that the chief physician happened to be nearby when the major collapsed—or so we all thought at first. But the major flatly refused to be treated by him, and banished him from the tent. *Get Nessa Shaw,* he said. *She's never flinched away from my wound, and she has more sense than half the doctors in the General Hospital.*"

"We are speaking of Major Elliot, I presume?" Nessa asked.

"Of course," said Captain Baker, as if there could be no other major worth mentioning. "He was having a private conference with the general when he slipped and fell, and the old wound opened up again. The major had his manservant, Scipio, attending him. The general called for me, and between the three of us we managed to move the major to the general's bed."

They had nearly reached the entrance to the sleeping marquee. The captain turned and faced Nessa with an almost pleading expression.

"The major's put his faith in you, miss," he said. "You must rise to the challenge and do what's needful for him without showing any sign of revulsion over his wound. He's sensitive about that. And if he sends you away too..." He trailed away as if the thing were too terrible to put into words.

"But what can I do for him that a surgeon or physician can't, other than keep my countenance?" she asked.

"What can anyone do for him at this point but make him as comfortable as possible?" the captain responded. "His wound's past curing—he knows that. But there's fight left in him yet, and he'll hold on as long as he can. He's a rare one, is the major."

She could hear the respect, bordering on reverence, in the man's tone. It was the same way everyone spoke about Major Elliot.

The soldier at the entrance stood proudly upright, holding his musket in his hand like a walking staff. The weapon's stock rested on the ground, and the razor-sharp bayonet was fixed to the muzzle, its point rising higher than the guard's head.

Nessa paused a moment outside the tent. She wasn't at all sure she could do what was required of her, but she had to do it. There was no other way. This wasn't the first time she'd had to reach down inside herself for reserves of strength that she'd never dreamed she possessed. She drew a breath, raised her head, and went in.

The general's sleeping tent seemed almost palatial in comparison to the tent Rory was currently sharing with August, with canvas walls dividing it into separate spaces and an actual bedstead holding the stacked mattresses off the ground. But the modest wooden folding table that served as a writing desk was no larger than the one Rory used, and the bed's canopy frame was angled to fit snugly under the slant of the roof, like an attic bedroom tucked beneath the eaves.

The bed was neatly made up with plain linens. On it, with his head and shoulders propped by pillows, lay Major Elliot. His face was pale and drawn, the mouth pressed into a tight line.

The stench was not overpowering at first, perhaps because the wound was covered with a towel, which the major clutched to his ruined side with his left hand. His frock coat and waistcoat had been removed and lay in a wet heap on the straw floor. The general's washstand had been moved close to the bed. It held a basin and pitcher on the top and a stack of towels on the lower shelf.

A dark-skinned man stood nearby, anxiously hovering as if he were desperate to help but didn't know how. This was Scipio, the major's manservant. Nessa had seen him before, waiting on the major.

General Greene sat beside the bed on a wooden folding chair. The general was stocky in build, with lowering eyebrows over shrewd, deep-set eyes. He wore the dignity of his office with easy assurance. The son of a Quaker merchant-farmer from Rhode Island, he'd been given no formal education, but had improved his own mind by means of voracious reading on a variety of subjects, including the Classics. Perhaps it was partly for this reason that he had taken such an interest in Rory. He was known to be carefully correct in following protocol, and scrupulously upright in all his dealings, as well as fair and just with his men. At times there had been a coolness between him and some of the officers from Virginia and the Carolinas, at least according to Rory, who'd had plenty of opportunities for observation. Even to Nessa's eyes, the general had the air of an outsider. There had been some grumblings about a New Englander's being placed in charge of the Southern Department—but it was General Washington, a Virginian, who'd made the appointment, and General Greene's performance had proven it to be the right one.

General Greene beamed a fatherly smile at Nessa as she entered.

"And here she is now!" he said heartily. "A most estimable and superlative nurse, as I have reason to know. She has treated my asthma many times. Her black walnut concoction gave me relief when nothing else could."

Major Elliot darted a gaze at Nessa. "Miss Shaw," he said, the words tight and clipped. "Thank you for coming."

He was clearly in agony, and Nessa pitied him from her heart, but she knew better than to show it.

"How could I possibly refuse a chance to be of service to everyone's favorite major?" she asked, in the breezy, cheerful, bossy elder sister air that had served her well at so many sickbeds. "Especially after you were good enough to cut through the red tape with that requisitions clerk earlier today on my behalf."

General Greene got to his feet. "I don't know what that means, my dear, but perhaps I should not inquire too closely. Scipio has prepared for you as best he could. We have a basin of water here, and more in the pitcher, and a full kettle freshly boiled, besides all these bowls and towels—and I see you have your basket of herbs and potions and such. If you need anything else, please don't hesitate to ask. I'll keep Baker posted just outside the tent, and Scipio will be here to attend you."

Scipio bowed his head to her.

The general turned to Major Elliot. "I leave you in excellent hands, Andrew. I hope and believe you will be resting comfortably soon. Please consider this tent to be your own for as long as necessary. My steward is arranging other accommodations for me for tonight."

"Thank you, General. I am sorry to turn you out of your own bedchamber. I'll return to my own quarters as soon as I'm able."

It was the longest speech he'd yet made, and clearly cost him considerable effort.

"Please think nothing of it, sir, and do not put yourself to any unnecessary strain," said the general. "I'm sure Miss Shaw will agree with me that you must conserve your strength."

Major Elliot gave the general a hard stare. "You will remember what I told you?" he asked.

A shadow passed over the general's face. "Be assured, Major, that I will give the matter all the attention it deserves. Now set your mind at rest, and allow Miss Shaw to take care of you."

As General Greene made his exit, Major Elliot shut his eyes and let out the sigh of a man who has done all he can and must now leave the outcome to others.

Nessa set her basket on the floor beside the washstand. She started taking out the herbs she needed—yarrow, plantain, comfrey, calendula, lavender—and placing them in a cheesecloth bag.

"Has the major had any laudanum yet?" she asked Scipio.

"Nay, nor will he," said Scipio. "Laudanum fogs the mind, and the major considers it unmanly. He prefers to keep his wits about him."

Nessa heard the tolerant exasperation in Scipio's voice, as if he were dealing with the whims of a headstrong but beloved child. Personally, she thought mental fogginess a small price to pay for pain relief, at least in a case like this, but she didn't say so. It was admirable of the major to wish to bear up well and maintain his soldierly standards of conduct.

The major opened his eyes long enough to exchange a brief wordless glance with his servant. Nessa got the feeling that there was a deep sense of understanding and trust between these two.

She tied up the sack of herbs, placed it in a bowl, and covered it with boiling water. A clean, wholesome, soothing fragrance rose up in the steam. She set the infusion aside to steep and took a seat on the chair the general had vacated. The time had come to see the wound.

At her bidding, the major unfolded his arm, and she removed the blood-soaked towel from his side.

The sight of the wound filled her with pity and horror, but she was able to keep her face calm.

"How did it reopen?" she asked.

It was Scipio who answered. "The major took a fall while rising from his chair in the general's office," he said, tilting his head toward the adjoining chamber where the writing desk was. "He was rather fatigued at the time. He's been overexerting himself of late."

"If he was fatigued, perhaps he should have postponed today's meeting," she said. "I'm sure the general would have been happy to accommodate him."

"The major had a matter of some urgency to discuss," said Scipio. "It could not be delayed."

Someone had had the foresight to cover the general's bed with a pitch-coated tarpaulin before laying the major there—a wise precaution, since the wound's exudations would otherwise have befouled the bedding and mattress. Nessa could smell the sharp piney scent of pitch, faint but pure, rising above the stench of putrefaction. It made her think of home, where her father and brothers drew the resin from colossal longleaf pine trees and turned it into turpentine and tar—or had done so, before the war had put an end to the naval stores trade with Great Britain. Growing up in a pine forest, she had taken the scent for granted. She'd never learned to love it until she'd gone away.

Nessa kept tight control of her face as she drained the wound into a metal pan. Her distress was less for the appalling stench than for the idea of all this having been inside the major's body, fomenting like poison. Physicians often spoke of laudable pus, and regarded its presence in a wound as a sign of healing, but in Nessa's experience it did not bode well for recovery.

Once she drained what she could, she sopped up the rest of the fluids with clean towels. Then she irrigated the wound with water from the pitcher, followed by the wound-wash infusion, while Scipio held another metal pan to catch the runoff. The raw flesh looked better now that it was cleansed, but it was still red and angry, and Nessa knew that even after a fragile layer of new skin closed over the gaping, ragged hole, more fluid would form beneath the surface. True healing for such a wound was beyond her skill—perhaps beyond the skill of any mortal physician.

All this time, the major didn't make a sound, though Nessa knew the pain had to be overwhelming. His face was the color of whey; he was breathing like a racehorse, and he gripped Scipio's free hand so hard that Nessa thought the bones must break.

She blotted the wound dry, then covered it with a fresh dressing. The sun-bleached linen looked clean and soft, but she knew it would not long remain so.

"All finished," she said.

The major let out a ragged sigh and released Scipio's hand. His breathing had almost returned to normal, and his face had lost some of its pallor.

Nessa drew herself up tall and stern, the way she had seen some of the doctors do when addressing their patients. "I've done what I can, Major. Now it is time for you to do your part. You must have complete bed rest for a month at least. Otherwise, your wound will have no chance to knit itself together."

His pale eyes regarded her calmly. No doubt he thought she was putting on airs, mimicking medical authority, when in fact she was nothing but a farmer's daughter with a strong stomach, a better-than-average knowledge of herbal lore, and a talent for telling people what to do.

"Impossible," he said. "My work—"

"Your work will have to wait, or someone else will have to do it. Come, Major. Surely the fate of the nation does not rest solely on the efforts of a single officer, no matter how capable."

His expression clouded, and for a moment she thought she had offended him. Then the ghost of a smile flickered at the corners of his mouth. "You probably think me foolish for not retiring from the army at once after receiving my wound at Guilford Courthouse."

She did think something like that. Viewed from a certain perspective, Major Elliot's persistence in service was admirable, but in her eyes it smacked of vainglory.

"I think you're a man of strong convictions, who is determined to do all he can to secure his country's future," she said.

"You're more right than you know," he said. "And there's plenty of work left to be done, even by crippled bureaucrats in the Quartermaster

Department. The war isn't over, Miss Shaw. There's time yet for all the Patriots' efforts to be undone—if not by open warfare, then by subterfuge."

A chill of fear stole over Nessa's heart. "Are you speaking theoretically, Major Elliot? Or are you aware of some specific threat?"

"It is too soon to tell the precise nature of what is being planned," said the major. "The conspirators are biding their time, keeping their mouths shut. But there is definitely a conspiracy afoot, both in the camp and in the town. Of that I have no doubt whatsoever."

Nessa began putting away her herbs and tidying her basket. The port city of Charlestown was a mere fifteen miles from the camp, just across the Ashley River, and had been in British possession ever since its fall two years ago. Through the port, it was possible for the garrison to be reinforced by the British fleet. Six months earlier, the Royal Navy had beaten the French fleet in the West Indies, restoring British naval supremacy after the humiliating defeat at Yorktown. At this very moment, a British fleet could be crossing the Bar, eager to reverse other losses and take vengeance on the Patriots.

There was a concourse across the river, in goods and intelligence, between the enemy in town and some of the so-called Patriots who lived on plantations west of the Ashley. It wasn't supposed to happen, but it did. Had the British leaders in Charlestown found a way to communicate with disaffected soldiers here in the camp as well? If so, they could lay their plans at their leisure and bide their time, waiting for the perfect moment to strike. It would not be the first time the Continental Army had been betrayed from within its own ranks.

"You look very thoughtful, Miss Shaw," said Major Elliot.

"Aye. I was just thinking that there is something especially sickening about treachery. An open enemy is bad enough, but for someone to pretend to be a friend, to smile and speak smooth words, only to stab you in the heart—" She shuddered. "It is despicable."

"And also effective," the major replied. "The weapons of open enmity are messy. Siege warfare, artillery barrages—they conquer by widespread destruction, turning the spoils of victory into a wasteland, with only an impoverished and embittered populace to tend it. Those who wish to preserve what they conquer must choose subtler means—and they can usually find some pragmatic person on the opposite side who is willing to open the wicket gate, so to speak."

Nessa didn't answer, and after a brief silence, Major Elliot changed the subject.

"General Greene seems to think very highly of your young brother. Before you arrived just now, he was entertaining me with the story of how his letter-writing business led him to become the youngest clerk in the Ashley Hill camp."

Nessa smiled. "Aye, the general has taken a great interest in Rory's education, and lent him many books. He's been most kind to us both, and of course we think the world of him. Do you know, I've often wondered what would have happened if General Greene had been placed in charge of the Southern Department two years ago, instead of General Gates. The defeat at Camden might have been a Patriot victory, and the war might have ended by now."

"Perhaps so. But Congress was determined to give the honor to General Gates—the Hero of Saratoga." His voice dripped with revulsion and contempt. "What nonsense. Benedict Arnold was the real Hero of Saratoga. He was ten times the field commander that Gates was. It sickens me to think of Congress falling over themselves in their haste to strike off a medal for Gates while Arnold lay grievously wounded with that mangled leg of his."

He smiled at Nessa. "Am I shocking you, Miss Shaw, by praising a traitor?"

"Not at all," said Nessa. "You praised his valor and ability, not his treachery. This is no more than simple justice."

"Very fair-minded of you to say so. General Arnold was indeed a valiant fighter and a brilliant commander, who deserved better than to be repeatedly passed over for promotion in favor of lesser men. But no grievance, however legitimate, can excuse what he did afterward. Conspiring with the British against his own people! Offering to hand over his own men to a foreign army, in exchange for money! 'Twas a betrayal most foul."

His voice rose on the last words, and he lay back, exhausted by his own vehemence.

"There, Major! You must compose yourself," said Nessa. "General Arnold has done harm enough. Don't let him impede your healing."

The major took a few deep breaths. "You are right, Miss Shaw. Hating Arnold is a waste of energy. Have you heard that he's been made a Brigadier General in the British Army? Quite a step down from the rank of Major General that he held with the Continentals. And whatever rank the British may bestow on him, whatever sop they may offer to his pride, his career is finished. How can they ever truly trust a man who has already turned his coat once? How can anyone? His reputation will precede him, professionally and socially, for the rest of his life. No one respects a traitor."

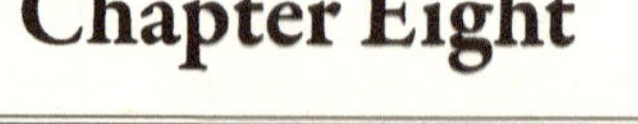

Chapter Eight

Nessa walked home in the twilight, limp with exhaustion. She'd done all she could for Major Elliot, and left him clean and relatively comfortable. But she had that awful sick feeling in the pit of her stomach, the feeling she always got when she knew a patient wasn't going to get better—the feeling of failure.

What if the same thing happened with August? What if he never got his memory back, and had to live the rest of his life without knowing who he was or where he'd come from? He would be trapped, unable to move forward without a past to ground him. Nay, the possibility was intolerable. She wouldn't let it happen. The three of them—August, Rory, and Nessa—would solve the puzzle of August's identity. They must—and soon.

It was suppertime in the sutler's row. The briny, greasy smell of salt pork in its various forms rose up from the cookfires to meet her. She and August would dine alone tonight. Rory was dining with the general, and helping him prepare for tomorrow's staff meeting.

Dining alone with August might be awkward, in light of their unfinished conversation about his potential wife. But he'd had time to compose himself, to put things in perspective—and so had she. The way forward was clear. She would forget the feeling she had for him, ignore it, pretend it had never been, and treat him as she would any patient.

She reached Rory's tent and drew back the flap.

August wasn't there.

She stood frozen in the doorway for one solid, blank moment before bolting back outside, where she spun in a slow circle, searching, and finding nothing but other camp followers going about their own business. August was nowhere to be seen.

Where could he be? She had told him how vital it was that he remain hidden while his attacker was at large. Surely he wouldn't have willingly left the safety of the tent. Unless...

Was it possible that his head injury had taken a sudden turn for the worse? She'd known that to happen once before in the hospital. A man who'd suffered a bad knock to the head had seemed to be recovering, only to abruptly lose consciousness and die. None of the doctors could explain why. Even in this enlightened scientific age, there were things beyond the understanding of the wisest, and the brain was especially mysterious. What if August had suddenly lost the new memories he'd made since his injury? What if he'd forgotten all about Nessa and Rory, forgotten his own name again, and wandered off? He might have strayed into the river, or collapsed. At this very moment he might be lying helpless and alone, easy prey to whoever it was that wanted him dead.

Panic rose, hot and fluttering in her throat. She turned back the way she'd come, took a few hurried steps—

And ran straight into August.

It was like running into a wall. His chest was solid, hard, and broad. She hadn't realized quite how tall he was, probably because she'd rarely seen him standing fully upright. Nessa was tall for a woman, but he loomed head and shoulders above her. He looked the picture of health, big and robust with bright eyes, and color in his cheeks, gazing down at her with a puzzled expression.

She sucked in a great strangled gasp of breath, threw her arms around his neck, and held him as if she would never let him go.

He stood still a moment before putting his own arms around her, tentatively at first, and then with increasing firmness. His hands were warm against her back.

They were attracting notice. People were staring at them in frank curiosity. Nessa tore herself loose from the embrace, seized August by the hand, and dragged him to the tent.

The tent flap had barely dropped shut before August asked, "Miss Shaw, whatever is wrong?"

"What's *wrong*?" Nessa cried. "How can you ask that? Where were you, August?"

"Nowhere," he said.

It was the instinctive, disingenuous answer of a small boy trying to evade punishment. Nessa made an indignant sound. August opened his mouth, closed it again, and finally said, "Well, if you must know, I had to ease myself abroad, as it were."

Ordinarily she would have smiled at the biblical euphemism, so typical of August, who seemed to have a quotation for every occasion. But fear had made her angry, and his light, humorous tone was fuel to the fire.

"That was careless and unnecessary," she snapped.

"On the contrary, I assure you 'twas very necessary."

"Don't be flippant! Didn't you hear anything Rory and I told you today? Someone tried to kill you, August. And as far as he knows, he succeeded, and you're dead and buried in a shallow grave in the woods, not strolling around the camp at your leisure. You can't show your face until we know who he is and how to protect you from him."

August gave her a calm smile. "Come, Miss Shaw. You cannot seriously mean for me to stay inside that tent every minute of every day."

"That is exactly what I mean. I didn't save your life only for you to throw it away. You're my patient—my responsibility. You will stay in the tent until I say you may leave."

The smile vanished. "And let you and your brother carry my slops and wait on me hand and foot? Nay, I won't do it. Not when I've got two perfectly good legs of my own."

They were indeed perfectly good, long and lean and well-muscled, the most perfect legs she had ever seen on a man. But she mustn't allow herself to be distracted by such thoughts.

"Listen to me, August. It is not safe for you in the camp. If your attacker sees you, he'll have the advantage over you. He'll recognize you, but you won't recognize him."

"You don't know that. Seeing him in the flesh might be exactly what I need to bring my memory back."

Nessa threw up her hands. "'Twill be too late by then! 'Tis probably too late already. He probably saw you just now and is planning how to finish you off at this very moment."

August's mouth flattened into a thin line. "I am not quite the helpless idiot that you believe me to be, Miss Shaw. I kept my wits about me, and no harm came to me, as you see."

"But you've been seen, August. You're a big, broad, long-limbed man. You'd be distinctive in any company, much less an army camp filled with emaciated men. All hope of keeping your presence a secret is gone now."

"Secrecy was never an option, Miss Shaw. Not really."

He took her hands in his and looked down at her. "Please try to understand. I cannot lie around your brother's tent, waiting for my memory to return, letting others bear the burden of my existence. 'Twould be unmanly and despicable. I must do something on my own account to get my memory back and learn what my mission is."

"And how do you intend to do that?" she asked.

"Simple. First thing in the morning, I'm going to the command center. 'Tis high time I made the acquaintance of General Greene."

AUGUST'S BODY SEEMED to know as well as his brain did that he was in the presence of Major General Nathanael Greene, Commander of the Southern Department, Washington's close friend and most trusted officer. The stiffening of August's spine, the crisp brevity of his speech as he answered the general's curt questions—he had never felt like more of a military man, at least within recent memory, than he did now.

But it was more than a trained response. Setting aside the reverence due his office, General Greene was a man worthy of respect. Since taking command in the South, he had brought back the Continental Army from the brink of disaster and set it on the road to victory—not only through his brilliant military leadership, as at Guilford Courthouse and the breathtaking race to the Dan, but through tireless administrative work and the delicate balancing of egos in the Continental Army and the militia. It was more than admirable. It was heroic.

The general was sitting at the head of the table in his dining marquee, with August and Rory on either side of him, and Nessa next to August. Nessa and Rory had done most of the talking, telling the general how August had been found, alone and hurt on the wooded trail, and what the two of them had found there when they'd returned for Nessa's basket. They'd told the general all that they had learned or deduced about August—his level of education, his fluency in languages, his wide knowledge of books. August himself had told of his apparent familiarity with military life and with principles of artillery warfare.

"But the clothing remnants you found in the fire were not from a uniform," said the general, addressing Rory and Nessa while keeping his gaze fixed on August. "Which would seem to argue against his being currently in the army."

"Not conclusively, though," said Rory. "Most of the men in the camp don't have uniforms anymore."

"True. But in my experience, officers generally manage to find a way. And I think it extremely unlikely that this young man, if he is or has been part of the Continental Army, would be anything less than a lieutenant."

It was unnerving, being spoken of in the third person before his very face. August struggled to keep his countenance as the general gave him a long, searching stare.

"There's another thing that's evident about him that you haven't mentioned," the general said at last. "I daresay you haven't noticed it."

"What's that, General?" asked Rory.

"He's a southerner."

"Oh," said Nessa. "Why...I never even thought about that."

"Because you're a southerner yourself," said the general. "It takes an outsider to recognize it—a certain something in the speech and bearing, a certain courtliness, a cherishing of one's honor. You don't see it, because you take it for granted. Fish are always the last to discover water."

Sighing heavily, the general turned his gaze on Nessa, then Rory, his stern eyebrows lowering even farther over his deep-set eyes. "You should have come to me straight away, as soon as he was found. The presence of an unknown man in the camp is a serious matter. There are a hundred questions to be answered, not the least of which is how he got past the pickets—assuming he hasn't been within the camp all along, which I believe is a reasonable assumption. I'll show him to all those who served on sentry duty the night he was discovered, and to my senior officers. Even if he isn't part of any regiment here, there's a chance one of them has met him on a previous occasion at a different command."

"But won't that put him in danger?" Nessa asked.

"Perhaps. But it is the best way of getting him seen by anyone, friend or foe, who might recognize him. We cannot afford to wait for his memory to return on its own. I would rather err on the side of more knowledge than less."

"*Scientia potentia est,*" said August without thinking.

General Greene gave him an inscrutable look. Belatedly, August remembered that the general was said to be sensitive about his own lack of formal education. Perhaps it would be wise to rein in the Latin quotations for a while. August knew he was far from earning the general's trust, but he wanted to do it, wanted it with urgent intensity.

What if the general doesn't believe me, doesn't trust me?

The question rose up in his mind, almost as if he were hearing an echo of his own voice asking it aloud, followed by another voice, answering.

You must make him believe you. You must, and you can. You have powers of persuasion enough, when you choose to use them. That's why I'm sending you. You mustn't fail me, August.

Was it a memory, or only a fancy? August couldn't tell. Scraps of dialogue, vague impressions, and quotations were constantly drifting to the surface of his memory, and he had no way of setting them in order, no fixed point from which to start.

The general's gaze drifted to somewhere past August's shoulder. August turned and saw an aide-de-camp hovering unhappily in the entrance to the tent.

"What is it, Captain Baker?" the general asked.

"Please forgive the interruption, General," said Captain Baker. "I thought you would want to know immediately. A man's been killed. Stabbed to the heart, right in the middle of the camp."

Chapter Nine

The dead man appeared to be from thirty to forty years of age by Nessa's estimate, though she had noticed that soldiers who had seen active service often looked older than they actually were. He had close-cropped dark hair, a large nose, and patches of dark stubble on his jaw. He was a big man, with rough, capable hands. His eyes and mouth were half-open, and he was raggedly dressed in worn breeches and a grimy hunting shirt.

Nessa was standing in a loose semicircle with General Greene, August, and Rory. After receiving news of the man's killing, the general had said that August might as well come along to view the body. Another act of violence in so short a time might well be related to the attack on August. Nessa and Rory had not been invited by name, but they'd come along anyway, and the general hadn't stopped them. Nessa was accustomed to dead bodies from her work in the hospital, and so was Rory, from his time in the militia.

A crowd had gathered at an uneasy distance. Nessa saw the familiar fresh face of Harry Beach, Rory's young friend. Rory raised a hand in greeting, but almost at the same instant, Harry turned away, and Rory disguised his wave by rubbing his hand along the back of his neck. Nessa felt sorry for him. Rory was so eager to be counted a man among men, and his intellectual capacity often made him seem older than he was, but he was still a boy, after all, with a boy's hopes and vulnerabilities. And no one liked being snubbed, even on accident.

The body had been found at a supply depot in the interior of camp, behind some crates at an unloading area, and moved into a more open space. The chief physician was already on the scene when General Greene arrived accompanied by August, Nessa, and Rory. This was the same doctor who'd been ordered away by Major Elliot, the one who was so fond of mercury ointment. The doctor was cool and collected enough now, hitching up the dead man's shirt and pointing out the thin, narrow cut just below the sternum.

"I would have to open him up to be certain," said the doctor, "but it is my judgment that the assailant's blade pierced the victim's heart."

"Wouldn't that cause a great effusion of blood?" asked General Greene.

"Not necessarily. Sometimes in a wound of this sort, the heart muscle seizes up and essentially quits pumping. In such a case, death is nearly instantaneous, and relatively bloodless."

"The killer smote him under the fifth rib," August said softly. "The same way Joab killed Abner in Second Samuel."

"Correct," said the doctor. "Such a wound would not be an easy one to inflict. It would have to be done at close quarters, clearly, by someone familiar with anatomy, and possessing great strength in the upper body."

"A prudent choice for a killing committed in a crowded camp," said the general. "No sound from a gunshot, and no chance for the victim to cry out before his heart seized up. Not much blood on the murderer's hand, either. How long has this man been dead, Doctor?"

"I would estimate between twelve and twenty-four hours, judging by the extent of rigor and lividity."

"Yesterday or last night, then." The general glanced at August. "And you were attacked some time the previous afternoon or evening, also in a stealthy manner, by someone who was able to get close to you. Well? Do you know this man?"

August slowly shook his head. "I wish I could be of help, General, but his face is not familiar to me. Of course it is possible that he was known to me before my memory was lost, but if so, I cannot recall him now."

The general gave a quick nod and turned to Captain Baker. "Has the man been identified?"

"Aye, General, by the supply clerk who found him this morning. The dead man is Walter Boyd, a sergeant under Major Bronson."

"A South Carolina man, then. Has the major been notified?"

"Aye, sir. He was here a moment ago, but I don't—ah, here he comes."

A tall, thin man in a threadbare blue coat approached the group. He bowed to the general, then looked down at his dead sergeant with an air of detached curiosity.

"Well, Major Bronson," said the general, "this is a strange business. What can you tell me about this Sergeant Boyd? Any complaints about him?"

"Nothing egregious," the major replied. "He's been reprimanded a few times for slovenliness in dress and for appearing drunk on the parade ground. Not a model soldier by any means, but far from my worst."

The general nodded grimly. Nessa knew how it must pain him for such behavior to be tolerated and considered not especially bad, but there was a limit to how much order could be enforced in a camp full of idle men with no pay and never quite enough to eat.

"When I got word of Sergeant Boyd's death, I immediately had his tent searched," said the major. "I supervised the search personally, and—well, General, I think you'll want to see what we found."

The general sighed. "Captain Baker, I think you'd better reschedule this afternoon's appointments. It looks as if I'll be occupied with other things for the rest of the day. Lead the way, Major. And August, you might as well come along again. I expect this will turn out to concern you also."

He didn't include Nessa and Rory in the invitation, but he didn't exclude them either. The two of them exchanged silent glances and followed the general to a tent the same size as Rory's. A guard had been posted at the entrance.

Major Bronson drew back the tent flap and fastened it back with a loop. The contents of the tent looked unremarkable—a blanket-covered straw tick, a rough wooden trunk, a mound at the foot of the bed that looked like extra bedding.

"'Tis all here," said the major. "Nothing has been removed, and everything has been put back as near as could be managed to the way it was before it was searched."

He reached inside, picked up what looked like an old tobacco pouch, and handed it to General Greene. The general opened it to reveal several folded papers. He took out the first one and unfolded it.

The page was covered with block letters, but the letters did not make words in any language that Nessa could recognize. The general opened the remaining pages one by one. These also contained mystifying combinations of letters, different from the first, but similar in overall form.

"Encrypted messages," said General Greene. "Interesting! It appears that Sergeant Boyd was involved in something of a mysterious nature."

"May I?" asked August, holding out his hand. The general gave him the sheets. August quickly scanned the first, then thumbed through the rest.

"Well?" the general asked. "Can you make any sense of them?"

"A bit," said August. "At first glance they appear to be written in a simple Caesar cipher that should easily yield to frequency analysis. Do you see this three-letter word here, and here, and down here? Judging from its position in the sentences, I would guess it to be the word *the*. This single-letter word either *I* or *a*—probably *a*, which would make this other three-letter word *and*. Then here's *in* and *an*, and probably *are* and *on*. That gives us several letters: T, H, E, A, N, D, I, R, and O. Nine letters—over a third of the alphabet. So if we were to write out the alphabet in order, and place the known substitution letters from the ciphertext underneath, we could see what pattern emerges, and extrapolate the rest."

"That all sounds encouraging enough," said General Greene. "Why are you frowning?"

"Well, sir, it all seems too easy. You see how the letters are grouped into word-sized units, and punctuated in what appears to be a reasonable way? A cautious coder would eliminate spaces and punctuation altogether, or perhaps add them at random to give a false impression. But as I've already recognized a few short words, that doesn't appear to be what was done here. It seems unconscionably careless. And a substitution cipher seems a poor choice for any enterprise in which secrecy is important. There are so many better choices available—mathematical ciphers with grids, Vigenère ciphers, steganography—"

"How long would it take you to decode these messages?" asked the general.

"No more than an hour, if they're as simple as they appear," said August. "But I can hardly believe that anyone with a message worth encrypting would choose so unsophisticated a method—unless there is a hidden layer of complexity, a message within a message."

"Perhaps there is no great secret to conceal," the general replied. "These may be playful letters from a sweetheart or a child, meant to be easy to decipher."

"Perhaps so," said August, but he didn't sound convinced.

General Greene studied him a moment. "You appear to know quite a lot about cryptography, August. Is it possible that you worked in army intelligence at some point in the past?"

"I cannot say, General. I don't know how I learned these things. I only know that I know them."

Major Bronson, still standing at the tent flap, gave a gentle cough.

The general turned back to him. "Did your search of the sergeant's belongings turn up anything else unexpected, Major?"

"It did, General. There might be a perfectly good explanation for it, but I thought it rather curious."

He stepped into the tent and turned over the folded blanket that had apparently served Boyd as a pillow. Underneath lay a brace of pistols, along with a bullet pouch and powder horn.

"Curious indeed," said General Greene. "Hand me one of the pistols, Major Bronson."

The major did so.

"Finely made," said the general. "Spanish, I daresay."

"Aye, from the Eibar region," said August. "Walnut stock, with mounts of chiseled steel and a miquelet lock."

He spoke lovingly, almost reverently, and his gaze was fixed on the beautiful weapon. The general's eyebrows lifted. "These pistols are familiar to you?" he asked.

"They're mine," said August. "I'm sure of it. I don't remember where I got them, or how long ago, but I know they're mine."

"Intriguing," said the general.

The major coughed again.

"More?" the general asked.

"Aye, General. Just one more."

The major crouched down to the bundle at the foot of the bed, and pulled back the blanket to reveal a saddle.

THE SADDLE WAS A FINE one, though worn and scuffed. The sight of it filled August with a kind of tingling excitement. The major picked it up and carried it outside the tent, where he set it on a tree stump.

A bag was fastened to the pommel. August knelt, opened the flap, and reached inside. Some part of him seemed to know what he would find there.

A spare shirt, clean and neatly mended. A pair of stockings rolled up. A straight razor with an ivory blade. A whetstone. A travel mirror of silvered glass, shattered into a spiderweb of cracks.

He took them out one by one and set them down. Small personal effects, of no great importance to anyone but their owner, and looking meager and pitiful huddled together around the base of the tree stump.

He picked up the razor again and turned it over in his hand, searching for...something. And there it was.

August held up the razor to General Greene, who took it and peered closely at the ornate initials engraved on the ivory handle.

"*A.F.*," the general read. "A for August. F for...?"

Desperately August riffled through his mind, searching for surnames beginning with F. Franklin? Farris? Forrest? None of them seemed quite right.

"I don't know," he said at last.

He looked down at the other things again, waiting for something, anything, to trigger his memory. Nothing.

He picked up the mirror and stared at a reflection still strange to him, now shattered into a fractured image. He longed to bring all the separate shards into alignment and see himself not as a collection of parts, but as a unified whole, a man with a past, a character, a purpose.

"There's a crumpled bit of paper on the ground," Rory said. "It came out of the saddlebag when you removed the shirt."

August picked up the paper. It was covered with writing. He smoothed it flat and read aloud.

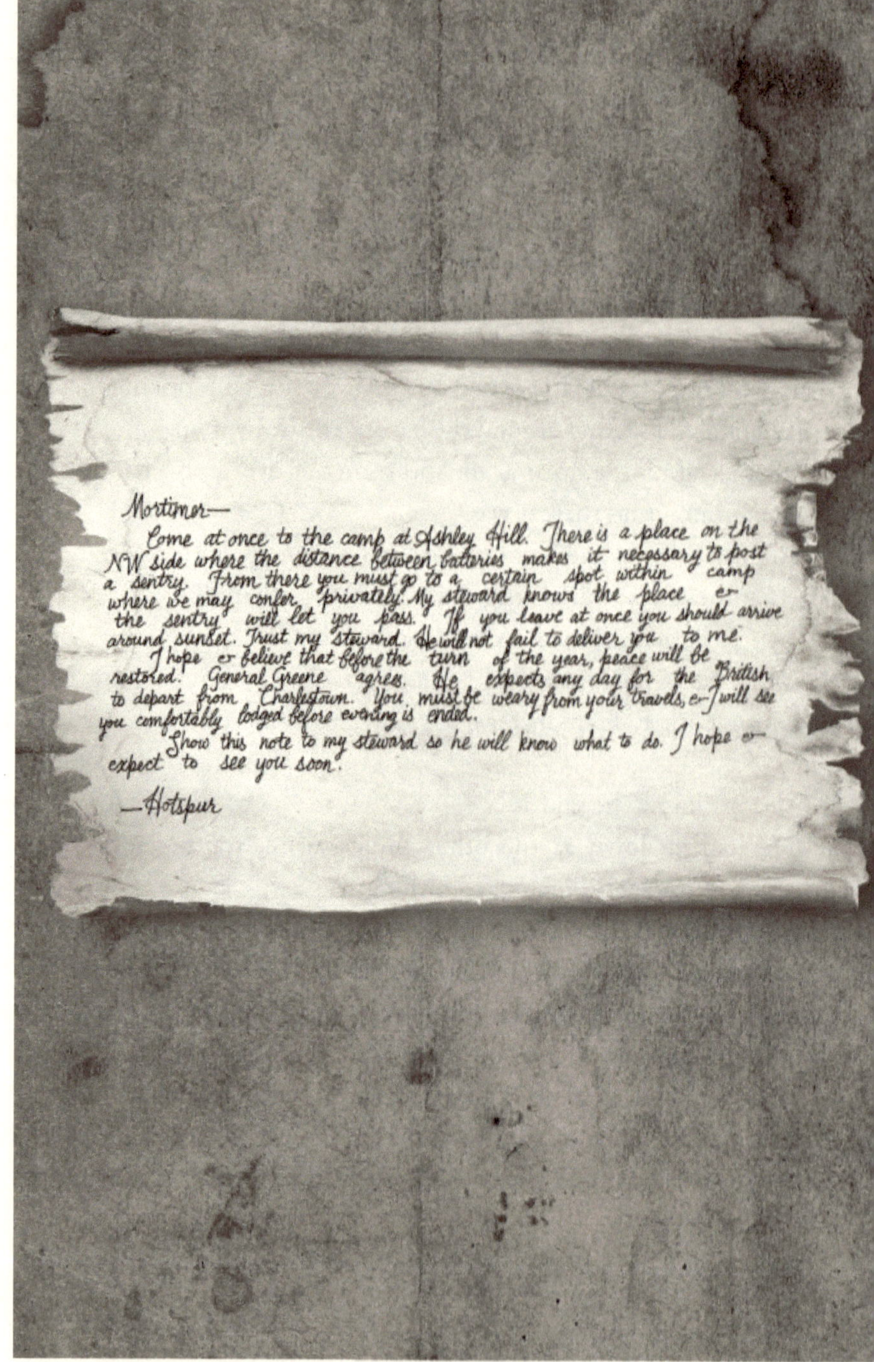

Mortimer—
Come at once to the camp at Ashley Hill. There is a place on the NW side where the distance between batteries makes it necessary to post a sentry. From there you must go to a certain spot within camp where we may confer privately. My steward knows the place & the sentry will let you pass. If you leave at once you should arrive around sunset. Trust my steward. He will not fail to deliver you to me.
I hope & believe that before the turn of the year, peace will be restored. General Greene agrees. He expects any day for the British to depart from Charlestown. You must be weary from your travels, & I will see you comfortably lodged before evening is ended.
Show this note to my steward so he will know what to do. I hope & expect to see you soon.
—Hotspur

Mortimer—

Come at once to the camp at Ashley Hill. There is a place on the NW side where the distance between batteries makes it necessary to post a sentry. From there you must go to a certain spot within camp where we may confer privately. My steward knows the place & the sentry will let you pass. If you leave at once you should arrive around sunset. Trust my steward. He will not fail to deliver you to me.

I hope & believe that before the turn of the year, peace will be restored to this land. General Greene agrees. He expects any day for the British to depart from Charlestown. You must be weary from your travels, & I will see you comfortably lodged before evening is ended.

Show this note to my steward so he will know what to do. I hope & expect to see you soon.

—Hotspur

He slowly lowered the paper, then handed it to General Greene, who studied it in silence.

"Well, August," the general said at last, "it appears that you came to the camp by invitation—assuming that Mortimer and Hotspur are pseudonyms inspired by Shakespeare, and not the given names of our correspondents. Do the names have any special significance to you?"

"Nay. I don't know why those particular names were used, or why the writer believed it necessary to use pseudonyms at all. Possibly he was concerned that the message might be intercepted."

"Who wrote this message? And what is the errand of which he speaks?"

"I don't know," August said again, weary of the words he had spoken so many times over the past day and a half. "I can't remember. But, General, I do feel certain that whatever it may be, it is of vital importance to the war effort."

A long silence passed. The general's gaze bored into August, and August stared right back at him.

"Very well," said the general. "Gather up these items and carry them back to the command center. Let's see what you can make of those encoded messages."

AUGUST SAT AT THE GENERAL'S dining table with several sheets of foolscap, a few quills, a bottle of ink, and the messages from Sergeant Boyd's tent spread out before him. His head was bent over his work, so low that his light-brown hair almost skimmed the tabletop. Nessa had watched him start by writing out the alphabet in one long line across the top of the foolscap. He'd been working continuously ever since, writing intently without looking up or speaking a word.

Rory sat across the table from him, flipping through a copy of *The Commentaries of Gaius Julius Caesar* that he had picked up from one of the bookshelves the general kept in the dining marquee. It had been his habit since childhood, whenever he went on a visit or paid a social call, however brief, to open up a book from his host's collection and read, or at least skim. Often he managed to finish an entire volume over one or more visits.

"How is the major today?" Nessa asked the general. "Is he still recuperating in your tent?"

"I believe he is better," the general replied. "He insisted this morning on being taken back to his estate. He departed just after breakfast."

Nessa frowned. "Is he well enough to travel?"

"I could not say. But he swore he would not rest properly until he was back under his own roof. He requested a leave of absence, which I naturally granted. I hope that being free from the cares and vexations of his work here will allow him to heal."

Nessa hoped so, too, though she privately believed that resigning his commission would have been a more practical step for the major at this point in his career, and she imagined that General Greene, though he could not say so, would agree.

"And how is Mrs. Greene?" she asked. "Have you heard from her lately?"

She had met the general's wife some months earlier. Caty Greene was a lively, playful lady, and devoted to her husband. Nessa liked her very much, and wished she could have spent more time with her, but Mrs. Greene had been sent to Kiawah, one of the Sea Islands, for her health.

The general's expression softened. "I had a letter not long ago from General Gist, who has been convalescing from fever and ague at Kiawah Island. He tells me that Mrs. Greene has become quite a gamester, having developed an immoderate passion for backgammon. She had a run of losses recently which led to her throwing the dice at General Gist's head." He chuckled. "My dear Caty! I do hope I shall have her with me again soon."

At that moment, August threw his quill to the table as if he had just finished a timed exam. He let out a long sigh and frowned down at his work.

"Well?" asked the general. "Have you got the message decrypted?"

"Aye. 'Tis a simple Caesar cipher, as I thought. I've copied the plaintext here, in this bottom paragraph."

He slid the paper over to the general, who scanned the paragraph, looked sharply at August, and then turned his gaze back to the paper.

"What is it?" asked Rory. "What does it say?"

"It is a demand for more money," said the general, "and a threat to reveal the entire plot, and betray the conspirators, if the demand is not met."

Nessa and Rory exchanged stunned glances. "So much for its being a playful exchange with a sweetheart or child," said Nessa.

"But what *is* the plot?" Rory asked. "What is it that the writer is threatening to reveal?"

August pushed the first encrypted message aside and picked up the next one. "Perhaps this will tell us."

Within a short time, August had decoded the entire stack of messages from Boyd's tent. This turned out to contain not only incoming messages, presumably intended for Boyd, but also copies of outgoing messages, written in a different hand, which he had evidently sent to his correspondent in Charlestown. Taken all together, they gave the broad outlines of a plot between the British in Charlestown and some agents within the camp, the main thrust of which was to kidnap and kill General Greene.

A shadow passed over the general's face in the shocked silence that followed the reading aloud of the final message. Nessa thought suddenly of the conspiracy that Major Elliot had warned him about.

"Why on earth did Boyd keep copies of his own messages?" August mused. "I can see why he would think it best to hold on to the incoming messages as future leverage or security for himself, though that precaution doesn't seem to have worked well for him. But what was the point of keeping copies of the messages he himself had already sent?"

"I think we can assume that Sergeant Boyd was no brilliant strategist," said General Greene. "Nor were his co-conspirators, I daresay."

"But the other conspirators did manage to kill Boyd," said Rory. "And from what the doctor said, the killing was very cunningly done."

"They didn't manage to get hold of the incriminating papers before Boyd's tent was searched, though," said Nessa.

"True," said August. "But then again, the papers are incriminating only to Boyd himself, and only because they were in his possession. We cannot tell from the messages who his co-conspirators are, only that there is a conspiracy."

"What I want to know," said Rory, "is where August fits into things. We all got a good look at Sergeant Boyd. He was a big man, and looked strong enough to have whacked August on the head, dug a grave for him, stripped him, and buried him without much trouble. And August's belongings were found in Boyd's tent. Which suggests that although he took precautions to keep August from ever being identified, he was greedy enough to set caution aside for the sake of a good saddle and a fine pair of pistols. But if Boyd tried to kill August, then who killed Boyd?"

"One of his fellow conspirators, I should imagine," said Nessa. "He threatened to expose them, and they quietly eliminated him."

"And how did the conspirator, or conspirators, get close enough to Boyd to kill him?" asked General Greene. "Either there are more conspirators in the camp, or our perimeter defenses leave much to be desired. Probably both."

"And why did Boyd try to kill me, if it was Boyd?" added August. "What threat did I pose to him?"

No one answered.

"I will follow up on this matter," said General Greene. "In the meantime, let us hope that the rest of the conspirators are as hapless and ineffectual as the unfortunate Sergeant Boyd. Master Rory, I require your presence this evening. I want you to go through written correspondence from all the officers in the camp, and from merchants, tradesmen, assemblymen—every man within a twenty-mile radius who has ever sent me a letter, a note, a bill, or a receipt."

"What am I to look for?" asked Rory.

"A handwriting match to the note from August's saddlebag. We need to know who invited him here, and why."

"Could Boyd himself have invited him?" asked Nessa.

"The handwriting on the note doesn't match that on any of the encrypted messages," said August. "A clever and cautious man could disguise his handwriting, but only if he thought there was reason to do so."

"Exactly," said General Greene. "We must also requisition a new tent so that August and Rory need not share any longer, and arrange for August to receive daily rations for as long as he resides in the camp."

The general rose, and Nessa, recognizing that she and August were being dismissed, rose also. August straightened his papers, got to his feet, and faced his host.

"General Greene, allow me to say how grateful I am for your fair and generous treatment of me. I realize that for an unknown man to suddenly appear in the middle of your army camp, without explanation and without antecedents, places you in an awkward position. Thank you for doing me the great courtesy of allowing me to take part in trying to unravel the mystery of my own identity. I understand, of course, that the Spanish pistols must remain in your possession until I can produce better proof of ownership than my own word. I look forward to finding that proof, and earning your trust."

It was handsomely said, and Nessa's heart warmed to hear it. The frank gaze of the steely blue eyes, the candid eloquence of the words—how could the general help but trust August? The loss of his memory was no fault of his own, and clearly he was doing everything he could to regain it, and freely sharing all the knowledge he did possess.

The general bowed his head in acknowledgment. "I will keep them safe until they can be restored to their rightful owner. In the meantime, you may take your saddle and personal effects. Good-bye, Miss Shaw. Good-bye, August. I expect I shall be in touch with you ere long."

August carried the saddle at his side, propped on one hip. He and Nessa headed back to the sutler's row together.

"If you have a saddle, you must at one time have had a horse," said Nessa. "I wonder what became of it."

"So do I," said August. "I wonder a great many things. Where I came from. Why I came. What happened to me. Whether anyone is awaiting my return."

They walked in silence a while. Then August said, "I'm glad we went to General Greene. I can see why Washington trusts him, why he values him not only as an officer, but as a friend, as a man. He is as intelligent and capable as he is virtuous."

"Aye, he is that," Nessa replied. "A lesser man could not have borne the strain of these past months of inactivity and suspense. I've heard him say that he looks back with longing on last year's actual military campaigns, as perilous and demanding as they were. The race to the Dan, the logistical tangles of moving armies here and there, the fighting at Guilford Courthouse, Hobkirk's Hill, Ninety-Six, Eutaw Springs—he says they are all to be preferred to sitting around having a staring contest with the British, waiting for them to leave, hoping they don't realize how fragile is our hold here, and trying to keep the army together long enough to uphold the illusion of superior numbers."

"I understand his feelings. I am in a similar position of enforced idleness. I cannot tell you how heartily I wish that I knew what this mission of mine was, and could get busy performing it. Time keeps slipping away, and perhaps at this very moment, some carefully constructed scheme is crumbling to dust for lack of action on my part."

"Aye, it must be hard. But you have not been idle, August. You're taking the action that is available to you. That is all anyone can do."

He turned and gave her a smile. "Thank you. And thank you for going with me today, and staying with me through all the coming and going. I cannot tell you how heartening it was, whenever I was being questioned, to see your face, and know that I had at least one ally—someone who believed in me implicitly, to whom I did not have to prove myself. Two allies," he corrected himself hastily. "You and Rory."

"Well, of course," said Nessa. It was strange to be thanked for something she hadn't thought twice about doing. She had gone because she wanted to, and stayed for the same reason. As for believing in August, she deserved no credit for that. She believed him, because she must. She couldn't help it.

They reached Rory's tent. Nessa drew back the flap and held it open while August carried the saddle inside and set it down on his bed.

"I'm afraid you sacrificed a great deal of time on my account this morning," he said. "Are you scheduled to work at the hospital today?"

"Evening shift. I still have a few hours before I start. I'm not sure how I'll pass the time until then. After the morning we've had, I feel too unsettled to begin anything."

"Well, I know what I'm going to do," said August, lifting the saddlebag's flap. "I'm going to have a shave."

Chapter Ten

August opened the razor and squinted down its edge. It was a fine blade—hollow-ground, concave on both sides—and well-maintained. Evidently he was the sort of man who took good care of his belongings, a thought which cheered him.

He laid the blade flat on the coarse side of his whetstone and drew it toward himself ten times, then turned it over and repeated the process on the other side. The movements felt familiar and right. He flipped the stone and went through the same motions on the medium grit side.

Meanwhile, Nessa was pouring water into Rory's basin and arranging soap and towels on the washstand. She propped the looking-glass against the pitcher, then gave the whole arrangement one final approving nod before turning to August.

"What are you smiling at?" she asked.

"Was I smiling? I was only thinking what a superb nurse you are, Miss Shaw, and how sorry I will be on the day you decide I'm fit enough to do without your solicitous care."

A faint blush rose in her cheeks, but she said only, "I don't deserve such praise. I can't bear to be idle, and when I see a job that needs doing, I do it, because I must. There's no special merit in that. And I think you might as well call me Nessa. It seems wrong for you to say Miss Shaw while I call you by your Christian name. It makes me feel as if I'm the mistress of a dame's school and you're a small boy I must teach to read and write."

August began soaping his face. "You could assign me a surname," he said. "You could call me Mr. Finkelblaffen."

Nessa laughed. "Nay, I don't believe I could call you that. Besides, the forced proximity and familiarity of our circumstances have made the observation of formalities rather absurd. Wouldn't you say so?"

"I would indeed. Very well. We will be August and Nessa to one another—like brother and sister."

He hoped his voice did not betray how very sweet was her name on his lips, or how very unbrotherly were his feelings toward her. He had in fact been longing to call her by her Christian name ever since he'd first heard it. *Nessa*—it was a fine, strong, beautiful name, and it suited her to the ground.

He drew the blade over his skin in short strokes. The edge was marvelously sharp, and habit helped him, guiding his hands, reminding him to change directions to accommodate the grain of hair growth and to hold his mouth just so to keep the flesh taut around the scar on his chin. He still felt as if he were inhabiting a stranger's body, with a stranger's face looking out at him from the glass, but at least the body knew what to do.

Nessa drew up a stool and sat down to watch. "'Tis wonderful how quickly you were able to decipher that pile of messages today," she said.

"I suppose," August replied.

"You sound doubtful."

"Because I am. I still think 'twas too easy. With so many sophisticated ciphers to choose from, why would a serious conspirator use a code so easy to crack?"

"Easy for you, but I don't think you can be taken as a baseline for the average man. Most likely our conspirators have never even heard of those sophisticated ciphers. They probably thought they were being quite clever."

August dipped his blade in the water and watched the whiskers float away. "Perhaps you're right. The most advanced ciphers were developed and perfected in France and Spain over centuries. It could well be that the British simply haven't had as much practice with court intrigue—and spycraft in the United States is still in its infancy, after all."

"What an awful lot of time those French and Spanish conspirators must have spent working their complex mathematical schemes, all for the sake of a few lines of communication," Nessa said. "It doesn't seem like the best use of resources for people who have ministers to topple and regimes to overthrow."

"True," August said as he inched the blade down his neck. "But there are ways of quickly encoding and decoding a message while still making it indecipherable to outsiders. The ancient Spartans used to wrap strips of parchment around rods and write their messages crosswise. When the strips were unwound, the characters were transposed, and the message couldn't be deciphered without a rod of the proper width. And a man in Florence invented a method of laying down a sort of stencil or mask, writing the plaintext in the openings, and filling in the rest of the page with other characters irrelevant to the plaintext. The decryptor had only to cover the ciphertext with a mask of the same size and shape, and the true message would appear."

"That does seem clever. I suppose that if the encryptor did a good enough job with the irrelevant characters, an outsider could look at the message without even realizing there *was* any hidden meaning."

"Exactly. And that would be the cleverest encryption of all."

Nessa sighed. "I wonder how you know all these things."

"So do I," August said. "I can't remember actually learning any of it. I simply know it—the way I know how to talk, and walk, and dress myself."

"Well, however you came by the knowledge, your being here now, when there is a threat to General Greene's life, is providential. I'm glad to have you on our side, and I'm sure the general is too."

August chuckled. "I imagine the general is hedging his bets. He doesn't know me, and I haven't yet proven myself to him."

"Nay, I'm certain you're wrong. The general can't help but see how honorable and upright and truehearted you are. Those things show through all the time, as plainly as your being able to speak French."

The fervency of her tone warmed him through. She sounded indignant at the very thought that anyone could doubt the sterling quality of August's character—and she had known him for less than two days, during part of which he had been unconscious.

"How strange it is to think of General Leslie over in Charlestown, acting as though he would like nothing better than to sail back to England with all his troops and leave us in peace, when all the while he is plotting to have General Greene assassinated," Nessa said. "I despise that sort of duplicity."

August's hand slipped, and he nicked his Adam's apple. A drop of blood splashed into the basin, tingeing the water faintly red.

"Your feelings do you credit," he said gravely. "For my part, I can see the necessity during war for sleights and stratagems that would be dishonorable at other times. I may not like it, but I do understand it. As for General Leslie, 'tis possible that he's unaware of the whole scheme. We cannot tell how far up the chain of command the conspiracy reaches. It could be the work of a fringe group within the British rmy."

"Well, however high up it goes, 'twould do harm enough if it took place. Did you ever hear the rumor of a failed British plot to kidnap General Washington early in the war? Imagine if it had been successful."

August shuddered. "I cannot bear to think of it. Without Washington, the Revolution would never have been more than a short-lived uprising, barely worth a footnote in a history book. He was the only man capable of uniting men from thirteen wildly disparate colonies into a single fighting force. He alone had the military experience, the reputation, and the character. New Englanders respected and trusted him, and he was fair and just in his appointments of officers, rather than giving preferential treatment to his fellow Virginians. He was—is—the man of the hour, the man of the century, called by a loving Providence to lead us to liberty. If the plot had succeeded—if we had lost Washington—the Revolution would have been lost as well."

"Aye, and much the same can be said of General Greene. I know he feels himself to be an alien among us, a New Englander in the South, and he has clashed with local militia leaders and government officials at times, but he has their respect and their loyalty. Losing him, even at this stage of the war, would be a death blow to the Revolution. There is simply no one capable of taking his place."

"Well, we won't let it happen. *Praemonitus, praemunitus*—forewarned is forearmed."

He turned his head, pulled at his cheek to tighten his skin, and shaved one final spot behind the corner of his jaw. Free from stubble, his reflection was sharper and clearer, and possibly more familiar, though it might have been merely that he was growing accustomed to his own appearance. He bent over the basin, rinsed away the last of the soap, and picked up a towel to dry his face and neck before turning toward Nessa.

"Well?" he asked. "How do I look?"

He regretted the words the moment they were spoken. They smacked of vanity, and more than vanity—of the wish to be assured that the object of his affection found him handsome.

A soft glow came into her expression as her gaze wandered down his face. His heart skipped a beat.

"Younger," she said at last in a light, playful tone, "but more resolute. And less like a Prussian grenadier."

He smiled, disappointed and relieved at the same time.

"*Je parle*," Rory recited, his gaze fixed in the middle distance. "*Tu parles. Il parle. Elle parle. On parle. Nous parlons. Vous parlez. Ils parlent. Elles parlent.*"

"Excellent," said August.

Rory cast a skeptical glance down at the *Table de Conjugaison* that August had drawn up for him. "And all the forms are pronounced exactly the same except for *nous* and *vous*? Even though the spellings are different?"

"That is correct," said August.

Rory accepted this linguistic quirk of the French language with a quick nod and moved on to the next verb in *Mode Indicatif, Présent*.

The two of them were in Rory's tent, which felt wonderfully roomy now that August's bed and belongings had been moved to a private tent in the sutler's row, not far from here.

Five days had passed since August had been presented to General Greene. Rory's search through the general's correspondence had yielded no match in handwriting to the note found in August's saddlebag. This had hardly been unexpected, but still it was disappointing. The general had shown August to all the senior officers, none of whom had recognized him. The officers had then followed up on reports of men who had gone missing from the camp, but those all seemed to be clear cases of desertion, and none of the missing men answered to August's description. None of the sentries had recalled letting him into the camp—or if they did, they hadn't admitted it. He had also been taken to Middleton Place and shown to the household, but no one there had recognized him either. And no one else had come forward claiming to know who he was, though he now moved freely about the camp. Neither had he regained any more of his memory.

The broken skin on his scalp had knitted back together, and the swelling had gone down. His head still ached, but only a little, not like at first. There was absolutely no reason for him to lie around all day while others waited on him. He was fitter than many of the men on active duty in camp.

But August had no duty, no role, no antecedents, no identity. He couldn't simply be assigned to a regiment. The general had no way of knowing his service record, whether it was honorable or otherwise, or whether he had in fact served at all. August understood. But he'd been driven half-mad by inactivity—until he'd hit on the idea of tutoring Rory in French. Here was something that needed doing, but was not official army business, and August was eminently qualified to do it.

Rory was a first-rate scholar, voracious for knowledge and quick to assimilate it. When he made a mistake, he didn't waste time or energy with self-recrimination or complaints about the difficulty of the subject matter. He simply accepted correction and moved right along. He was humble enough to know that mastery would take time, and confident enough to believe he could achieve it. Teaching him was a genuine pleasure.

Nessa thought August was pushing himself too hard, that his mind needed rest to put itself back in order. The trouble was that August's mind refused to rest. It kept going whether he wanted it to or not, around and around in endless circular arguments, or twisting tortuously through mazes of unanswered questions, past the point of exhaustion, like a rat chewing on coca leaves. And the subject it returned to again and again was Nessa herself.

Even now, she was in his thoughts, hovering behind the vocabulary and verb conjugations—her proud red head, her warm brown eyes, her wide, full-lipped smile. She was no delicate blossom of a woman, but tall and strong, and at the same time graceful and feminine, moving with a competent energy that wasted no movements and shirked no effort. Opinionated, and unafraid to make her opinions known, but never overbearing. Firm, but tenderhearted, gentle. She was the most beautiful and desirable woman that August, with his considerable range for imagination, could imagine—and if he were free to pursue her in all decency and decorum, he would do so in a heartbeat.

But he wasn't free, as she herself had so scrupulously reminded him. That unknown past of his separated him from her as surely as a verified marriage would have done. He could not court Nessa Shaw until and unless he learned that he was not already a married man.

And if it turned out that he did have a wife—well, at least then he would have his answer, and be released from the agony of uncertainty.

How would his supposed wife feel, assuming her existence, if she knew how cleanly she'd been erased from his memory by a simple knock to the head? It wasn't as if he'd meant to forget. He couldn't even remember his own surname, his own birthday. But surely that potential shadow-wife would feel, as August himself could not help but feel, that love should be more indelible than that. Rightly or wrongly, he believed that love would leave its mark, independent of intellectual knowledge, and safeguard his heart against forming a new attachment.

He could be wrong. It was possible that he loved his wife devotedly, and that once his memory was restored, his present feelings for Nessa Shaw would vanish like morning mist, like a dream, and he would be amazed and ashamed that they had ever existed.

But he didn't believe it.

Was it a sin for a married man to feel the way August felt about a woman who wasn't his wife, when he couldn't remember that wife's existence? That was not for him to say. But while his marital status remained in doubt, it was his clear duty to keep himself above reproach.

All this August thought while another part of his mind attended to Rory's recitation and occasionally corrected his pronunciation. When Rory reached the end of the table, he immediately started again. The boy was indefatigable, and August was proud of him.

Rory finished the table again and began a third time, faster than before, and hardly pausing to look down.

"That's enough for the present," said August after the third pass. "You've been studying for two hours now. Give your mind a chance to consolidate what it has learned."

Judging from the look on Rory's face, he didn't like the idea of mental rest any more than August did, but he made no protest.

"Is your sister working the afternoon shift at the hospital today?" August asked. He felt self-conscious even speaking of her to Rory, as if Rory would see right through his pretended nonchalance.

"Aye," Rory replied. "The men miss her when she isn't there. They ask for her by name. Some of the doctors, too—the sensible ones, at least."

"Naturally," said August. "I imagine she excels wherever she goes, in whatever she does."

"That's true. Of course, she already knew much about herbal lore, and had plenty of brothers and sisters to look after for practice. It didn't take long for her to become a highly sought-after nurse—only a week or so after we joined the army's camp at Bacon's Bridge, in the spring."

Some bit of memory niggled at August's consciousness. He tried to catch it, but it eluded him.

"You have that look that you get whenever you're trying to remember something," Rory observed.

"'Tis something to do with Bacon's Bridge," August replied. "Something happened there, did it not? Something to do with the army—something bad."

"You're thinking of the Gosnell mutiny," said Rory.

The words connected like a puzzle piece sliding into place. "That's it," said August. "I don't remember the details, but I remember the name."

"There aren't many details to know. The mutiny was discovered before it could properly begin. The ringleader, Sergeant Gosnell, was tried in a court martial and executed the next day, and that was the end of it. Gosnell was a Pennsylvania man, part of the regiment that got reconstituted and sent to the South after an earlier mutiny in Morristown."

"I remember that mutiny," said August. "'Twas in the winter of...eighty-one, I believe."

"Aye, that's right. Sergeant Gosnell was actually one of the Morristown mutineers who was pardoned and reenlisted. I guess the army should have taken a harder line with them. The trouble was, the men had legitimate grievances. They had received no pay since the twenty-dollar bounties they'd been given upon first joining the army three years previously, though they'd been promised wages. Other states paid more, and even Pennsylvania was by then giving bigger bounties to their newer recruits. It must have been rather hard for the men who'd served so long, and borne the brunt of the fighting, to see the new men paid so well—all while suffering through a New Jersey winter with constant heavy snowfall and shortages of food and clothing."

Rory's description of the Morristown mutiny stirred August's own memories of the event—secondhand memories of Washington's frustration over the deplorable living conditions at the Morristown camp, and charges of corruption and indifference among state governments and members of Congress in allowing those conditions.

"Hard indeed," said August. "But they took an oath. They swore to support the American cause, fight for the liberty and independence of the United Colonies, and faithfully serve in the Continental Army until the end of the war or until their terms of enlistment expired. They swore to obey the orders of their superiors—"

"—and uphold the principles of freedom and democracy," Rory finished with him. "I know. But—"

"But nothing. The oath wasn't conditional on Congress doing its part, or pay being given promptly, or the orders being the right ones, or the superiors being particularly competent. It was a unilateral vow, one that they undertook voluntarily."

Rory sighed. "You're right. I suppose an oath is a dangerous thing."

"It is. If there were no risk of living to regret an oath, there would be no reason to take one in the first place. That is what oaths are for, to hold the oath-maker to his purpose after the first flush of fervor has passed."

"I saw Gosnell's execution," Rory said quietly. "He behaved well, giving away his possessions to his friends, and expressing a proper remorse at what he had done. He didn't blame the court martial. He said they had no choice but to find him guilty. He was shot by a firing squad from his own regiment."

August didn't reply. It seemed a horrible thing for a teenage boy to have witnessed—but Rory, too, had taken an oath, and so, in all likelihood, had August, at some point in his past. Perhaps more than one. Oaths of allegiance and fidelity, which he was honor-bound to uphold, whether he remembered them or not.

"Well, sir," August said briskly, "you have made an auspicious beginning in your study of French, and I expect your progress to be rapid. You have a remarkable facility for languages."

"I know it," said Rory without guile. "I like language study. A foreign language is like a code to be broken."

"All language is a code, when you think about it," said August. "Letters are symbols for sounds, which when put together in a certain order form words, which in turn are symbols for things, both concrete and abstract. By the time those words are written down, you have something several degrees removed from the original—and that's before considering metaphor, idiom, poetry, satire, and the like."

"Not to mention actual code," said Rory.

"Aye," said August with a chuckle.

Rory thought a moment, then said, "I got to see an interesting bit of code some months ago. You'd have liked it, August. A patrol on the far side of the Cooper River found a man heading northeast. He said he was a merchant on his way to North Carolina to visit his sick mother. The patrol searched him and discovered a paper covered with an odd sort of writing. It looked like a cipher."

Instantly August thought of the paper he'd seen tucked inside Rory's Vauban book. "Really? Did it look like the papers from Sergeant Boyd's tobacco pouch?"

"Nay, there were no spaces between the letters, and the line lengths were all the same length, like they'd been made with a grid."

With difficulty, August suppressed his excitement. "And what account did the traveler give of this mysterious paper?"

"He said it was a game he played with his brother in North Carolina, encoding messages for each other and then decoding them. The messages were nothing important, only nonsense verses or comical stories. So the soldiers told him to decode this one for them. Then his story began to fall apart. He backtracked, saying that he hadn't actually written this one and hadn't yet had time to decipher it. In that case, they asked, why was he taking it with him to North Carolina? Well, suddenly it appeared that there was a third brother from Georgia, and the letters were sent by round-robin. When they asked him the names and addresses of these brothers, and of the sick mother, he refused to say another word. So they brought him to the camp and put him in confinement until they could figure out what to do with him. But when morning came, he was dead."

"That all sounds highly suggestive," said August.

"Doesn't it, though? Army agents made inquiries about him, but no one had ever heard of a man by the name he'd given, which was no more than they expected at that point."

Keeping his voice light, August asked, "And the message? What happened to it?"

Rory shrugged. "Lots of officers studied it, but none of them could break the cipher. Eventually it was passed on to me, but I couldn't make anything of it either."

"How long ago was this?"

"Oh, months ago. Nothing came of it that I know of. 'Tis possible that the message really was something of no great import—personally embarrassing or compromising to the bearer, perhaps, but of no significance on a larger scale."

August thought otherwise. From what he'd seen, the cipher was an advanced piece of encryption, not a cheap parlor trick. With the original messenger dead—he was clearly only a courier, not a principal—the sender could easily try again. By now the message might well have reached its intended recipient. And just because nothing had yet come of it didn't mean that nothing would.

A drumroll sounded from somewhere outside.

Rory jumped to his feet. "Is that the noon tattoo already? I've got a meeting to go to."

He picked up his satchel and stuffed it with quills, a bottle of ink, and a small hand blotter.

"Whatever happened to the cipher?" August asked. "Were you given a copy?"

He was skating rather close to the edge now, but Rory didn't seem to suspect anything. "I was, but I don't know what's become of it. I must go now. I wanted to arrive a few minutes early."

"Go," said August. "I'll straighten up here. Oh, and Rory?"

Rory stopped halfway through the tent flap and looked over his shoulder. "Aye?"

August opened his mouth and hesitated for half an instant before asking, "Might I borrow some reading material from you?"

"Of course!" Rory replied. "Anything you like."

He was gone without another word, leaving August alone in his tent. August waited a minute or two, then pulled out the Vauban.

The book immediately fell open to the page where the cipher was kept. It was like a sign—or a temptation.

He could break this encryption. He knew he could. He didn't know how he'd come by his knowledge of the Vigenère cipher, or the cipher of Suarez de Figueroa, or the Imperial cipher of 1555, or any of the other ciphers currently rolling around in his head, desperate to be put to use—but he had that knowledge. It was his to employ in service to his country. At this particular time, in this particular place, he might be the only one capable of deciphering this particular message.

He laid the paper on Rory's desk, took out a fresh sheet of foolscap and a spare bottle of ink, and began to write.

Chapter Eleven

"**I** don't wish to alarm you," said Nessa in a low voice, "but I think we're being followed."

It was a fresh, crisp Sunday afternoon. Nessa and August had just been to divine service and were now taking a walk around the camp. Several minutes earlier, she'd turned around to answer a greeting from another nurse, a cheerful, hardworking woman who had a grown son in the army. As the three of them chatted, Nessa happened to notice a man a few yards behind them. There was nothing remarkable about his appearance; he was of medium height and build and had a bland sort of countenance. She probably would have forgotten all about him if she hadn't noticed him a second time when she'd stopped to remove a stone from her shoe. There he was again, ten feet or so away, casually observing the crowd, the sky, anything but Nessa and August. And just now, when she'd stolen a quick look over her shoulder and seen him a third time, she could no longer believe that his presence at the same distance could be coincidental.

She wished she could believe that she was being irrationally anxious, but in fact there was nothing irrational in thinking that whoever had tried to kill August would be keeping a close eye on him now.

August didn't break his stride or turn his head. "Sandy-haired man with a narrow face, wearing a hunting shirt? Sort of a medium, nondescript fellow? He's been following me for days. I don't know his name, but in my mind I've been calling him Sandy Slinkalong."

Nessa stopped in her tracks. "Why didn't you tell me?"

He smiled down at her. "Why should I tell you? Are you my bodyguard as well as my nurse?"

"Don't be flippant, August. This is a serious matter. In case you've forgotten, a man tried to kill you not long ago."

August took her arm and started walking again. "We must keep moving. Standing still makes things awkward for Mr. Slinkalong. Aye, Nessa, I'm aware that someone tried to kill me. It may have been Sergeant Boyd, or someone in league with Boyd, or someone else altogether. 'Tis quite possible that that individual, or some person or persons connected to him, knows that I survived the attack and is currently planning how to get rid of me. But I doubt very much that anyone is going to try to whack me on the head on a Sunday afternoon in the middle of a promenading crowd."

"Boyd wasn't whacked on the head. He was stabbed by someone who knew how to quietly pierce a man's heart with a single knife-stroke. A cool-headed assassin like that would have little difficulty killing a man in a crowd. He could melt away before you hit the ground."

"He's had ample opportunity before today, and he hasn't struck yet. Whatever his motive, Sandy Slinkalong is merely keeping an eye on me, as I am keeping an eye on him. Please don't worry about me, Nessa. I have my wits about me and I'm on my guard."

Don't worry? There had already been one attempt on his life, a man had been tailing him for days, and he told her not to worry?

Before she could think of a sufficiently indignant reply, a voice called out, "Make way!"

The crowd parted, pressing itself to either side of the wide track. Nessa and August drew near to a large supply tent. On the track's other side, Sandy Slinkalong climbed onto a tree stump and shaded his eyes with his hand to see what was happening.

A horseman was coming, with a second horse tied by a lead rope with its head close to the rider's leg. As they passed, Nessa saw that a third horse was tied to the second horse, and on and on in a long procession. A few additional horsemen, armed with whips, followed to keep order, but their presence hardly seemed necessary. The horses being led, like those being ridden, were all lean, gaunt creatures with jutting hipbones and dispirited walks. It made Nessa's throat hurt to see them. She thought of the horses at home, Bran and Hector and Boudicca, and sent up a quick prayer that the war would end soon and all the army's horses could leave this place and go to good pasture and good homes.

The final horse in the procession was not tied to another horse, but was being led by two handlers, one on either side, each holding a lead rope. This animal was a dark buckskin with a deep-brown coat. His legs and muzzle were black, as were his mane and tail, and the dorsal stripe running down his broad back. Thick bands of muscle laced his neck and chest. He was a strikingly handsome beast, clearly the product of distinguished breeding, and just as clearly out of humor with his current situation.

As he drew near to them, he lifted his proud head and let out a long whinny.

It was a startlingly loud, plaintive cry that went straight to Nessa's heart. She had been around horses all her life; she knew the sounds horses made and their meanings. The squeal of aggression. The blow of affection. The snort of alarm. The low, breathy nicker that meant, *Come here to me.* And the whinny—the searching, questing call of a horse that is lonely for his friends, or summoning his friends to him, or seeking any as yet unknown horse who might consent to become his friend. It started high in the horse's vocal register, descended through a middle range of multiple shuddering notes, and ended in the low, guttural range of the nicker. Each horse's whinny was distinctive, absolutely unique, and recognizable by other horses—and people.

The buckskin was straining against its handlers now, trying to free itself. The crowd jostled to move farther back. Nessa turned to August and saw him staring at the horse, his eyes wide, his face white.

"Arion!" he said in a breathy undertone.

The buckskin started to rear. Cutting through the crowd, August went to him quickly and took his halter. Almost immediately, the horse settled down. August laid a hand on the powerful neck, making low, soothing sounds. The buckskin let out a soft blow of breath.

For a long moment August and the horse stood still, with eyes only for one another, as if they were in their own private world together, feeding one another's calm. The handlers waited, exchanging puzzled glances.

Then August turned and asked, "Where are you taking this horse?"

"To the pen near the grand parade," one of the men said. "This whole lot was rounded up on James Island ten days ago. They're to be sold at auction on the twenty-third of this month."

"Sold?" August repeated. "You cannot sell him. He's mine."

ARION. It was the name of a marvelously fast, black-maned horse of Greek mythology, said to have saved the life of his master, the king of Argos, in battle. August knew this, the way he knew left from right, and how to walk and talk and shave himself—the same way he knew that the buckskin gelding whuffling against his shoulder was his.

The handler did not seem perturbed by August's claim of ownership. "You'll have to take it up with the Deputy Quartermaster General," he said. "Here, read this."

He handed August a grimy paper, written in a close, clear hand that August recognized as Rory's. It was dated Sunday, October 20, and signed by General Greene.

To be sold on Wednesday the 23rd instant on the grand parade, by the D.Q.M.G. at eleven o'Clock, about twenty horses, lately taken from the enemy, for ready money; should any of them hereafter be claimed, and proved as the property of any inhabitants of this State, and Congress should determine, that such property shall be restored to the former owners, they are to be given up, and the purchase price will be returned by the public to the purchasers.

As he scanned the advertisement, he became aware of someone drawing near to his side. It was Nessa. Wordlessly, he handed the page to her and turned back to the man who had given it to him.

"You say they were found on James Island?" he asked.

"Not just found. Captured," said the handler. "There are some British parties on Charlestown Neck and James Island that retire under the guns of their redoubts each night. They drive out their cattle and horses to pasture overnight, then bring them back again in the morning. Colonel Kościuszko and his men watched them for a while and learned the routine. They captured the horses the night of the tenth. They'd've liked to capture the cattle as well, but the cattle were under too heavy a guard."

August's eyes briefly met Nessa's. He knew she was thinking the same thing he was—that the horses had been captured the day after she had found him on the trail.

Arion nudged August in the shoulder. August knew at once, without knowing how he knew, that Arion had often nudged him that way to get his attention. A memory flashed through his mind of a long-legged tan foal munching green grass, and a voice—August's father's?—saying, *You'll be responsible for the training of him. He's yours.*

Arion was his horse. The two of them were bound by ties of affection and trust that transcended memory. Part of August wanted to fight to the death any man who tried to take Arion from him. But a visceral sense of belonging was not proof of ownership. Neither was Arion's own reaction to seeing him, or August's fragments of memory.

He took the advertisement back from Nessa and glanced over it again. "The twenty-third. How long away is that? What day is this?"

"The twentieth," said the man.

Three days. Would it be enough?

August folded the paper and put it in his pocket. "Give me those lead ropes," he said. "He may stay in the pen until I am able to prove ownership, but I will take him there myself."

Half an hour later, August leaned against the rails of the rough wooden fence that surrounded the pen where the twenty horses were being kept. Nessa stood behind him. Arion, freshly brushed with a borrowed currycomb, was prancing around the enclosure with his neck arched and his tail carried high, showing off to the other horses, who weren't paying attention. August had given Arion a thorough going over and had found him in good health and good spirits, though he was missing a shoe and his coat had been caked with mud. The entire exercise had been a revelation of sorts, with bits of memory bursting forth in quick flashes—too brief and too disconnected to reveal anything concrete about August's identity, but dazzling nonetheless. These were memories not of distinct events, but of long rides, quiet rubdowns in a roomy box stall, buckets of hot bran mash steaming in wintry air, and the ring of the farrier's hammer.

"I wish I had some oats to give him," August said now. He did not want to see Arion grow gaunt and discouraged like these other animals. But there was no grain, and precious little grass or hay, for the horses of the Continental Army. And in accordance with Section 13, Article 20 of the *Articles of War*,

Arion, like a captured supply wagon or artillery piece, had been secured for the service of the United States.

"He's so beautiful, August," Nessa said.

August's throat tightened, and for a moment he couldn't speak. Sunlight gleamed on Arion's glossy golden-brown coat, rippling over curves of muscle as the horse continued running around the enclosure in a breathtaking display of grace and strength.

"He's been separated from me for eleven days now," August said. "Or perhaps more. I don't know that he was with me on the night I was attacked. I wonder what has been happening to him, and how he managed to fall in with the horses at James Island."

"However he came there, the British must have been delighted to add such a fine, proud animal to their stock of horses," Nessa said. "They're probably still lamenting his loss."

"Aye, and in three days' time he'll be taken to a sale ring and led around while an auctioneer sings his praises and the members of the crowd make their bids. I'll have to stand by and watch my own horse being sold out from under me before my very eyes. I would gladly spend my own money to buy him myself, if I had any money to spend. But I haven't so much as a single copper coin or even a Continental paper note to my name—or at least in my current possession. I might well have money enough back in whatever place I came from, but 'twill do me no good as long as I remain ignorant of it."

"Three days isn't a fast deadline," Nessa said. "According to the advertisement the horse handler showed us, you should be able to get Arion back even after the sale, once you can prove ownership."

"But a lot could happen in the meantime. Arion might be sold to a brutal man, or ridden into a skirmish. He could be recaptured, or shot, by a British soldier. He could stumble and break a leg while trying to retreat over rough ground. I could lose him forever. Nay, I cannot allow that. I must get him back."

He struck the fence rail with the heel of his hand. "But how? I cannot prove that Arion is mine without first proving who I am—and I've made precious little progress on that front."

Anger rose up in him against the man who had done this to him—the nameless, faceless man who had meant to take August's life, and had succeeded in taking his past, his mission, his horse, and quite possibly his future. He had treated August like a piece of refuse, to be knocked on the head and dumped in a hole in the ground.

"You know that isn't true," said Nessa. "Think of all we've learned about you since that first night. We've found the place where you were attacked, and the remains of your clothing, and your saddle and pistols, and the note that brought you to the camp. That's all hard physical evidence. And now you have Arion—at least, he's here, and he clearly knows you."

"But that isn't enough."

"Nay, but taken all together, 'tis quite a lot. We just need to find a few more missing pieces, and the whole structure will show through and make sense."

He turned and looked at her. She was facing him with her chin lifted high and her brown eyes bright with determination. Sunlight shone on her red-brown hair, giving it a warm glow. He ached to take her in his arms, but he had no right, and he was beginning to fear that he never would.

"What if we cannot find those last pieces?" he asked. "What if they're lost forever?"

She cocked her head. "That's rather defeatist talk for a man who crawled out of his own grave."

He smiled. She was so beautiful when she was stern—and when she was tender, and thoughtful, and exasperated. And she was right. He thought of the old homestead, and the hearth where his belongings had been burned, and the ground he'd been unceremoniously dumped into, and the rough track he'd made when he'd crawled away. The land had told its story, but it had nothing further to tell. What he needed was fresh ground—and with Arion's return, he knew where to go to find it.

Chapter Twelve

"This is the Ashley River," said Rory, drawing a long, waving diagonal line across an Imperial-sized sheet of paper from the upper left corner to somewhere just below the middle of the page. "And this, to the east—" he added another line that started near the center top and wriggled its way down before meeting the first in a V shape "—is the Cooper. Charlestown is here, at the tip of the peninsula." He drew some hash marks in the point of the V to represent streets and wrote *CHT* above them. "Then we have the Ashley River Road, running to the west of the Ashley River, and more or less parallel to it, like so." He sketched it in. "Here's Middleton Place, about midway between the river and the road." He drew a blob and labeled it *MP*. "And here's the army camp on Ashley Hill—" another blob, labeled *CAMP* "—and the forest where Nessa found August, close to the remains of the old hunting lodge." Some scraggly trees were roughed in, along with a trail and a crude hut.

At this point Rory saw fit to add an arrow with a large N by way of a compass rose. Then he sketched some cannon at intervals around the camp's border to represent the artillery batteries, along with some V-shaped redans.

"For heaven's sake, Rory, that's quite enough detail to be going on with," Nessa burst out. "Next you'll be drawing all the individual tents, and each piece of laundry hanging on the lines."

Rory gave her a haughty look. "I am the one doing this," he said, "and I will do it in my own way."

He laboriously labeled the rivers and the road, working more slowly than ever, while Nessa tried to keep from screaming. She stole a glance at August to see how he was bearing up. He was staring down at the map as if his life depended on committing it to memory.

Rory added another line for the Ashley River's west bank, widening it near the end of the peninsula for Charlestown Harbor, then curving it around to the southwest in a vague outline of the collective coastline of the Sea Islands. He labeled the harbor, and the Bar, and drew a tiny ship surrounded by tinier waves. Nessa ground her teeth.

"Here's the Stono River," Rory said, starting low on the left side of the page and drawing another lazy undulating line that went from west to east, then abruptly turned south and met the sea. "And here—" he pointed to the mass of land south and west of Charlestown Harbor "—is James Island, where Arion and the other horses were found. What makes it an island rather than a peninsula is this." He connected the Stono to the Ashley with a line that slanted from southwest to northeast and emptied into the harbor. "This," he said, tapping the line, "is the Wappoo Cut. It was made in the last century as a more direct water route between the Ashley and the Stono. There used to be a bridge over the Wappoo at the western end, but it was dismantled some time ago in the war, and James Island has been in British possession for two years or so, since the siege of Charlestown. The British soldiers pasture their horses and cattle there—although I suppose they won't be doing that any longer after Kościuszko's latest capture."

Nessa looked at August again. "Is any of this familiar to you?"

"Vaguely," he said. "Like a place I've heard of but never seen."

"James Island would be an ideal place for August's attacker to dispose of a very conspicuous horse," Rory said. "Though it must have caused him much anguish to part with such a fine animal."

"And August's saddle was found in Boyd's tent," said Nessa. "But not his bridle. The ostler said Arion hadn't a strap of tack on him when he was captured. Nothing that could identify him."

"What I don't understand," said August, "is how whoever it was managed to get Arion across the Wappoo Cut to begin with. Arion hates crossing water in ferries or boats. I don't know how I know that, but I do. I would be able to get him into a boat and keep him calm enough for the passage, but I doubt very much whether a stranger could manage it."

"Maybe the stranger didn't manage it," said Rory. "Maybe Arion made the crossing on his own. Say he was with you when you were attacked. He probably didn't take kindly to your being whacked on the head. What if he bolted, and ran south? Once he cleared the camp, 'twould be only fifteen miles or so to the Wappoo Cut—the work of less than an hour at a full gallop. Even if he slowed to a walk, he could easily reach the crossing sometime that night and join the other horses in the British herd."

"That would also explain why the saddle was found in Sergeant Boyd's tent," said Nessa. "August must have unbuckled Arion's girth to give him a rest at the old homestead. When Arion ran, the saddle was left behind."

August nodded. "And naturally the British would have taken off his bridle after he joined the other horses."

He gazed down at the map. "It all sounds plausible enough. I must go to James Island myself, and see what clues I can find along the way."

"You can't go to James Island," said Nessa. "'Tis in British hands, as Rory said."

"Kościuszko and his men just got back from James Island," Rory objected.

"They went there on a raid. But they're cavalrymen in the Continental Army. August is—well, we don't know what he is. And General Greene isn't going to give him leave to traipse about the countryside and venture into enemy territory."

"The general might give him leave to go as far as the Wappoo Cut," said Rory. "That isn't enemy territory. Kościuszko's men patrol that area all the time, and Captain Wilmot has a camp at the Stono."

Rory turned out to be correct. General Greene did give August leave to go to the Wappoo Cut in the company of no less a person than Colonel Kościuszko himself, who had recently come to the camp to confer with the general face to face and was now returning. August was even allowed to ride Arion.

They would travel down the Ashley River Road until it took its easterly curve toward Charlestown, then continue to the Wappoo Cut on the trail used by Kościuszko's men. That was the route that Arion had most likely taken.

Nessa saw August off the next morning before sunrise. He was alert and restless, clearly impatient to be gone. Nessa knew how he had chafed at inaction, and how glad he must be to leave the confinement of camp for a ride through open country on his own excellent horse—not to mention the chance to find some clue to his identity.

"'Tis good of General Greene to let you go," she said. "He must believe you to be trustworthy."

August chuckled. "I'm sure he is almost as eager as I can be to learn who I am and what I'm doing here. It cannot be agreeable for him to harbor in his camp a stranger who can give no rational account of himself. As to my trustworthiness, that's neither here nor there. I have no doubt that Colonel Kościuszko and his men are under orders to shoot me dead if I should try to break free."

At that very moment, Kościuszko glanced their way, almost as if he had heard his name, though he was standing several yards off. He wore a sword belted along one thigh and a carbine—the preferred firearm for dragoons, short-barreled and easy to maneuver from the saddle—hanging at his back from a shoulder strap. He had a striking, strong-boned face with jutting cheekbones, a cleft chin, sharply angled eyebrows, and piercing dark eyes that missed nothing.

Nessa was startled. "Do you really think so?"

"'Tis what I would do in the general's place," August replied cheerfully. "I've spent the past twelve days in his camp. If I were to try to escape, I would be as good as declaring myself a spy. And my death would simplify things for him in a way. He might never learn who I am, but I would no longer be a potential threat."

"Nay, I cannot believe that of General Greene. He couldn't be so cold-blooded."

August smiled at her. "If he were truly cold-blooded, he'd have had me shot days ago and washed his hands of me. He's a fair and just man, but he is still a man of war. I know he's been like a father to you and Rory. But depend upon it—he didn't get to be a major general without spilling blood."

"You don't seem very concerned about it," said Nessa.

"Why should I be? I have nothing to fear, because I have nothing to hide."

"Nothing to fear? How can you say that? Someone tried to kill you, August, and we still don't fully understand who or why. All we know is that there's a conspiracy afoot. It might very well have penetrated to one of Kościuszko's dragoons, or all of them, or even Kościuszko himself."

August laughed softly. "Colonel Kościuszko, a traitor to the cause of American independence?"

"Don't laugh! There's been treachery in our ranks before, by men whose honor as Patriots was as unquestioned as his."

"I know it," said August, his smile fading. "General Arnold, General Lee, Dr. Church—their betrayals are more hurtful than any outward action by the enemy. Treachery is like acid eating away from within. It makes us doubt everyone around us, even those nearest to our hearts. We dread laying ourselves open to more betrayal. But if we give in to fear and mistrust, we might as well surrender to the British right now. And that is something I will never do."

His expression was deadly serious now, eyes narrow, jaw hard. Staring into the middle distance, he said, "I may not know the date of my birth, or where I come from, but I know who I am. I am a Patriot. I believe in man's God-given right to life, liberty, and the pursuit of happiness. And I know just as surely that I came to Ashley Hill for a purpose. I feel that in every fiber of my being. I must learn what that purpose is, and accomplish it, before time runs out and the Patriot cause is lost forever."

"But you don't know who tried to kill you, or who else might still wish you dead," Nessa said. "You don't know whom you can trust."

"In that, I'm no different than any man in the army. Betrayals come from those we believe to be friends. You know this as well as I do, Nessa—and you cannot truly want me to refuse to do my part while other men venture their lives. You may say that you do, but you know in your heart that you would be ashamed of me."

Nessa swallowed over a painful lump in her throat. "It feels like sending you into battle blindfolded," she said.

"I don't need to see my way forward," he said. "God will guide my steps. The truth will out—it always does in the end. The memories I've lost will be restored. And then—"

She could see the effort it took him to stop speaking, to bite down on whatever words he wanted to say to her, but could not.

"Well," August said at last. "That is a conversation for another day—but one that I hope and believe will take place, and soon."

He slid the toe of a worn secondhand boot into the stirrup, and in one fluid, effortless movement, swung himself onto Arion's back. He had no hat to tip, but he touched his hand to his brow and gave Nessa a deep nod.

"Until we meet again," he said, and rode off to join the other horsemen.

THE MOOD AT THE GENERAL Hospital was somber that day. It had been widely hoped that fall's cooler weather would bring about a great improvement in the patients, but that hadn't happened, and Nessa hadn't really expected it to. Many of the men were already too far gone to recover quickly, or at all. She could tell by the dull, hopeless look in their eyes.

Sergeant Philips was feverish again. Nessa knew it, even before she laid a hand on his brow, by the flush in his cheeks and the unnatural brightness to his eyes. He denied it at first, and claimed to be feeling quite well, only a bit fatigued, but then a shivering fit took him, and he could no longer pretend. By the end of her shift, he was soaked in sweat and shaking so hard that his teeth rattled in his mouth. There was no trace now of the optimistic Sergeant Philips who had invited Nessa to call him Ned.

Two patients died that day. Nessa did all she could for them, until there was nothing more to do but draw the threadbare sheets over the gaunt, wasted bodies and pinched faces that still bore the harsh marks of their suffering.

It wasn't until she had left the hospital for the evening that she remembered the man who had been following August yesterday—Sandy Slinkalong, as August had called him. She had forgotten all about him in the excitement of Arion's appearance. August had made light of the situation, but to Nessa it seemed ominous—and August had said the man had been following him for days. She hurried to the general's quarters to tell him.

Happily, there was no official dinner or staff meeting going on. Captain Baker, the general's aide, consulted briefly with the general and then admitted Nessa to the office tent.

The general was alone, sitting at his folding desk, frowning over some documents. A tallow candle shed its yellowish glow over the linen ceiling and walls.

"I hope I'm not disturbing you, General Greene," Nessa said as she came in.

"Not at all, not at all. I'm glad to have an excuse to set aside this tedious paperwork for a while. Have a seat, my dear."

Nessa sat on a wooden stool as the general pushed his pile of papers off to the side and rubbed his eyes. He looked tired and discouraged.

"Are you unwell, General?" Nessa asked.

The general let out a sigh. "I'm well enough—only worried about how I'm to continue feeding the troops. You've probably heard of my long struggles with the South Carolinian commissary, trying to get them to provide provisions for the Continental Army. If they don't come through for us soon, I'm afraid we'll be forced to start impressing food from the populace."

Nessa stared. "Taking it by force? From ordinary citizens? But most of them barely have enough for themselves. Surely there's another way."

"I wish there were. Believe me, I've tried to find one. The men under my command have suffered great hardships, and many of them are half-starved. I will do what I must to see that they are properly fed."

A cold pit formed in Nessa's stomach as she thought of the British raiding party that had come to her family's farm the previous year. She could still remember the sick feeling of watching the jeering red-coated soldiers carry off the small stores of ale, flour, salt pork, and the rest. It grieved her to think of Patriot soldiers going to farms in the countryside and taking away the sacks of cornmeal and potatoes laid carefully by from scant harvests. With most of the men away fighting, or dead, it was hard to keep a farm productive. And how long would it be until the cellars and pantries emptied by the impressing parties could be replenished? It wasn't even winter yet. There were months to go before spring planting, let alone harvest.

The general must have read her silence. "It seems harsh, I know," he said steadily. "But the soldiers are hungry too. They have left their own homes and neglected their livelihoods in the cause of liberty. We cannot call upon men to defend their country without providing them more than a bare subsistence."

"I know," Nessa said miserably. "But it is hard. I just wish the British would go away and leave us alone, so the men could go home to till their crops and tend their stock."

"I wish that as well, and pray for it daily. There will be a great deal of work to be done once peace is declared—planting and mending and building up. I for one am eager to get on with it."

He clapped his hands to his knees. "Is there something I can do for you, my dear?"

Nessa had almost forgotten the purpose of her visit. "I came to tell you about something that happened yesterday. I ought to have told you right away, but then Arion was found, and I forgot all about it. I was walking with August after divine service when I noticed a man following us. He didn't approach us—in fact he stayed well back—but I saw him three different times that afternoon. When I mentioned him to August, he said the man had been following him for days."

"Can you describe the man?" asked General Greene.

"Sandy haired, medium height, medium build. Altogether a rather medium fellow."

General Greene chuckled. "A fitting description of Corporal Ballard. There is nothing striking about his appearance, but his wits are sharp, a combination that fits him well for the duty I have assigned to him."

Nessa drew back a little. "Surely you don't mean..."

"That I ordered Corporal Ballard to follow August and keep me apprised of his movements? I did. And I have a different man watching his tent at night. The two of them have been shadowing August ever since I was first made aware of his existence."

"You've been spying on him?" Nessa asked.

"I have been surveilling him," the general corrected her.

"But why? You don't think...You can't suspect..."

The general sighed. "Try to consider my position, Miss Shaw. A man shows up unannounced at the headquarters of the Continental Army in the South—a camp that for months has been beset with intrigues and haunted by attempted mutinies. This man can give no name—or no more than half a name—nor any explanation for his presence. No sentries remember admitting him, which suggests that he entered by stealth. Is this not reason enough for caution, if not skepticism?"

Stung, Nessa said, "But you know why he can't tell you his full name or where he came from—because he was knocked on the head. His memory was stolen from him."

"So he claims. But until I am presented with verifiable evidence of who he is and what he is doing here, I must take reasonable precautions."

"If that's what you think, then I wonder that you didn't lock him up to begin with," said Nessa. "Unless...Nay, you wanted to draw him out, to see where he went and what he did."

"Precisely. Thus far, ever since he was given the liberty of the camp, he appears to have rarely ventured beyond his own tent and that of your brother. He may well prove to be an honest man and a Patriot, but I cannot take that for granted. He must be watched. And if someone in the camp did try to kill him, then we may expect another attempt to be made on his life—in which case, his surveillance detail will be on hand to defend him."

Nessa didn't answer. She suddenly felt that she had been ridiculously naïve. August had known all along that the general had reservations about him. It was a reasonable thing to think, and everything the general had said just now was sensible and just. But somehow she had imagined that the general could not help seeing how good and honorable August was.

General Greene pushed his chair back from his desk. "Miss Shaw, may I speak freely?"

Nessa nodded, though she had a foreboding that she wouldn't like to hear what he was about to say.

"It appears to me," the general said carefully, "that you take a great interest in what happens to this young man."

He stopped and waited.

"He is my patient," said Nessa without meeting the general's eyes. "I found him. I took care of him. I'm responsible for him."

"I think it is more than that."

"Well, I don't deny that I take a—a friendly interest in his future. Anyone would."

She tried to keep her tone light, but she could feel her cheeks flaming, betraying her. It was humiliating to be seen through so completely.

"You mustn't suppose that I'm scolding you, dear girl," the general said gently. "As far as I have observed, and as far as my surveillance agents have reported, there has been nothing improper in your behavior—and in an environment such as this, where the absence of normal familial structures makes it difficult to preserve the boundaries of decency and decorum, that is commendable. I am only trying to do as your good father would do if he were here, and as I would hope any man of sense and principle would do for one of my own girls in a similar case, if I were not there to help and guide her."

"And what would you wish that man to say to your daughter?" Nessa asked, looking down at her folded hands in her lap.

"To be careful," the general said simply, "and to guard her heart."

A long silence passed. Finally General Greene said, "I hope you do not resent my interference, and that I have not overstepped. You must know that you and your brother are very dear to me. I hold you both in the tenderest regard, and I want only what is best for you."

She lifted her head, looked the general in the eye, and tried to smile. "How can I resent what is clearly so kindly meant? You have been so good to Rory and me, General, and I thank you for your concern. But I assure you that it is needless. August is the soul of honor. You only suspect him because you don't know him."

The general smiled sadly at her. "You're quite right about that, Miss Shaw. I don't know him. And neither do you."

Chapter Thirteen

Not far from the camp's border, Kościuszko's company met a fatigue detail busily digging what appeared to be a trench for a new latrine—two feet wide, several yards long, and already three feet deep. The men stopped digging a moment and stared, no doubt quick to grasp at anything that broke up the monotony of the work. If the British left within the next few days, as seemed not unlikely, the new latrine would be unnecessary and the men's labor wasted. But it was impossible to know exactly when the British would leave—and though a new latrine might be laborious to build, an overflowing old latrine had its own evils. Better to have it and not need it than the other way around. Also, it was good for the men to have work to do rather than sitting idle and nursing grievances.

One member of the fatigue detail stood out in particular because he was young and relatively fresh-faced. He stood to his full height, rested his pickaxe on the ground, and arched his back. When he saw Arion, his eyes widened and his mouth dropped open. August felt a surge of pride in his handsome mount. Of course, any well-fed horse was a wonder in this place, but Arion would be striking wherever he was seen.

Once beyond the confines of camp, Kościuszko's party set off on the Ashley River Road at a brisk canter. The river was perhaps a thousand feet away to their left, visible only as pale mist behind the dark silhouettes of the trees along the banks. Not long after the sun came up and burned off the mist, the river pulled away from the road in a wide arc. Some miles later, it began to curve back toward them, and the road veered left to meet it, at which point the horsemen abandoned the road to continue their southeasterly course.

This was the South Carolina Lowcountry of which August had heard, but which was still new to his eyes—or so he supposed. It was low-lying, marshy country, with broad, level land stretching out as far as the eye could see, and only a few swells and bluffs varying the elevation along the river's edge.

It was a chilly morning, but windless and clear. The road was mottled with shadows cast by trees—live oaks, mostly, wider than they were tall, with heavy branches trailing to the ground, and long grey tassels of Spanish moss showing against the deep-green foliage. The feathery needles of the bald cypress trees had turned golden brown, and in the branches of the sweetgums, red and yellow leaves stood out like five-pointed stars against other leaves that still held to their green. Some sort of shrubby aster grew in mounds three feet high, densely covered with small cheerful lavender blooms with bright-yellow centers. Bare-limbed persimmon trees clung to their soft globes of orange fruit, and muscadine grapevines twined around the trunks and branches of sturdy hardwoods and spilled their dark-purple clusters.

Then the trees gave way to an open field with grasses ranging from dark brown through deepest russet and palest gold, with here and there a patch of vivid green. As the riders passed, a flock of red-winged blackbirds rose up with a rushing sound, their shoulder bands like showy red-and-gold epaulets on officers' uniforms.

It didn't take August long to realize that he was being closely shadowed by one rider in particular—Agrippa Hull, a young, free black man from Massachusetts who worked as Kościuszko's aide. Apparently Hull had been tasked with keeping an eye on the mysterious rider.

The dragoons offered August no conversation, and he wanted none. He wanted only to think of Nessa as she had looked at their parting, in a faded homespun gown the color of butternut hulls and a worn brown shawl drawn around her slender shoulders, her sweet, solemn face turned up to him. He knew that he would always remember her so. He had precious few memories right now, and this one was the brightest of all. It cast a glow over the entire morning, sharpening his senses into exquisite clarity, magnifying the day's glory to an almost unbearable radiance.

He was no longer afraid of finding out something that would keep Nessa from him. Perhaps it was only the beauty of the day and the pleasure of the ride acting on his emotions, but he felt a deep-down certainty that the truth, once discovered, would only bring them together.

They reached the Wappoo Cut when the sun was still low in the sky. As they approached, August could see the glint of water beyond the pale-barked trunks of a line of sycamore trees.

August sat deep in his saddle, and Arion came to a smooth halt without need for rein pressure or a verbal command. The trust and understanding between the two of them was a palpable thing, a bond that had survived the loss of August's memory.

Several trails led down to the water, showing where horses had gone to drink. August dismounted and took Arion's reins in his hand. Arion seemed very much at ease in this place and walked with confidence down one of the trails.

A flash of light close to the water's edge drew August's eye. Coming closer, he saw that it was a used horseshoe, caught against a rough rock. August picked it up and turned it over in his hand. Five bent nails stuck out of the holes. The shoe's bottom surface showed signs of wear, but the corrosion was minimal.

A shiver of anticipation went down August's spine. He went to Arion's near fore and ran his hand down the leg until he reached the fetlock. Arion lifted his foot without waiting for a verbal command, and August set the shoe against his hoof. It was a perfect fit.

The discovery of the horseshoe raised a mild excitement in the company. The colonel came over and personally tested its fit, then stood and gave August a brief nod, as if to acknowledge that so far, at least, August's account of himself was not inconsistent with physical evidence. Clearly Arion had come this way not long ago, as would be expected if he'd fled from the ruins of the old house to James Island, and then thrown his shoe while coming to the water to drink and, most likely, to cross. The water's level was low enough for Arion to easily ford.

It wasn't much, but it was a start. It was as if a well-oiled key had slid into a lock, and the first pair of tumblers had shifted into place along the shear line, ready to part when the key was turned.

August's heart soared. The other clues would come in due time—he knew they would. He would learn not only who he was, but what he was supposed to do. And once his work was done, he would turn his energies toward more congenial pursuits, like finding himself a wife.

NESSA DRAGGED HERSELF back to the sutler's row, drained and exhausted by her anxiety over August, her day at the hospital, and General Greene's exhortations. The fact that the general meant his warning so kindly made it all the harder to take. She could have borne up under false accusations of impropriety, but his fatherly concern had nearly undone her.

Everything he said was reasonable in itself. She would have agreed wholeheartedly with him, had the girl in question been someone other than herself, and the man anyone but August. Which perhaps suggested a lack of impartiality in her thinking—but she was right. She knew she was right. August was a good man, an honorable man, and a Patriot. Soon the truth would come to light, and everyone would know it.

She wondered if August had returned to the camp yet. Kościuszko had said that he planned to take his men on a patrol west of the Ashley and then cross the Stono to visit Captain Wilmot's camp on Johns Island, and it hadn't been made clear how long August was to remain with them before being sent back to Ashley Hill with a detachment of riders. Anything might have happened in the hours since she'd seen the dragoons ride away that morning. August might have recovered his memory. He might have discovered something that proved his identity. Or Kościuszko's company might have encountered the enemy and gotten into yet another pointless skirmish.

Most of the tents in the sutler's row glowed with candlelight, but August's tent was dark. Nessa passed it and went to Rory's tent, where she stood a moment outside the closed flap. She could hear Rory's voice reciting French verb conjugations. Was August there with him, returned safe and sound from his expedition? Or was he out somewhere in the darkness, unarmed, being fired upon by the British?

"I can see your shadow through the canvas, you know," Rory called. "Are you going to come in, or stand there skulking?"

Nessa drew back the tent flap and went inside. There was Rory, sitting at his desk...

And there was August, stretched out full length on the floor, face down, with his toes braced and his palms flat on either side of his chest, which was an inch or so from the ground. He straightened his arms, pushing himself up, his body maintaining a wonderfully straight line from heels to head. Then he lowered himself again, making another straight line from elbow to elbow across his back. Up and down he went, swiftly and surely, over and over, the wings of his golden-brown hair hanging over the sides of his face.

Nessa stood there a moment, speechless with relief at seeing him safely home again, before asking, "What are you doing?"

"Keeping fit," he replied without a break in the up-and-down motion. "A few brief walks a day and a thirty-mile round-trip canter on horseback are not enough. An idle, sedentary life causes the muscles to weaken and the blood to thicken, but physical exercise strengthens the body, making it firm and active."

Nessa didn't know whether to laugh or scream. Here was more evidence, if any was needed, that August was not a laborer, or else he would take physical exercise for granted and not speak of it in such elevated terms, much less put himself through a program of structured calisthenics.

"*Mens sana in corpore sano,*" said Rory matter-of-factly.

"Aye, and *la medicina è niente altro che una sostituzione dell'esercizio e della temperanza,*" August replied, still doing his push-ups.

Rory turned to him. "You know Italian."

August froze with his arms fully extended and lifted his head.

"I do! What was it that I just said? I believe it was a quote from Francesco Petrarca. Do I know any more Italian? Do I know any Dante?"

He lowered his chest to the floor and pushed up again while rattling off some lines that sounded like Latin with extra flourishes and a peculiar lilt.

"I do know Dante," August said triumphantly. "That was from his *Divine Comedy.*"

"Do you know any German?" asked Rory.

Without hesitation, August recited something incomprehensible with lots of harsh consonants in the back of the throat, still continuing his exercises. "Schiller," he said. "*Ode to Joy.*"

"Very well," said Nessa impatiently. "We all know that your education has been exemplary. But what I want to know is, what happened today at Wappoo Cut?"

August gave one final push and sat up, one arm resting on a bent knee, his face flushed with exertion, his eyes shining with gladness. "What happened is that I found a horseshoe on the north bank of the Cut—Arion's missing horseshoe."

Nessa dropped to the floor and knelt across from him. "Oh, August! That's wonderful!"

He shrugged. "'Tis not much of a discovery—we already knew he must have gotten to James Island somehow. But it does suggest that he came from the direction of the camp."

"Aye, exactly as we supposed. It supports your story. 'Tis one more piece of the puzzle fitted into place."

He grinned at her. "I know. 'Twill not be long now, Nessa. I know it—I feel it. Before this week has passed, I will know precisely who I am, and why I'm here."

Chapter Fourteen

He was trapped underwater and couldn't get free. Someone was holding him there, someone he knew and trusted, who would surely let him come up soon. But he was taking a long time about it, and August was growing frightened. He'd expelled all the air from his lungs in his first shock at being pushed under, and now there was a vacuum in his chest aching to be filled. His head felt tight with pressure, ready to burst, and spots danced before his eyes. Another moment and he'd have to take another breath, he wouldn't be able to stop himself, and his lungs would fill with water and he'd die.

A glint of light flashed in his eyes, inches from his face. He reached for it—

And came awake with a ragged gasp to find himself alone in his tent, sitting up on his bed. His heart pounded, his skin clammy with a cold sweat, and his coarse blanket was twisted around his legs.

With a groan, he lay back again. His mattress was thin and lumpy and smelled of mildew, but it was solid and dry, and he could breathe again.

He'd had the water dream, with variations, every so often since his arrival at the camp. While it was going on, it felt horribly real, and fraught with significance. But as soon as he woke, the portentousness melted away, and it became nothing more than the confused offering of a mind wracked with anxiety, with a sick fear of being unable to breathe.

Either way, he doubted he'd be able to get back to sleep. It was still dark, but he could feel that dawn was not far off. Groping the crude wooden crate that served him as a bedside table, he found his tinderbox and lit his candle. Then he reached inside one of the worn boots he'd been given, formerly the property of a malarial soldier now buried in the camp graveyard. He lifted the felt insole and took out the carefully folded paper that contained the copy he'd made of the cipher he'd discovered in Rory's Vauban book.

So far, all his attempts to decrypt the cipher had failed. Theoretically, this was progress, and by the process of elimination he should eventually be able to arrive at the solution, assuming he lived long enough. But it was slow, discouraging, tedious work.

By the time he began to hear signs of life at the campsites around him, he was ready to lay it aside. He refolded the papers and stowed them back beneath the insoles of his boots—the copy of the original cipher in his left boot, and his scribbled notes and outworkings in the right. Then he dressed himself, snuffed out his candle, and headed out into the morning.

The encampments of the Delaware, Maryland, and Pennsylvania regiments were astir with more than their usual level of morning activity, along with an air of excitement and bustle. These troops were scheduled to depart the camp today for the long march north. August had mixed feelings about this. Their going would mean less crowding in the camp and fewer mouths to feed, but also fewer men to fight if fighting men were needed. The British hadn't yet left Charlestown, and whether they were on the brink of boarding their transports and sailing away, or preparing to renew hostilities with fresh vigor, was the subject of constant conjecture and debate. The whole situation was like a game of nerves, and August couldn't help but feel that in making the first move at demobilization, the Patriots had put themselves at a disadvantage. On the other hand, there wasn't much to be gained by keeping all the troops in the camp to slowly starve to death.

The morning star shone bright and clear in the deep-blue sky as he made his way to the pasture where the horses of the Continental Army were kept.

Nearly four weeks had passed since August had gone to Wappoo Cut with Kościuszko and his men. How sanguine he'd been when he'd found Arion's missing horseshoe on the bank of the channel! It had seemed a good omen for his investigation into his own origins. He'd ridden back to camp full of confidence and told Nessa that he expected to solve the mystery of his identity, and his mission, within a matter of days. His hubris had been thoroughly punished. Not a single clue had come to light in the weeks since, and other than some lines from Cicero and Shakespeare, his memory hadn't returned.

The horseshoe itself did not prove August's ownership of Arion. It showed only that Arion had lost a shoe at the Wappoo Cut. Accordingly, Arion had been included in the horse auction held as scheduled on the 23rd of October, and had been purchased by General Greene himself. August had tried to feel glad about this and mostly succeeded. As the property of the commander of the Southern Department, Arion would get the best possible care—and once August was able to prove his ownership, it would be a simple matter to have his horse restored to him. The general even allowed August to groom and exercise Arion himself—a favor for which August was deeply grateful.

The horses were huddled together for warmth at the most sheltered part of the pasture. At August's whistle, a shape detached itself from the dark mass and ambled toward him with an eager step and a soft nicker. The darkness was melting into grey light, and as Arion drew near, August could see his hipbones beginning to show through his coat. Arion put his head over the top rail and nuzzled August's pocket with his black nose, hoping for a treat that was never given. It pained August to have nothing better to offer his horse than tired-looking hay from the deflated communal stacks. It pained him still more to think of Arion slowly wasting away like the other horses in the camp. The buckskin still had a spring in his step and a decent amount of flesh covering his bones, but with winter settling into the South Carolina Lowcountry, the remaining forage was scarcer than ever—and hotly contested between the Patriots and the British, who had their own thin horses and lean cattle to feed.

August ran his hand down Arion's neck and scratched under the thick black mane. The solace of his company seemed a poor substitute for adequate food, but it was all he had to give.

He could sense the presence of his constant shadow, Sandy Slinkalong, also known as Corporal Ballard. He now knew, because Nessa had told him, that General Greene had ordered Ballard and another man to tail him, and had not been particularly surprised by the news. It was a sensible precaution for the general to take, and August had been glad to learn that the man he'd observed following him was surveillance detail rather than someone who was watching for an opportunity to kill him. He hadn't often glimpsed the man who had the night shift, but he was familiar enough with Ballard, though August feigned unawareness as a professional courtesy. He had a grudging respect for Ballard, who performed his duty with diligence and managed to preserve a discreet distance that allowed them both to pretend the surveillance wasn't happening at all.

When the first hints of rose appeared in the eastern sky, August said good-bye to Arion and headed back to the sutler's row to make breakfast. Since Nessa and Rory spent most of their waking hours at work, and August had no official occupation, he had volunteered to take over the cooking duties from Nessa. After an apprenticeship period that had seen its share of mishaps, he had become reasonably competent at brewing chicory coffee and boiling rice with pieces of salt pork. The three of them took most of their meals together in Rory's tent, or in the open space between their tents when the weather was fine.

Rory had gathered firewood the night before. August crouched down at the charred remains of their shared cookfire and scooped the ashes into an ash can. He was arranging kindling when he heard a sound like the cry of a hurt animal.

He stood, looked around, and saw Nessa standing behind her tent with her back to him and an empty water pail in her hand. Her head was bowed, and a red-brown curl trailed loose from the knot of hair on her head. She was crying.

His heart dropped like a stone. Had something happened to Rory? Had she received bad news from home?

He crept over to her. "Nessa?"

He gently laid his hands on her shoulders. She spun around and with a great wrenching sob fell into his arms. He held her close, breathing in the scent of her hair, relishing the feel of her against him even as his dread grew.

"What is it?" he asked. "What has happened?"

She was weeping too hard to speak clearly, but in her answer he discerned the name Wilmot.

"Captain Wilmot?" he said. He had briefly met the Maryland officer the day he'd gone riding with Kościuszko and his dragoons.

Nessa nodded. "He's dead," she managed to say. "Killed two weeks ago. The general just received word from Colonel Kościuszko."

With his arm around her, August guided her to a seat on a tree stump and sat down beside her. Gradually, through tears and ragged breaths, the story came out. Apparently Captain Wilmot and Colonel Kościuszko had been aware for some time of an enemy foraging party that came regularly to James Island to cut wood. The two Patriot officers planned an attack on the woodcutters, but instead fell victim to an ambush by a British force that outnumbered their own by four to one. A Patriot lieutenant was wounded, and Captain Wilmot was killed.

"Did you know the captain?" August asked.

Nessa shook her head again. "I never saw him."

"Then why—"

She sniffed. "I know you must think I'm being ridiculous, making such a fuss over the death of a stranger. Heaven knows we've suffered plenty of other casualties over the past seven years, some of whom were men known to me, though I let those losses pass without much notice, because I had to. But this—oh, August, what was the point of it? Poor Captain Wilmot died over *firewood*—just like Colonel Laurens, who was killed in a paltry little skirmish over horse fodder. And that was three months ago!" She waved a hand impatiently. "I understand the reasoning, that we must starve out the enemy so they will go home. But they aren't going home. Do you realize that over a year has gone by since Cornwallis surrendered at Yorktown? The peace talks in Paris have been going on since April—and we don't appear to be any closer to expelling the enemy from our country than we were then."

Her eyes filled with fresh tears. "What if the war isn't ending at all? What if the British have been stalling for time for their conspiracy? Can they truly mean to go on fighting? Both sides are exhausted—at least, our side is, and their side appears to be, but maybe that's part of their plan, to make us think that, when in fact they're just gathering their strength to strike again."

She was gripping his hands with both of hers. "I can't do it anymore, August. I can't keep changing sheets in the hospital and spoon-feeding broth to men who are never going to get better. I want to leave this dirty, overcrowded camp forever, and go home to my family, and breathe the clean air. I can hardly remember what peace is like. It seems to belong to some mythical past. I want to get up in the morning and make a good breakfast, eggs and porridge and milk, and real coffee, and not a scrap of salt pork in sight. I want to buy dress goods, and make new gowns, and not mend the same shirts over and over until there's nothing left of them but patches. I want to plant a garden without wondering if British raiders will come and destroy it. I want to see cattle and horses grazing in green pastures, with plenty of flesh covering their bones. I want to lie down at night in a soft bed with a real roof over my head, and hear the wind in the pine trees, and not be afraid."

He put his arm around her again and drew her to him. She clung to him and wept. He wished he had words of comfort to offer, but what could he say? That everything would turn out all right in the end? That he wouldn't let anything hurt her? He hadn't even managed to discover something as simple as his own identity. Nay, he would not insult her with empty promises. Action, not speech, was what was needed. *Rem non spem, factum non dictum, quaerit amicus.*

At last she pulled back. "Forgive me. I ought not to have given way like that. 'Twas weak."

August took a ragged handkerchief from his breast pocket and gave it to her. "Dear heart, you have nothing to apologize for. You've been carrying heavy burdens for far too long—burdens you shouldered willingly, with a smile on your face and a word of cheer for everyone you meet. I cannot begin to express how brave and splendid you are, coming to this camp of your own free will, not only to look after your brother but to spread comfort wherever you go."

Slowly and deliberately, she blotted her face with his handkerchief. The storm was spent; she was regaining control of herself.

"Thank you, August," Nessa said.

"You're most welcome," August replied. "I only wish—" He swallowed over a painful lump in his throat. "I wish I had something more to give you—something real."

"You do," Nessa said. "You have."

Noises were beginning to fill the air—the clatter of cookware, the sizzle of pork fat, the voices of men and women—all the familiar din of a busy army camp in the morning.

"Back to work," Nessa said with a self-conscious laugh. They got to their feet and stood awkwardly a moment before making their way around to the front of the tent.

As August started on breakfast, he thought of the cipher hidden inside his boot. Could it be the key to exposing the British conspiracy? He had to find out. He would crack that cipher if it was the last thing he ever did.

Chapter Fifteen

If only the British would leave. That was the thought that kept running through Nessa's mind every waking hour of every day of the month of November. If only they would get into their transports in Charlestown Harbor and sail past the Bar, across the Atlantic, and all the way to England. Then the Patriots would be free to depart from the dirty, overcrowded camp and go home to their families, their farms and shops, their warm, clean beds.

Sometimes, when she was taking a load of refuse out of the hospital, Nessa would spend a few idle moments staring across the Ashley River in the direction of the town. *Go away,* she would think. *Forget your conspiracy and leave us alone.*

The weather had turned brutally cold, and the blue wool uniform coats that had arrived in the camp just in time for summer, to the disappointment and derision of all, were now distributed and gratefully accepted.

It was a bleak time in the hospital. Scarcely a day went by without at least one death. For a while, it seemed as if Nessa was hearing the funeral march all day long. General Greene had to issue an order that it not be played anymore because of the depressing effect it was having on the men. After that, the bodies were carried in silence to the camp graveyard, but Nessa continued to hear the grim march in her head.

Sergeant Philips slipped away one night after Nessa went home. She gave him his broth and changed his sheets that evening and came back in the morning to find his bed empty.

As the malaria patients succumbed at last to their long struggles, their beds were gradually filled with victims of seasonal colds and influenza. Nessa boiled elderberries into a thick medicinal syrup and brewed pot after pot of sassafras tea. Weakened by malnutrition, the men and women of the camp had no defenses against common ailments that would have been no more than minor nuisances to robust constitutions. Nessa became acutely alert to any sign of cough or sore throat in August or Rory. So far, they all continued to enjoy excellent health, but she wondered how much longer that could last.

In spite of bitter cold, the haunting anxiety, and the dreary toil, they had good times—wonderful times. Nessa's hours of leisure were generally spent in Rory's tent, where the three of them went on testing August's memory. It was entertaining, figuring out what he did and didn't know. He seemed to have read everything. Every quote they started, he could finish. He knew music, as well. Nessa loved to sing, and although she'd had no formal training, she knew dozens of songs—the popular tunes and folk songs that everyone knew, a few Mozart and Haydn airs she'd learned from her city-bred sister-in-law, and even some melancholy Gaelic ballads she'd picked up from an old admirer of her sister's. August didn't know a word of Gaelic—it was one of the few subjects about which he was completely ignorant. He knew all the other songs and sang the tenor line, or made one up, while Nessa carried the soprano. But whenever Nessa sang in Gaelic, he listened with his head to one side and a rapt expression on his face.

Those evenings were treasures of incalculable worth. For a short while, it was as if the three of them were in a crystal bubble, safe from the war, untouched by its cares. Wit and music, mirth and fellowship were woven together in a rich tapestry, and the cramped little tent was transformed into a warm, gracious parlor. Nessa went to bed with songs and laughter echoing in her head, and the memory sustained her through the next day.

During those hours when Nessa was free from work and Rory was away, August kept to his own tent, which Nessa chastely avoided. If Sandy Slinkalong and his nighttime counterpart were still surveilling August, they would have nothing untoward to report to General Greene. She and August had not had a moment alone together since the day when he'd found her weeping over Captain Wilmot's death and comforted her. All told, August spent more time with Rory than with her, diligently tutoring him in French during Nessa's shifts at the hospital.

Rory and August seemed to genuinely enjoy one another's company. Nessa was glad of this. It was good for Rory to have a friend. Harry Beach had all but disappeared, and when she'd asked Rory what had become of him,

Rory had replied that Harry was always on work details and they hadn't seen each other in weeks.

Whenever August and Nessa were together, his behavior toward her was scrupulously correct, as was hers toward him. It was as if they were playing an elaborate game. No observer could have guessed that there was anything but friendly regard between them—but *they* knew. August had never even come close to speaking of his feelings for her, not since the morning before he'd ridden to Wappoo Cut with Kościuszko's men, and she had certainly never broached the subject to him. But she knew that she loved him, had known it for weeks now, and she was almost certain that he loved her. She could feel it in the air, and see it in occasional brief glances that set her heart racing and flooded her face with heat.

There could be no formal declaration between them until he learned the truth about himself, but she felt an unshakable conviction that when the truth did come to light, it would lift the cloud of suspicion from him and reveal him to be not only a Patriot, but a single man, free to honorably bestow his love where he wished.

A FEW ORANGE LEAVES still clung to the twigs of the sassafras tree. Nessa knelt beside the trunk and dug carefully with her trowel to expose some mature roots about an inch or so in diameter. Using her knife, she cut off several pieces, then put them in her herb basket. The fragrant sap made her fingers sticky. Later, she would wash the roots, cut them into smaller sections, and spread them to dry on a clean cloth in her tent. Within a week or two, they would be ready for use. She had already harvested some this fall, but with all the sore throats and coughs in the camp, her current stores were running low.

When she had enough roots, she tucked her tools into her basket and got back on her feet. The December sunshine couldn't penetrate the shade, and she drew her worn brown shawl around her shoulders as she leaned her back against the sassafras tree and shut her eyes. Her shift at the hospital had ended a quarter of an hour ago, but she was in no hurry to go back to the sutler's row. The clean, quiet woods were a hushed haven from the noise and stench of the camp. She'd been back several times over the two months since she'd first found August unconscious on the trail—sometimes to harvest herbs, and sometimes just to clear her head.

As the weeks had passed, she'd been growing increasingly worn down by a sense of futility and hopelessness in her work, and she'd needed time to herself before she could be fit company for Rory and August. It was disheartening to spend her days giving her patients the best of care, or at least the best she could manage with her limited resources, only to lose them in the end. She'd watched three men die that morning—a cavalryman from South Carolina, an engineer from Delaware, and an infantryman from New York. She couldn't even remember the last time she had seen a patient leave the hospital on his own two feet rather than on a bier.

She left her herb basket beside the sassafras tree and followed the trail another few yards to the track she and Rory had made to the old homesite. It was still visible, and the surrounding herbage had died back, making passage easier. Stepping carefully, Nessa walked through.

The shallow grave where August had been temporarily buried alive was like a scar on the ground. Nessa did not linger there. She skirted the innermost part of the clearing where the returning trees were thinnest, stepped over the fallen chimney crane, and stooped down in front of the hearth. Among the ashes and cinders was a small metal object. She picked it up. It was one of the buttons from August's burned frock coat—brass, with a chased copper sunburst design.

If August were courting her, she might have a lock of his golden-brown hair to cherish, or a scrap of his writing, or a dried flower pressed between the leaves of a book. But he was not courting her. He could not honorably pursue her until his memory was restored, or at the very least he learned the facts of his personal history.

She picked up the button and held it a moment in the palm of her hand. Then, on a sudden impulse, she plucked some grass blades, threaded them through the button's shaft, wove them into a ring, and slipped it onto her finger.

She felt a little flustered at the thought of what General Greene, or Father, or even Rory would say if they could see her now, making a love token like a starry-eyed girl. But they weren't here. There was no one to see, no one to know, no one to reproach her. Before returning to camp, she would take it off and put it in her pocket, and there it would stay for as long as she wished. She could slip her hand inside her pocket whenever she liked, and touch the little half-globe that had once been part of the claret-colored frock coat August had been wearing when he was attacked, on the evening when he first came into her life. She was not free to touch his face, to kiss his mouth, to speak to him from her heart, but she was free to keep his button in her pocket, and she would allow herself this luxury.

She went back to the sassafras tree, picked up her herb basket, and started back to camp.

As she neared the edge of the woods, she heard the rumble of wagon wheels. She emerged from the trail onto a rough road, where she stopped and stared. Several wagons were being hauled into camp by oxen.

"Miss Shaw!" a voice called.

She turned to the man who had spoken. She didn't recognize him at first, but there was something vaguely familiar about the straight black brows, long nose, and deep-set, grey-blue eyes.

"Major Elliot!" She hurried toward him, unable to believe her eyes. "Is it really you?"

He smiled. "In the flesh."

It may have been the major's flesh, but it was far healthier flesh, and there was considerably more of it, than when she had seen him last. He was still lean, but no longer gaunt, and his face had lost its unhealthy pallor.

"But you're looking so well!" Nessa said.

"I had a wonder of a nurse," he replied.

She waved this off, but the words pleased her, nevertheless. It was so good, after the day she'd had, to see a former patient who had actually gotten better.

"General Greene told me that you were taken back to Magnolia Grove to recuperate," she said. "Have you been there all this time?"

"Aye, with my man Scipio as my caretaker. It was touch and go for a while, and I was confined to my bed for weeks. But then the wound began to heal, better than it ever did with that mercury ointment smeared all over it. I feel better than I have in years, Miss Shaw, and I have you to thank for it."

"I didn't do much more than clean it and dress it," Nessa said.

"Perhaps that was all it needed."

Perhaps it was. Nessa had often wondered if some of the more elaborate treatments she'd witnessed did more harm than good. It was deeply gratifying to think that her care might have saved a man's life.

"I'm very happy to hear of your recovery, Major Elliot," she said. "What are you doing back in camp? I heard that you had taken a leave of absence. Have you come to resume your work in the Quartermaster Department?"

He chuckled. "As a matter of fact, I'm working with the Commissary Department today, but in a civilian capacity. Do you see these wagons? They've come from Magnolia Grove, bearing provisions for the army—some grain, rice, sweet potatoes, animal fodder, and a few steers. I heard that General Greene has had to resort to impressing foodstuffs from the populace and decided to bring a voluntary offering."

"How very generous of you!"

The major waved off her praise. "'Tisn't much, I'm afraid. But it may save some small farmer from having his seed corn and breeding stock taken away from him. I don't like to think of American soldiers going through the countryside, forcibly carrying off goods from law-abiding American citizens."

"I couldn't agree more. My own home was once raided by the British, back when Henry Craig was occupying Wilmington. I would hope that our own men would not be as brutal as those men were, but I imagine that the overall effect of having your food stores and livestock taken from you is much the same, regardless of the manner of those doing the carrying off."

The major looked at her, a light of interest in his eyes. "I had forgotten that you came from Wilmington. My grandfather had land in the New Bern area. My mother and father and I used to visit him for a month every summer. Such good times I had there, playing with my cousins—fishing, swimming, riding horses. The plantation lay in Craig's path during his campaign to subdue the countryside, as he put it. The house and fields were burned, and my grandfather was shot in cold blood—an old man on his own land. The British knew he was a Patriot, of course."

He spoke with the measured calm of a man who had himself under regulation, no matter what depth of resentment might lie beneath the surface.

"I'm sorry," Nessa said. She had heard countless similar stories of atrocities carried out against known Patriots during Major Craig's campaign in the countryside of North Carolina that summer.

Major Elliot gave a half-shrug with his good shoulder.

All this time they had been walking alongside the supply wagons. As they drew near an expanse of bare ground, the major said, "I see that the northern regiments have started their march home at last."

"Aye, they departed a few weeks ago, but General Greene halted them at Camden until he can be certain that the British are truly leaving Charlestown. 'Tis being said that the British are actually preparing to board their transports and sail away."

"I'm sure no one could be happier to see the backs of the British than I," replied the major, "but I'll believe it when I see it."

They continued chatting until they reached a parting of the ways.

"This is my turn," said the major, stopping. "I'm off to see General Greene."

"And I'm going home to my dinner," said Nessa. She turned to face him. "Good day, Major Elliot. I'm very happy to have seen you, and to find you in such good health."

He opened his mouth as if to reply, but then froze, his words forgotten. His attention appeared to have been caught by something in her herb basket. Nessa glanced down and saw her own hand on the handle, still wearing the grass ring with August's button.

She had meant to take it off before now and stow it in her pocket, but had been distracted when she'd met the major. Now his gaze returned to her face, with such a searching, knowing expression that she felt her cheeks growing warm.

"I see you have a signet ring," he said, holding up his left hand. "Like mine."

It did look something like a signet ring, with the button's domed shape.

"Where did you get it?" the major asked. "From a sweetheart?"

"Not a sweetheart," she said, trying to sound as if it were the truth. "Only a very good friend."

Of course, August hadn't actually given her the button ring, but the truth was too complicated—and embarrassing—to share.

Major Elliot frowned in mock sternness. "A very good friend indeed, to raise such a blush. Come, Miss Shaw. Let there be no pretense between us. Who is the man? Is he in the army? Where is he from?"

"I don't actually know where he's from," Nessa said.

"He is a stranger to you?"

"Nay! That is—he doesn't know where he comes from, either."

"*He* doesn't know? What can you mean? How can he not know where he comes from?"

"Because he's lost his memory."

Major Elliot's eyebrows lifted. "Lost his memory?"

"Aye. I'm sure you've heard...Nay, perhaps you haven't. It all happened around the time you became ill, and then you were at Magnolia Grove."

He stared at her a moment, then said, "Clearly I have missed a great deal while I was away. Would you be good enough to enlighten me?"

So she told him how she'd found August, unconscious and with a wound to the back of his head, on the wooded trail two months earlier, and taken him to her brother's tent, and looked after him. How he'd woken with no memory of who he was or where he'd come from. How she and Rory had gone back later to where she'd discovered him and discovered a shallow grave where he'd been temporarily buried, and the remains of the fire where his clothing had been burned.

"That's where the button came from," she said. "We took him to General Greene and told him everything—this would have been four or five days after he was found. The general showed him to the officers, but none of them recognized him. You'd already begun your leave of absence and gone home by then, so you missed all that. Then about a week later, some horses that Colonel Kościuszko and his men had captured from the British were auctioned off in camp. One of the horses knew August, and August knew him."

"August?"

"That's his name—his Christian name. He remembers that, but not his surname. Most of his memory loss is of his personal history. He can remember events from the war, and historical events, and literature."

"I see. Go on. You say he recognized a horse?"

"Aye, a fine, well-fleshed horse, which suggests he hadn't been around here for long. Whoever attacked August must have realized he had to get rid of such a conspicuous animal, and James Island was a good place to take him, since the British were keeping their horses there. He couldn't have guessed that Kościuszko would capture them all so soon."

"Nay, I suppose he couldn't," the major said. "It must have come as a nasty shock to the man, to see the horse brought into the camp—assuming the attacker was in the camp at that time."

"We think he was. You see, the same day we told General Greene about August, a sergeant called Boyd was found dead near a supply depot—stabbed in the heart. And when Boyd's tent was searched, some coded messages were discovered, along with a saddle that had been hidden at the foot of the bed. Which certainly suggests that it was Sergeant Boyd who tried to kill August, but gives us no idea who killed Sergeant Boyd."

"He kept the saddle?" asked Major Elliot. "That was foolish. I suppose he thought he could wait a few years and then sell it, or even keep it for himself. Petty villains are often greedy fools."

"He may not have been so petty a villain," said Nessa. "The coded messages connect him to a conspiracy with the British."

"Did they? Well, I daresay he was a minor player in that particular drama. He doesn't sound as if he had the brains for a larger role."

He thought about that for a moment, then looked at Nessa again. "What else has been learned about this August fellow?"

"Not much, except that he's very well educated and appears to have a military background. Naturally his memory loss is terribly frustrating for him. He's certain he came to Ashley Hill for a purpose, and of course he wants to remember what that purpose is."

Hearing it all outlined in broad strokes, Nessa realized what a fantastic story it must appear to be. Major Elliot seemed understandably taken aback, but he was an intelligent man with a wide range of experience, and did not take long to assimilate it.

"So this is the young man—forgive me, I'm guessing that he is young, as I would suppose a man of riper years would not be walking around and having an audience with a major general so soon after having his head bashed in and spending some time buried alive."

"He doesn't know his age," said Nessa. "I would guess him to be around thirty."

"Thirty," the major repeated. "An age of great possibility. Old enough to have a good store of experience and to have gotten over being a complete fool, but young enough to have decades of strength and vigor ahead of him—assuming that he still has his health. It may surprise you to learn, Miss Shaw, that I myself am only thirty-two. But to return to the matter at hand—this is the young man whose frock coat button has been fashioned into a ring to adorn your hand."

"I was only playing," said Nessa. "You must think me foolish, but with so much solemnity around me from morning to night, I do long for a bit of gaiety at times. And the button is such a pretty thing, with that copper sunburst design."

"Aye, very distinctive. You deny, then, that you care for this man?"

"Of course I care for him. I'm his nurse, or I was."

Major Elliot held up a hand. "Please don't equivocate, Miss Shaw. You're better than that. Do yourself and me the compliment of returning a truthful answer."

Nessa lowered her head. "I do care for him in the sense that you mean. I don't know how I could not care for him. He is everything that is noble and good—brilliant and accomplished, yet playful as a child. I've known men with far less intellect and far fewer attainments show a much higher opinion of themselves. August is never arrogant. He loves knowledge, he delights in it. He doesn't use it to set himself apart from others—he wants them to enjoy it with him. He is brave and patient and kind, and as ardent a Patriot as I ever met."

Major Elliot listened quietly to all this. Then he said, "Far be it from me to mar any pleasure of yours, or to sully a man's name, without cause. But for your sake, if for no other reason, I must speak freely. I am afraid, Miss Shaw, that you have been blinded by your partiality to this man. You are trying to fit the facts to support the solution that you wish to be true—a natural but dangerous mistake in reasoning. Consider, please, that there are other conclusions to be drawn from the facts you have presented. You say that this August is a military man?"

"I said he appears to be. He's familiar with army procedures, and he is very knowledgeable about artillery."

"But the remnants of burned clothing you found—including that charming button—were not from a military uniform."

"That's right."

"Do you see what that means?"

"I take it to mean that he had resigned from military service prior to traveling to Ashley Hill."

"Possibly. But my dear Miss Shaw, is it not also possible that the man is a spy? A Tory, out of uniform, behind enemy lines—just like Major André."

Nessa knew about Major John André, the Adjutant General of the British Army, who had acted as Benedict Arnold's liaison in Arnold's plan to weaken the defenses of the fortress at West Point and hand it over to the enemy. Dressed in civilian clothing, Major André had met with General Arnold in secret to go over details of the surrender, then attempted to return to British lines. But he was stopped by some Patriot militia soldiers and searched. Inside his boots he had hidden a set of plans of the fortifications at West Point, along with other documents that showed Arnold to be a traitor. Because he was out of uniform, André was considered to be a spy, and he was ultimately executed as one, by hanging.

The decision to hang André had caused distress among Patriots, many of whom not only recognized that he had simply been following orders as a soldier, but had come to like and admire him during his captivity. General Washington was reported to have exerted considerable effort to have André returned to the British in a prisoner exchange, but the British refused. So André was hanged, and Arnold escaped to be made a Brigadier General by the British.

"Consider," said Major Elliot. "He traveled here from I know not where, dressed in civilian clothing, pretending to be I know not what—perhaps a merchant offering to supply the army. What his real plan was, I cannot say. He met with a confederate somewhere in the camp. The fact that he got struck on the back of the head suggests that the meeting went awry. However badly his mental processes may have been affected, he was coherent enough to understand that he was too unwell to get away. He would need help, and a good deal of time, to recover from his injury. Rather than risk being recognized as a spy, he burned his own clothing and presented himself as an amnesiac."

Nessa started shaking her head partway through this supposition and continued doing so to the end. "I tell you it is not so. August is not, he cannot be a British agent. He is a Patriot. The way he spoke of Yorktown, of General Washington—"

"Of course he spoke like a Patriot. He was in a Patriot camp."

"But he could not have been so calculating about it! He was not capable of being so. He was hurt, disoriented. His wound—"

"Just because a man is hit on the head does not mean he loses his memory. Most of the time he does not. But a clever man might feign memory loss or mental confusion in order to give himself time to rest, recover, assess his situation, and plan his next move. Or it may be that he was genuinely muddled at first, but soon got his wits back and pretended to be so still."

"It is not possible. I could not have been so deceived. August is a Patriot, and an ardent one. He spoke in perfect sincerity."

"So he may have done. He might well have been a Patriot at one time, but later found occasion to turn his coat. And once his memory is restored, so will his new allegiance be."

The major sighed. "I don't wish to vex you, Miss Shaw. Please believe that. I only want to put you on your guard. It seems unconscionably reckless of General Greene to allow this fellow to be at liberty in the camp, free to come and go as he chooses, and meet with whom he will. He could be doing all manner of mischief right under the general's nose."

"That is not possible. 'Tis true that he is free to move about, but he is being followed day and night by a protection and surveillance detail assigned to him by General Greene. Any clandestine meetings would surely be reported, if not prevented—but there have been none. He goes to see the general, and to visit his horse, and to divine service—and that is all."

Major Elliot thought a moment. "But the surveillance did not begin until after you presented August to General Greene. And you say the man Boyd was killed on that day. Is it possible that August killed Sergeant Boyd himself?"

Nessa opened her mouth and shut it again. She had been about to say that prior to his meeting with General Greene, August had never been left unattended—but that was not so, because she had come home from tending to Major Elliot's wound to find August missing from the tent. And the period when he was unaccounted for did overlap with possible times for Boyd's murder.

The major was watching her closely. "Be assured, Miss Shaw, that this man is doing more than you suppose. He has some sort of work going on of which you are not aware."

Then he checked himself. "But what business is it of mine? I am not currently a part of the Continental Army, and no one has asked for my opinion. General Greene must of course do what he thinks best. But I feel certain, Miss Shaw, that there will be more blood shed over this man—aye, and by his own hand—before all is said and done."

After they parted, she stood a while, thinking of all he had said and watching the laden wagons go past. Doubt and suspicion burned in her like poison. Was it possible—? Nay, she did not believe it. She knew August—not his origins or his full name, but the man himself. She could not be so wrong.

She took off the button ring, slipped it into her pocket, and walked slowly home.

Chapter Sixteen

A wisp of memory swept over August—of a kitchen paved with flagstones, and himself perched on a dishes dresser, short legs swinging in new linen breeches with stockings and buckled shoes, savoring the mouthwatering aroma of roast goose. Quite a contrast to his actual state—making yet another batch of salt pork and rice over an open fire, outdoors, in clothing that was coming apart at the seams. Nevertheless, he felt cheerful. He had spent a very profitable morning with the cipher, ending on the verge of a breakthrough.

After hours of tedious work that had produced one dead end after another, he had determined that the message had been encrypted with a Vigenère cipher. Close examination of the ciphertext had revealed some repeating sequences of letters, indicating the length of the keyword. He had then divided the text into groups of the same length as the keyword and had begun performing frequency analysis for each group.

Having come so far, he'd found it wrenchingly difficult to put down his pencil, fold up the papers, and return them to his boots in order to prepare the midday meal. But he had done it.

Nessa was scheduled to work a second shift at the hospital today, and Rory was putting in a full day at General Greene's command center, organizing paperwork for transport to Charlestown, assuming that the British really were about to sail away. That would give August a whole afternoon to finish the frequency analysis and come up with a likely keyword for the cipher. Then he would attempt to use that keyword to decrypt the message. If the decrypted message didn't make sense, he would try another keyword of the same length. Once he had the right keyword, decryption would not take long at all.

Nessa was a bit later than her usual time, so he set the three-legged covered pot to the side of the cookfire to keep warm. He put his nervous energy to good use, gathering firewood, drawing water, and tidying the camp area. Tent stakes tended to loosen over time, so he inspected the stakes around his own, Nessa's, and Rory's tents, re-driving and reinforcing where necessary.

At last Nessa came, walking briskly with her brown shawl around her shoulders and her herb basket hanging at her arm. A wave of fragrance, sharp and sweet, wafted out from the basket. For a moment he was back in that kitchen, with his bare feet on the flagstone floor, drinking something fizzy and cold with a pleasant bite to it.

"Are you remembering something?" Nessa asked. "You've got that look again."

"Aye, but nothing of import—only that someone in my household used to make small beer out of sassafras, and that I used to drink it on hot summer days. Most of my memories seem to be of the food and drink variety, or of vague horseback rides or travel by sea. They are interesting, but I would be better pleased with a sudden recollection of full name, date and place of birth, name of mother and father, military service record—and, of course, the reason I came to Ashley Hill."

"Don't forget the name of the man who hit you on the head," Nessa added as she set her basket inside her tent.

"Ah, but I did forget, you see. That's the trouble."

She smiled at the clumsy joke and took a seat on the stool he had brought out for her. Because Rory was not joining them today, the two of them would take their meal in the open air. It was a sunny day, though a bit breezy, and the cookfire was still warm.

He poured some boiling water from the kettle over some dried gingerroot in the chipped brown teapot and dished up some food for them both. They ate quickly, since Nessa had to return to the hospital soon. When they'd finished, Nessa poured them each a mug of ginger tea.

"We ought to offer a cup to Sandy Slinkalong," she said. "It must be dull, lonely work following you day after day, watching you live your blameless life and waiting in vain for you to do something worth reporting to General Greene."

"I would not dream of insulting Corporal Ballard by acknowledging my awareness of his presence," said August. "One day, when the war is over and I am known for an honest man and a Patriot, I will take him out for a drink. Until then, he must pretend that he is not following me, and I must pretend that I do not see him. That is the code we follow."

Her face turned sober. "Perhaps the end truly is in sight. They say the British are actually boarding their ships in Charlestown Harbor. Perhaps they really will just sail away and not come back." She sighed. "But I don't know. It may be that they have given up on the conspiracy—and it may be that they are biding their time, waiting for an opportune moment to strike. With the regiments from Maryland, Delaware, and Pennsylvania gone, we're more vulnerable than before. And I keep remembering something that happened when the British and the Tories were evacuating Wilmington, after Cornwallis surrendered at Yorktown. The Patriot militia was on a hillside just outside the town, watching them board their ships—my brother Fergus was among them. Suddenly a group of rogue Patriot dragoons rode down the slope and started slashing with their swords."

"I think I've heard of this," said August. "The dragoons didn't attack British soldiers. They attacked Tories."

"That's right. Do you know, I've heard a great many horrible stories of things that have been done in this war, but I believe the worst of them are the stories of Americans fighting Americans. The brutality, the viciousness, seems magnified when the fighting is between fellow countrymen." After a brief pause, Nessa went on, "The ship's cannon fired. There was a column of British soldiers on the dock, and the Patriot militia on the hillside. It could easily have turned into a messy battle, with both sides getting drawn in. But it didn't. The Patriot general kept control of his men, the rogue dragoons rode off, and the British got on their ships and sailed away. It came within a hair's breadth, though. And I keep wondering—what if a fight breaks out just when we think the British are about to leave Charlestown? What if that's their plan? What if they take advantage of the upheaval to strike? At that crucial moment, if anything happened to General Greene—oh, I can't bear to think of it. I wish we knew more about that conspiracy and their plans."

For an instant he was tempted to tell her about the cipher—in fact, he'd been tempted to tell her about it for weeks. An encrypted message of such complexity might well contain more pertinent and specific information than the simple Caesar ciphers found in Boyd's tent. And his excitement over the good progress he'd made on it today was something he longed to share with her. But he held his tongue. There would be time enough to explain later, after the message was decrypted—assuming the content even turned out to be useful. There was a chance—a miniscule chance that he hardly dared acknowledge—that it would have nothing to do with the conspiracy at all.

Instead he said, "God has guided and upheld us throughout this conflict, and he will not abandon us now. Within a few days, I hope, the British will be gone, and General Greene will be safely lodged in John Rutledge's house in Charlestown."

"I hope that also," said Nessa.

August stretched his legs out, crossed them at the ankles, and took a sip of tea. "Have I told you how grateful I am for your knowledge of herbal lore? I don't know if I ever had ginger tea before, but I love it now. It warms me up from the inside out."

Nessa wasn't listening. She was staring down at his feet, a furrow forming between her brows. "What is that sticking out of your boot?" she asked.

His heart gave a great painful throb in his chest. With a calm that he did not feel, he bent down to examine his feet. At some point in the past hour, some of the stitching in one of his boots had given way. For a length of a few inches, the sole had detached from the upper, leaving a gap that exposed a paper closely written with block letters.

"Only paper," he said. "The soles of my boots have been wearing thin, and I've had to stuff them with paper for insulation."

Her eyes met his, and there was something in them that he had never seen before. "That doesn't look like just any paper," she said. "It looks like a cipher."

She was watching him, waiting for him to explain. He opened his mouth, closed it, and finally let out a sigh. "The game is up," he said. "I'm caught, just like poor Major André."

It was another clumsy joke, but this time she was not amused. She actually looked a bit sick. "August," she said sharply, "what is that paper, and why is it in your boot?"

He told her.

"You copied a document you found in Rory's room?" she asked. "And went to work on it secretly? Without asking permission from General Greene?"

"I was afraid he wouldn't give me permission," August replied. "This isn't a simple code I can knock out in a single session in the general's command center, like the ones from Boyd's tent. This is a complex cipher. I still don't know what it says. It may turn out to be nothing. Asking permission would have slowed me down—assuming it were granted at all."

She was on her feet. "You have to tell the general today—now. We must go to him at once."

He stood. "Nessa! What's wrong?"

The expression in her brown eyes was desperate. "August, please. If you are what you say you are, an honest man and a Patriot, then prove it. Come with me to the command center and tell General Greene the truth. 'Tis the right thing to do, and you know it."

"But don't you have to be back at the hospital soon?"

"Never mind. We have to take care of this first. Please, August."

"All right. We'll go."

But when they arrived at the command center, they were not allowed to see the general. He was in a meeting with General Wayne, who was to lead an American party into Charlestown early the next day.

"I have to go to the hospital now," Nessa said. "Promise me you'll tell the general everything as soon as he gets out of his meeting. Promise me, August."

"I promise," he said.

As he walked back alone to the sutler's row, his feelings were rather mixed. He could see the situation from Nessa's point of view, but was not convinced that forthrightness on his part from the beginning would have been the correct choice. When he imagined himself telling General Greene that he had happened to find a mysterious encrypted message while poking around unattended in Rory's tent, and requesting official sanction to work on it, his mind could not conceive of a scenario in which he would receive a favorable response. It was far more likely that additional suspicion would have fallen on him, and blame on Rory for leaving the message where it could be found. If August did manage to decrypt the message, and the content turned out to be something of import, most likely all would be forgiven. If not, no one need ever know.

It was Nessa's distress that had wrested the promise from him. For a moment it had almost seemed as if she suspected him of something—or, rather, was trying not to suspect him.

A knot of people had gathered at a sort of alleyway running between the backs of two rows of tents. They were standing around, murmuring uneasily in the way of people who feel that something ought to be done about something and are waiting for someone else to do it. August shouldered his way right through to the center of the crowd.

Looking down on the ground, he saw the sandy hair, narrow face, and medium build of Corporal Ballard, lying on his back with one leg bent awkwardly beneath him, a small bloodstain on his hunting shirt just below the sternum.

"He can't have been here for long," someone was saying. "Ten minutes, maybe? Seems like I've seen him around before. His face is familiar, but I couldn't tell you his name."

A one-eyed man with a burn scar on his face—once a soldier, now a tinsmith in service to the army—gave August a hard stare. "You're that fellow who just turned up in camp one day with no explanation. I don't believe we've met."

"Is that so?" August asked, evading the implied question with an actual question of his own. More people in the crowd glanced at him and started to ease away from him.

August thought fast. Corporal Ballard had been a bodyguard of sorts, protecting him as well as monitoring his movements. Now Ballard was dead, killed in the same manner as Sergeant Boyd. General Greene's attitude toward August thus far had been as fair-minded as could be hoped, but for August to remain at liberty after this second murder seemed a lot to expect. He would have to be confined at the very least—and he couldn't afford that. There was too much at stake, and clearly August was dealing with a clever foe.

There were no notable athletes among the camp followers. Their numbers comprised women, children, and men who by reason of age or infirmity were unfit to be soldiers. A couple of the stouter men made uncertain movements as if to grab him, but when he turned on his heel and ran away, no one followed him.

Chapter Seventeen

A raw north wind blew through the woods, rattling the bare branches of maple and hickory trees overhead, driving the last of the year's dead leaves down the trail, and cutting through the brown shawl that Nessa held tightly around herself. She walked into the wind, head lowered, body tilted forward, welcoming the cold, wishing it could reach inside her to numb the pain.

Two days had passed since August had run away following the murder of Corporal Ballard. The entire camp and its environs, including the woods, had been searched, to no avail. According to Rory, General Greene went about looking grim and spent much time in conference with Major Elliot. Sources in Charlestown reported that the British and their allies had finished boarding their transport ships and were only awaiting favorable conditions to sail, but of course no one could be sure. Tension in the camp had reached an almost unbearable pitch.

Nessa carried no herb basket today. She wasn't even pretending to be doing anything other than walking alone in the place where she'd first found August.

Her thoughts were in turmoil. In spite of all that had happened, and everything Major Elliot had said, she still believed that August was no spy, but a true man and a Patriot. But was that only because she had been fooled? Had the whole of his interaction with her been a mere screen over what he truly was? Had he been preying on her feelings for him, using her to get what he wanted, while secretly carrying out his plot to overthrow the fragile republic?

Her heart told her that it was not so. But wasn't that exactly what it would say, if she had been fooled?

She reached the old homesite and halted there. Beneath the wintry sky grey hanging low overhead, it looked more desolate than ever, with dried tendrils of bindweed twining around the fallen timbers of the house, and the eerie ring of sassafras trees creeping back into the cleared land. This must once have been a cheerful, hopeful place. She wondered about the man who had first carved it out of the woods, perhaps in the early days of the South Carolina colony—laying his foundation, building his cabin, fetching rocks for his fireplace. Had there been a wife who'd cooked over the open fire at the cozy hearth? Had they survived on berries and wild game, spending their evenings dreaming of plowed fields, sturdy barns, and contented livestock? Judging from the state of the woods, they hadn't ever managed to clear any additional land for farming. Now they were in their graves, and the forest was taking back their home, erasing their hard work, making a mockery of their dreams.

She sat down on the cold ground before the old fireplace. The chimney shielded her a little from the wind. There were no scraps of charred fabric or tarnished buttons left in the hearth now, only ash.

"Don't turn around."

Her breath caught in her throat, and a wild spasm of unreasoning joy passed through her, because the voice was August's voice. He was here, close by, within reach. She had only to turn her head to see his face.

But he had said not to, and like a silly lovestruck girl, she obeyed.

"If you're asked if you saw me, I want you to be able to say that you didn't," said August. "I understand that you might choose to tell them anyway. I wouldn't blame you if you did. But they won't find me. They've already beaten these woods once. I kept myself hidden then, and I can do it again."

"Why did you run?" she asked. "It looked black against you, August. You could have gone to the general and told him the truth."

"You know I couldn't. Even if he believed me innocent of killing Ballard, duty would compel him to place me in confinement at the very least. And I could hardly expect to be allowed to go on decrypting the message if I were being held on suspicion of murder."

"Why? What would be the harm in allowing you to work on the cipher? Once it has been decrypted, we'll know more about what the conspirators are planning."

"That's assuming that the message was written from one conspirator to another, and that it ultimately reached its intended recipient. There are other possibilities that would occur to someone who isn't convinced of my fidelity. The author of the message might have been a Patriot who suspected treachery within the Continental Army and didn't know whom he could trust. Or if it was the work of traitors, the information in it could be something previously unknown to me as a fellow traitor, and valuable to me. And we don't have time for the matter to be debated. I simply must get the decrypting done without a moment's delay. I told you I'd determined that it is written in a Vigenère cipher that has a keyword of thirteen characters. I've been racking my brain trying to come up with words or phrases that might work, but so far—"

"Where did you sleep last night? It was so cold. I thought about you all night long, out in the open with no shelter, not even a blanket."

He paused, and when he spoke again there was a wonderful tenderness in his voice. "Dear heart, don't fret over me. I'm an old soldier, remember? At least I think I am. If my brothers in arms endured winters in Morristown and Valley Forge for the sake of independence, then surely I can suffer through a cold night in South Carolina. I have my army greatcoat, anyway. 'Tis a good thing I was wearing it when we went to call on General Greene. 'Tis a better thing still that I got away with the papers in my boots and a bit of pencil in my pocket."

"Are you hungry?"

"Not very. Don't worry about that, and don't try to bring out any food for me. I don't want to cause any trouble for you."

"Then why are you risking talking to me at all?"

"Because I had to tell you that I love you."

It was done. The words were spoken. They were out in the open where they could never be taken back. Sitting there on the cold ground, in the midst of all her troubles and worries, Nessa felt a wave of perfect happiness wash over her.

"I think this can come as no great surprise to you," August went on. "I have loved you almost since the moment I first saw you. Perhaps it is wrong for me to say so, when I don't even know if I am free to love in that way. But now, with my very life in the balance, I don't know when or if I'll have another chance."

Nessa swallowed over a tight lump in her throat. She was trembling all over, and the rocks in the empty chimney turned blurry with tears.

"You don't have to say it back," August went on. "You don't have to say anything at all. You don't owe me anything. It is I who am indebted to you. If I had a thousand lives to live I could never possibly repay—"

"I love you, too," she said. "I can't help it. I love you, August."

He didn't answer, but laid a hand on her shoulder, and she covered it with her own. Neither of them was wearing gloves, and she could feel how the cold had chapped his skin.

"I told myself I wasn't going to touch you," he said in a voice thick with emotion. "I was afraid that if I did, I wouldn't be able to let you go."

"I don't want you to leave," she replied. "But you've got to."

"I know it. And I will. But first I want to capture this moment in my heart to hold onto later, to keep me warm. Nessa—Nessa, I love you so. I will not urge you to trust me. I will show you that I may be trusted, and do all that is within my power to make myself worthy of you."

He drew his hand away. She kept still a minute or so longer, and when at last she turned, he was gone.

SOMEONE WAS HOLDING August's head underwater, someone bigger and stronger than August, someone who always got his own way. The two of them always did what *he* said, because he was older smarter and usually right, and most of the time August didn't mind. But this time August had resisted. He didn't want to get out of the water yet—he was enjoying his swim. So his companion had pushed him under the water and held him there, and August was frightened, because he didn't want to die and he could feel his life about to slip away, but he was also angry, because it wasn't *fair*. Above him, sunlight glinted off some small metal object that hung around his assailant's neck. He closed his hand on it and pulled with all his might.

Next thing he knew, he was gasping and coughing, with his hair plastered to his skull and his shaking legs feebly churning water beneath him, struggling to keep his head above the surface. And directly across from him was an indignant face with a pair of steely-blue eyes like his own.

With a great gasp, August came awake in the platform-like pocket formed by the spreading branches of the hospitable live oak tree where he'd been spending most of his hours since leaving the sutler's row. In an instant, the summer afternoon had changed to a bitter December morning, and he nearly pitched himself out of the tree before coming to himself.

He lay still, holding fast to the branches of the tree, his breath making a cloud of fog. He no longer believed that the drowning dream was only a dream. It was a memory, and an important one—possibly the key that would unlock all the other memories. He sensed that he was on the verge of something, right on the cusp of remembering. At the same time, he felt a great dread, as if part of him didn't want to remember.

He stayed there a while, motionless, desperate to grab hold of what it all meant, but the dream, or memory, had already turned to vapor.

With a sigh, he shifted his weight, trying to ease some of the soreness out of his body, only to put stress on another set of muscles. He had spent most of the past two days here, reasoning that any search parties would concentrate on the forest floor and not bother climbing every tree. His precarious perch had allowed only brief snatches of fitful sleep, and at night he'd heard scrabbling sounds from some sort of varmint, perhaps a hibernating squirrel having a meal in its periods of wakefulness. He was cold and exhausted and covered with scratches. Hungry, too, but the hunger pangs had lessened after the first day.

He took the sheaf of papers out of his greatcoat pocket, along with his bit of pencil, and went back to work.

He'd been working on the cipher hour after hour after leaving the sutler's row, and still he didn't have it solved. He was weary to death of letters and calculations and wanted only to find some warm, quiet place where he could hide himself and sleep for years and years. He kept telling himself that every failed attempt brought him closer to success, which was theoretically true, but only if he had unlimited time, which he didn't. If he didn't decrypt the cipher soon, he might as well not decrypt it at all. Perhaps all this effort was a waste.

But he took hold of those thoughts and put them aside as if he were clearing rubbish from a work surface. After all, where would the Revolution be if people gave up when a thing was impossible?

He glanced over the scribblings that filled the pages in his hands. Ever since leaving the camp, he'd spent most of his waking hours attempting to use frequency analysis to determine the cipher's keyword, filling in various spots with some of the more common letters in different combinations, but that approach hadn't yielded anything useful thus far. There were simply too many possible combinations, and thirteen characters made for a fairly long word, if it was only one word. He had even tried bypassing the frequency analysis by coming up with several thirteen-character words and phrases, which he then used one by one as the keyword. Achieving success with that method would have been no more than blind luck, and he was not surprised when he failed. Rows of block letters, struck through with angry horizontal lines, marched down his paper.

~~RULEBRITANNIA~~
~~TOWNSHENDACTS~~
~~ENLIGHTENMENT~~
~~HANOVERSHOUSE~~

Of course, he had no reason to suppose that the keyword should have anything to do with royalist philosophy, or make any sense at all. It could just as easily be a line taken at random from a farmer's almanack, or from a tradesman's bill. Indeed, for security purposes, the more random the keyword, the better.

If it had been August himself making the cipher, however, he would have found it nearly impossible to resist the temptation to choose a keyword of some special significance to himself or to his cause. He was a romantic at heart, and he couldn't help but believe that the encryptor would turn out to be one, as well—as if his foe were merely a dark reflection of himself.

Most likely he was just being fanciful, trying to impose a semblance of order on a problem of incalculable complexity.

His fingers were so numb and shrunken with cold that they could barely hold the pencil anymore, and he was running out of space on his sheet of foolscap. He dug into his pocket and pulled out all the paper scraps he had been using in his decrypting exercise. Most of them were fairly covered with writing, but he did manage to find one small piece, folded down the middle, that appeared blank.

He unfolded the page. Nay, not entirely blank. It had writing, but on one side only. The handwriting was not his own.

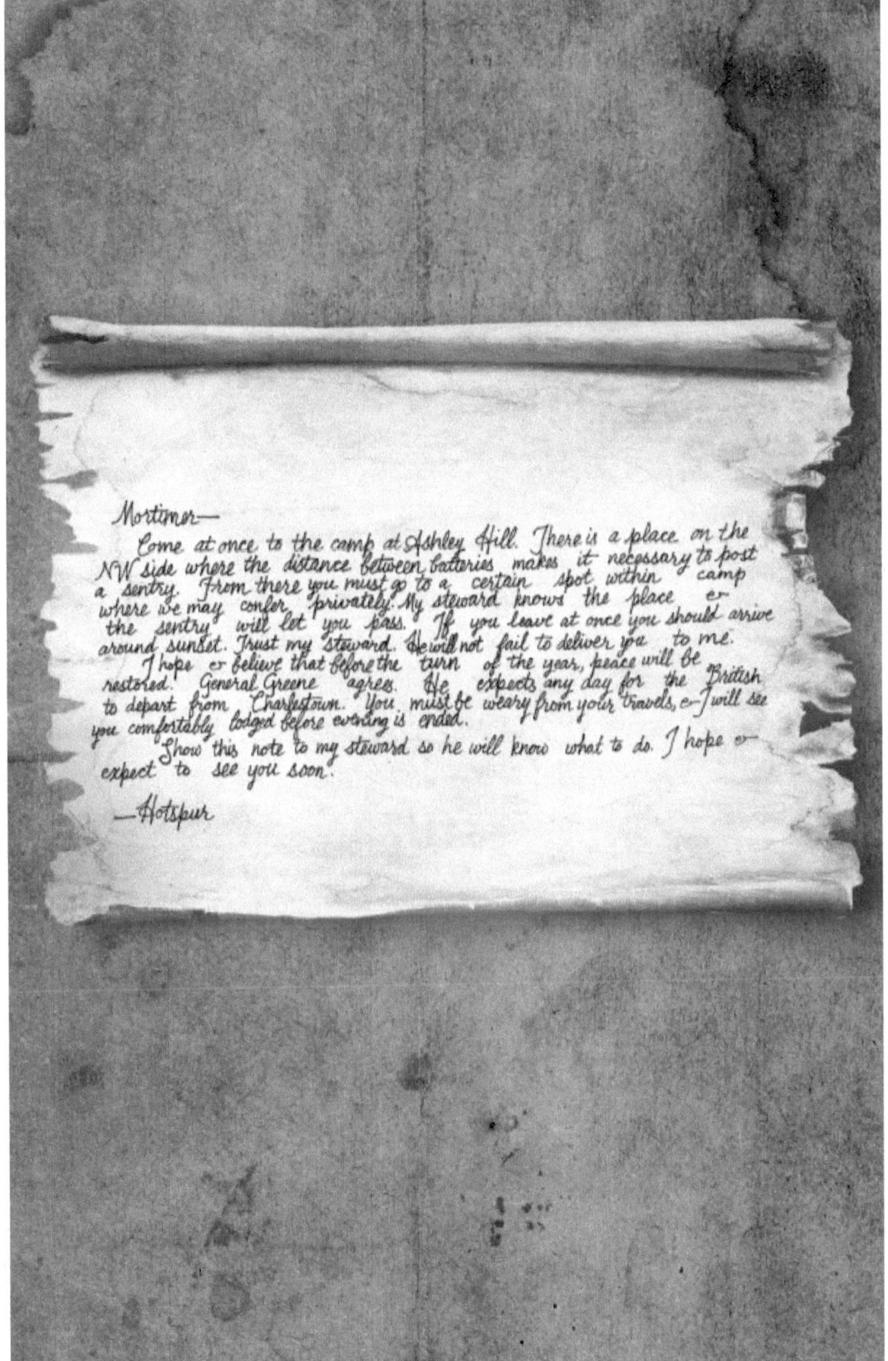
Mortimer—
Come at once to the camp at Ashley Hill. There is a place on the NW side where the distance between batteries makes it necessary to post a sentry. From there you must go to a certain spot within camp where we may confer privately. My steward knows the place & the sentry will let you pass. If you leave at once you should arrive around sunset. Trust my steward. He will not fail to deliver you to me.
I hope & believe that before the turn of the year, peace will be restored. General Greene agrees. He expects any day for the British to depart from Charlestown. You must be weary from your travels, & I will see you comfortably lodged before evening is ended.
Show this note to my steward so he will know what to do. I hope & expect to see you soon.

—Hotspur

Mortimer—

Come at once to the camp at Ashley Hill. There is a place on the NW side where the distance between batteries makes it necessary to post a sentry. From there you must go to a certain spot within camp where we may confer privately. My steward knows the place & the sentry will let you pass. If you leave at once you should arrive around sunset. Trust my steward. He will not fail to deliver you to me.

I hope & believe that before the turn of the year, peace will be restored to this land. General Greene agrees. He expects any day for the British to depart from Charlestown. You must be weary from your travels, & I will see you comfortably lodged before evening is ended.

Show this note to my steward so he will know what to do. I hope & expect to see you soon.

—Hotspur

It was the note that had been found in his saddlebag, addressed to him by some unknown compatriot, presumably writing from Ashley Hill. After all the hours he had spent poring over combinations of letters that made no sense at all, it seemed strange to look on a piece of straightforward writing with no hidden meaning.

He remembered something Nessa had said about how time-consuming it must have been for agents of espionage in French and Spanish courts to painstakingly encrypt their messages. He had replied that there were some encryption methods that were quick and easy to encrypt and decrypt, while also being quite secure—like the Greek scytale rod and the Florentine mask. Then she'd said something about the possibility of making an encrypted message look as if there were nothing encrypted about it, to which he'd responded that that would be the best encryption of all.

He sat there, thinking of Nessa, wishing he were with her in some warm, comfortable parlor far away from here, in a place safe from war. The dark-green leaves of his live oak tree rustled overhead and all around him. He had one leg braced against a branch, with the note from the saddlebag resting on the thigh. The page had a crease running down its center. Idly he stared at it.

Then he sat up straight and held it in front of his face. It was as if an actual mask had been laid over the page, covering all the words except for some of those in the center, which formed an undulating symmetrical shape on either side of the crease.

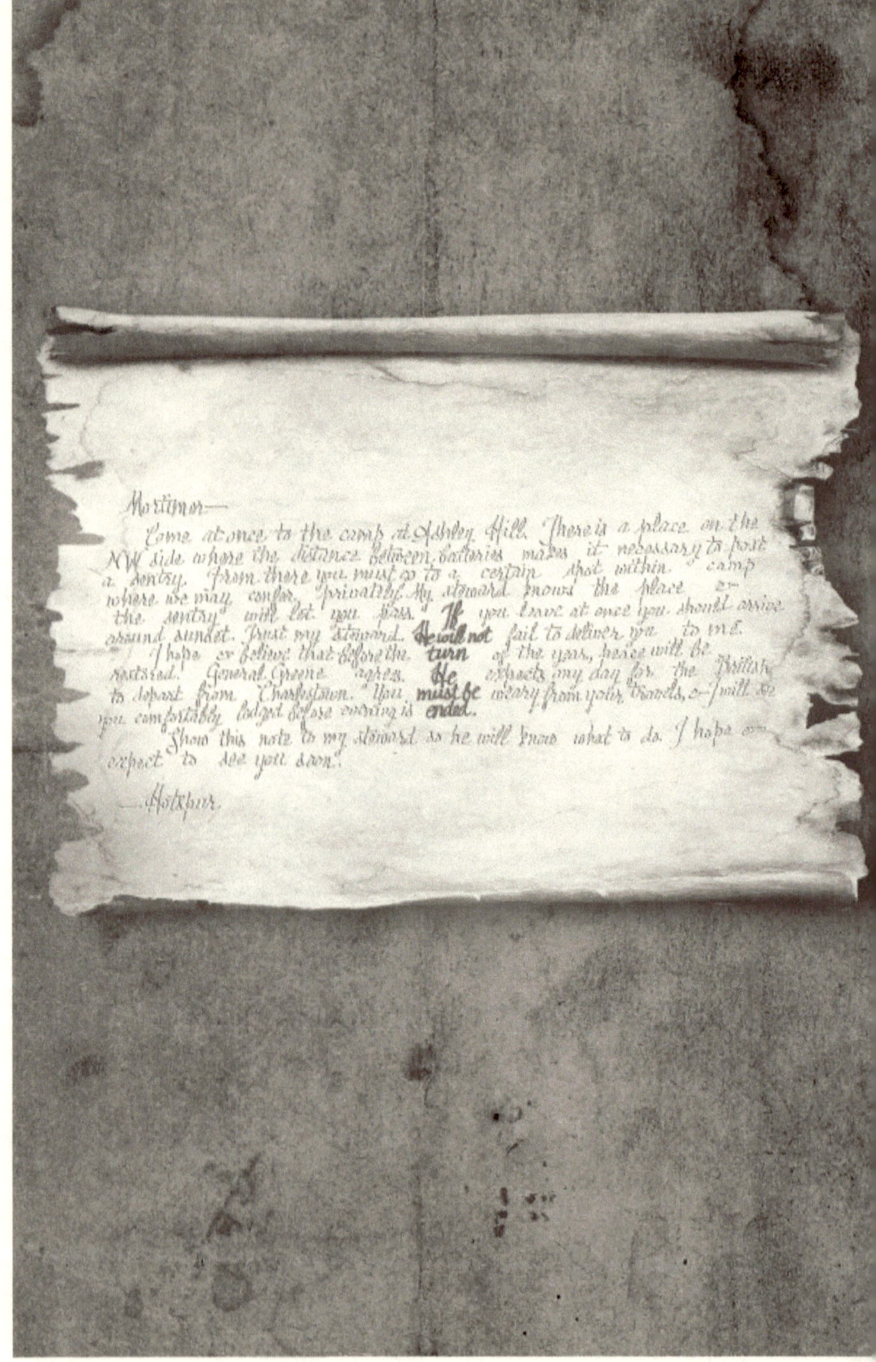

Mortimer—
Come at once to the camp at Ashley Hill. There is a place on the NW side where the distance between batteries makes it necessary to post a sentry. From there you must go to a certain spot within camp where we may confer privately. My steward knows the place & the sentry will let you pass. If you leave at once you should arrive around sundet. Trust my steward. He will not fail to deliver you to me.
I hope & believe that before the turn of the year, peace will be restored. General Greene agrees. He expects any day for the British to depart from Charlestown. You must be weary from your travels, & I will see you comfortably lodged before evening is ended.
Show this note to my steward as he will know what to do. I hope & expect to see you soon.

—Hotspur

If he will not turn he must be ended.

He slowly lowered the paper, his mind racing. Things he had barely noticed before suddenly came into view and made sense—the ragged margins, the uneven spacing, the occasional awkward phrasing. How could he have missed it? There were two messages here—one to him, and one to another person. The full-page, seemingly innocuous text, inviting August to come to the camp to discuss some errand, and that narrow, sinister, brutal sentence, ordering someone else to kill August if he couldn't be persuaded to do something. August had been tricked by a mask cipher.

A great stillness settled over him, and his mind's eye turned to some long-past day. He saw a worn deal table, and a piece of paper covered by another paper with an oblong opening cut out of the center. In the open space, in short, uneven lines, August had written his message on the bottom page.

Meet me at the gatehouse at midnight. Bring twenty gold doubloons and a map of the palace. Also some cream puffs from the kitchen.

"Very good," said a voice—deep, and grave, and kind. Then a hand—long and lean, with ink stains on the fingers—drew the mask away, leaving the bottom sheet with its narrow oblong of writing. "Now you must disguise your plaintext by filling up the rest of the page with words—and not just any words, but words that will combine with your plaintext to form an intelligible, rational communication that may be looked upon without suspicion by anyone who sees it. You mustn't crowd your words, or spread them out too thin, or make your margins too ragged."

August looked across the table into a pair of deep-set, grey-blue eyes in a seamed face. *Grandfather.*

A boyish voice called from another room. "August, hurry up! Let's go swimming."

Then his world was spinning, tilting, and he was back in the pond, desperately sucking in breath after breath of sweet, clean air and peering up into his cousin's face. It was a strong face, old for its age, with a long nose, a firm mouth, and straight brows over blue-grey eyes—eyes that at the moment looked indignant and slightly hurt. The chest and shoulders were bare, and laced with stringy adolescent muscle. The dark hair was shoulder length, in the fashion of an earlier decade, but tossed back to reveal a thin line of blood around the back of the neck. And August had in his hand a hard lump of metal with the ends of a dangling chain drifting in the water around his closed fist.

"Give it back!"

The shout was a boy's shout, not yet changed to a man's deeper pitch, and what was meant to sound imperious was merely petulant. Moving more quickly than he would have thought possible in his current state, August scrambled out of the water and onto the bank before dropping the thing he held in his hand.

His companion followed him out of the water and picked up the metal heap—a signet ring on a heavy chain. He examined it greedily, then turned his gaze back to August with a scowl. "You broke the clasp. Why would you do that?"

August's jaw dropped open. "Why would I...? What else could I do? I had to get free of you somehow. You were holding me underwater! You nearly drowned me—and all because I wasn't ready to finish my swim!"

"Don't be ridiculous, August," said Andrew, in a voice that suddenly sounded patient and grown-up. "I was only playing. I was going to let you up—I was just about to do it. You didn't think I was actually going to drown you, did you?"

He looked so puzzled and hurt that August began to doubt himself, and even to feel guilty. The outraged part of him that knew he'd been wronged was not assertive or articulate enough to stand its ground.

"You—you held me under!" August sputtered. "I couldn't breathe!"

His cousin smiled, a fond, patient, indulgent smile. "Poor old Auggie. Were you frightened? I should have gone easier on you. I forget sometimes how much younger you are than I am. Go on back in the water now and finish your swim. There's no real harm done, and I won't tell Grandfather how the chain got broken."

But swimming had lost its charm for August, for that day and forever. He never again went into that clear green pond on his grandfather's property, and he continued to have an abiding horror of drowning and suffocation. But for the rest of that year's visit, his cousin was so winsome and charming, so downright deferential to August's wishes, that the two of them were soon as good of friends as they ever had been.

August closed his eyes and leaned his head against the oak. Something hurt deep inside him; something had broken that would never quite heal.

But he didn't have time to mourn now. He opened his eyes and shuffled his papers until he found the one with the long row of scratched-out, tried and rejected keywords.

He stared at them. "Can it really be that simple?" he said softly.

Then he laid the page down, and at the very bottom he wrote MAGNOLIAGROVE.

Chapter Eighteen

I t was another cold night. Nessa could hardly sleep, thinking about August, out in the woods with only a greatcoat to shield him from the biting wind, trying to wrest sense and meaning out of that confounded paper with its baffling collection of letters.

She wished Rory would come home, but he was busy at the command center, working late hours to prepare for the removal of General Greene's papers to the Charlestown house of John Rutledge, former governor of South Carolina. Perhaps it was just as well that there was no opportunity to discuss the situation with him. If he knew that August was hiding out in the woods, he might feel obligated to tell General Greene. It might be best to spare him from having to make such a choice.

When she got up in the dreary grey morning, Rory wasn't there. Either he'd come home late and left early, or he'd stayed all night at the command center. Probably the latter. Nessa made her solitary breakfast over the cookfire where August had cheerfully prepared so many meals for the three of them. He must be famished by now. Maybe she would take him some food, although he'd told her not to. But what if she herself were being watched? Her attempt at kindness might lead to his capture.

There was an air of hushed excitement in the sutler's row that morning. The word from town was that the British transports had left their docks and were sailing toward the Bar. The camp followers didn't seem to know quite what to do with the news. It was what they had been looking forward to for so long, and now that it had happened, it didn't feel real. Some of the camp followers weren't ready to believe that the ships had actually sailed away. Others thought maybe it was a trick. Maybe the soldiers hadn't really gone on board the transports, or maybe they'd crept off again in the middle of the night and were now hiding in the town, waiting for the American party to enter, at which point they'd attack, and seize General Greene.

Nessa was too tired and worried to venture an opinion. She listened to the various theories for a while, then went to work. No matter what the British were doing or not doing in their transports, there were still sick men in the hospital who needed care.

When she arrived, she was surprised to see a new face among the patients—new to the hospital, at least, but familiar to her.

"Why, Harry!" she said. "Is that you?"

It was indeed Harry Beach, Rory's one-time friend, but terribly changed. He was thinner, and flushed with fever, but there was something more, a sort of vacant, haunted look that Nessa had seen a thousand times on the faces of men whose souls were scarred by combat, though Harry had been confined to camp for the entirety of his brief military career.

"Hello, Miss Shaw," Harry said. His voice sounded rough and raw, but it was still a young man's voice.

"I haven't seen you in weeks," said Nessa. Since the middle of October, in fact, not long after August had been found—about a month and a half ago. It seemed a short time for so profound a change.

"What brings you to the hospital?" she asked.

Silently, Harry held up his right hand. It was grossly swollen, fingers, wrist, and all, with an angry red hue, and dark streaks radiating from an abscess in the meaty base of the thumb. Nessa went cold inside. She had seen enough dirty wounds to recognize gangrene when she saw it, and she knew that Harry was most likely going to lose that hand, and possibly the lower arm as well.

"Oh, Harry," she said. "How did this happen?"

He gave a brief twitch of a shrug. "I got a splinter one day while gathering firewood. It was a big one, a good half-inch. I tried to dig it out with my knife, and I thought I got it all, but it didn't get better."

Nessa could hardly stop herself from groaning aloud in frustration and grief. He should have reported to the hospital at once, and had the wound properly cleaned and dressed, and rested long enough for it to heal completely. Instead, he'd evidently carried on with his usual routine—in fact, now that she came to think of it, she recalled hearing Rory say that Harry had gone out of his way to get assigned to extra work details, which clearly had kept the tissue irritated and driven new contaminants into the raw flesh, day after day and week after week. Now an otherwise healthy young man was about to lose his hand, not to a combat injury, but to a simple wood splinter that would have healed cleanly with proper care. This was one of the more maddening parts of her job—the preventable tragedies.

She wanted to rail at Harry, scold him, lecture him on everything he'd done wrong. But the time for lectures was past, and Harry already appeared to be overflowing with misery.

Often during her hospital work, Nessa would keep a stream of light chatter going, to give the patient something to think about other than his own suffering. Other times she was silent, sharing space and giving wordless sympathy. This time, she sensed that the right thing to do was to listen. Harry wasn't talking much, but she suspected it was not because he had nothing to say. She would have to draw him out.

"Rory tells me one of your brothers was at Camden," she said. "Our brother Fergus was there also, with General Caswell's militia. I think Rory said your brother was a Continental?"

"Aye," said Harry. "That was Hugh, the eldest. He was with the Fourth South Carolina, under Colonel Buford. Killed in action. My second brother, Joseph, died at the Siege of Savannah with Father, both on the same day. They were in Gadsden's regiment. Thomas was the one next to me in age. He was at Guilford Courthouse under Colonel Laurens. So then there was just me left, and when I turned sixteen, I joined up to do my part."

"I'm sure your father and brothers would be very proud," Nessa said.

Harry's face stiffened, then collapsed. His shoulders hunched, and he hung his head and sobbed—loud, wrenching, violent sobs.

Nessa didn't think twice. She took his head on her shoulder as if he had been Rory, and he did not resist. He wept long and hard. And when at last his tears had been spent, he lifted his face and said, "Oh, Miss Shaw, I've done a terrible thing."

It took some time to get Harry's whole story straight, but eventually it transpired that some months earlier, Harry had been assigned sentry duty at the low spot on the west side of camp between the two artillery batteries. This was to be his first time acting as a sentry. He had gone to his post well before twilight, and a sergeant in his regiment had given him some extra strong coffee to help keep him alert. Harry had appreciated the gesture, though he hadn't expected to have trouble. It was only First Watch, after all. But the sergeant had warned him that the solitude and boredom made it hard for a man to keep his eyes open, and he'd been right. Harry hadn't been on duty long when a powerful sleepiness came over him, in spite of the coffee. He'd done all he could to stay awake, walking briskly around, jumping up and down, and trying to recite the Articles of War from memory, but his sleepiness was like a heavy weight pressing down on him, and he finally couldn't bear it anymore and sat down to rest his eyes for a few minutes. He fell asleep instantly and began to have strange dreams, beautiful and terrifying, ending with a sort of vision of a huge dark horse, without saddle or rider, that galloped past in a thunder of hooves, barely a foot away from his head. He then came awake with a start. He could see by the position of the moon how much time had passed—about three hours. He had slept for nearly his entire watch.

Nessa listened to all this with outward calm, prompting and clarifying when necessary. A horrible suspicion was forming in her mind. The seemingly generous offer of coffee; the deep, heavy sleep; the fantastic dreams—they all pointed to a conclusion that seemed plain enough to her, with her hospital experience, though their meaning had escaped poor Harry. Now she asked, although she already knew the answer, "Was this the night that the sentries were questioned about afterward, whether any man had passed or anything out of the ordinary had happened?"

Harry flinched. "Aye. I lied and said none had passed. I had already lied once, you see, to the sentry who relieved me and to my commanding officer. I thought—I hoped—that it was true, and that no harm would come, and no one would ever know. And for a while it appeared that way. That entry point is considered low risk, and there were no reports of enemies sneaking into camp. But then the inquiries were made about that very night, whether anyone gave admittance to a tall man in civilian clothing, probably on horseback, and I said nay. I was afraid. And not long after that, when I was helping dig a new latrine, I saw a tall man leaving the camp with Kościuszko and some of his men, and he was riding the horse from my dream! A buckskin with a dark face and points, very distinctive. There was no mistaking him. So then I knew my dream hadn't been a dream at all."

"And still you didn't tell the truth?"

Harry shook his head, refusing to meet her eyes.

"But Harry, don't you see how serious this is? There's no telling who came through while you were sleeping. And 'tis important that the general know who came and went that night—not only for the security of the camp as a whole, but for specific reasons. The tall man you saw riding the buckskin—he's been accused of terrible things. But no one knows what really happened that night. And by giving false information, you've muddied the waters."

"I know it, miss," Harry said wretchedly. "But the penalty for falling asleep on sentry duty is death. I'd be shot—or hanged. And what would my poor mother do then? She's lost so much already. How could she bear it if her last son turned out to be a miserable failure?"

This, of course, was why Harry had been throwing himself into extra fatigue details, trying to make up for this one terrible lapse. But it hadn't worked. He had only driven the infection deeper, body and soul. She pitied him from her heart, but she was also angry. He had lied, and trouble had followed—for himself and others.

Oh, Harry, she thought. *You poor, foolish, trusting boy.*

But all she said was, "I don't think you'll be hanged or shot when the circumstances are known."

"What circumstances?"

"Harry, there isn't enough coffee in the whole of the camp to keep one sentry awake for a single turn at guard duty. Whatever that man gave you, 'twas not coffee. He drugged you—probably with laudanum. That's why you fell asleep and had strange dreams. Chicory would disguise the bitter taste, and you wouldn't know the difference because you've never had real coffee."

Harry sniffed. "Why would he do that?"

"Because he wanted to get someone into the camp secretly." And because he knew that Harry was a weak link, easily manipulated, and certain to keep quiet afterward out of fear. If only Harry had spoken up earlier! Things might have been so different. But none of this was Harry's fault. He was only a pawn.

Nessa turned and faced Harry head-on. His eyes were puffy and his nose was swollen.

"Tell me the name of the man who gave you the drink," she said.

"'Twas Sergeant Boyd. Him that was found dead not long after."

No surprise there. Nessa let out a grim sigh.

Harry must have misinterpreted her sigh, and immediately added, "Wait. You don't think that—that I killed him?"

"Nay, of course not," Nessa said hastily. "But, Harry, Sergeant Boyd was conspiring with the British in a plot to kill General Greene and conquer the South. There were papers discovered in his tent after his death that prove it."

Harry frowned. "That can't be right."

"Oh, Harry, I know you thought he was being kind to you, but he was only tricking you for his own purposes."

"Aye, I believe that part," said Harry. "But he couldn't have been conspiring with the British—leastways, not with papers. Sergeant Boyd couldn't read nor write."

Nessa opened her mouth, then shut it again. She remembered what August had said about the coded messages found in Boyd's tent, how absurdly simple the coding method was. Too simple to be the work of the mastermind of an actual complex conspiracy, but exactly the sort of thing that would seem believable for a man of little education to have managed, assuming he could read. Those messages were meant to be found, and meant to be decoded. Sergeant Boyd, whatever other moral failures he might have been guilty of, had not been a major player in a treasonous plot. He had been used as hired muscle by someone far cleverer, and set up to deflect suspicion from that person, and killed before he could give up the truth to the Patriots, or threaten to do so.

But what *was* the truth that the clever puppet-master was so zealous to conceal? What could be grave enough to screen with an elaborate fiction about a fake conspiracy?

And who was the puppet-master?

THE NEW KEYWORD FIT.

August transcribed rapidly, letter by letter, no longer feeling the cold, until the entire plaintext was written on the back of his cousin's note.

The day the British cross the Bar, General Greene and Governor Mathews will be killed, and agents will be sent to kill select members of the legislature. As soon as Greene and Mathews are dead, I will send you an express. When you receive it, you must immediately kill Governor Martin and those assemblymen you deem prudent to eliminate. Blame David Fanning or other firebrands as needed. A similar express will go to Savannah at the same time. With the civil government in disarray, our people will step in and take control. I will be appointed acting governor of S. Carolina. Stage 1 will then be complete and we will begin on Stage 2. Time is of the essence so hold yourselves ready to act.

He sat there a moment, stunned. He'd had it all wrong. They all had—including General Greene. August had to reach him now and tell him the truth while there was still time—if indeed it was not already too late.

He folded the papers, carefully placed them in the pocket of his greatcoat, and climbed down from the tree. He could feel the stitching in his boots coming apart from the strain, and by the time he reached the ground, the soles had split from the uppers at the toes. Running as best he could, he hurried down the trail, out of the woods, and into the sutler's row.

As a known fugitive, he expected to be arrested at once, but that was perfectly all right with him. He didn't care if he was seized, beaten, and manacled, as long as he was taken to General Greene, and quickly.

But the camp seemed strangely empty, and of those who remained, no one had attention to spare for him. He made it all the way to the command center—or what had been the command center—unchallenged. General Greene's sleeping and dining marquees had been emptied and were in the process of being taken down. Only the storage tents were intact—one for tack, luggage, and miscellaneous gear, and another for documents. Sentries guarded the entrances.

Beyond the storage tents lay the fenced pasture where the horses were kept. August crossed behind them, avoiding the guards. There was no point in getting himself captured if General Greene wasn't in the camp, and it was beginning to look as if this was the case.

"You're back."

The voice was quiet and calm, and August knew it well. He turned to see Rory, bleary-eyed and bedraggled, standing at the corner, just outside of the document tent.

"I didn't kill Corporal Ballard," August said. There was no time to waste on niceties.

"Oh, I know that," said Rory. "If you were going to kill him, you'd have managed to do it in a way that didn't make you look so guilty. The real clincher was when a knife with a long, thin blade was found in your tent after you'd run away. 'Twas a clumsy contrivance, far too convenient to be believable, but the sort of thing that had to be acted on. You were right to get out while you could."

Some of the tension left August's body. "I've decrypted the cipher," he said. "Where is General Greene?"

"He departed earlier this morning."

"For Charlestown? Governor Rutledge's house?"

Rory looked around before answering. "Most of the camp thinks so, but nay. You know of the threat to his life mentioned in the messages found in Boyd's tent. At the last minute it was decided that the general should go to a private residence in the countryside instead."

"Magnolia Grove," said August.

"Aye, that's right."

A soft nicker and a nudge at his shoulder told August that Arion had heard his voice and come to greet him. August lifted a hand to his horse's neck in an automatic caress.

"How long ago did they leave?" he asked.

"Half an hour, perhaps. They took a coach so the general would not be seen. No one would think it odd for Major Elliot to travel by coach. His injury makes it impossible for him to ride a horse."

"I know about his injury," August said shortly. "They would have left the camp by the sentry post on the western side of the camp, in the low spot between the two batteries, and then followed the Ashley River Road north for a couple of miles before turning west."

"I would assume so," said Rory. "There's a good east-to-west road that leads from there to Magnolia Grove."

"I remember," August said.

It was coming back to him—his journey from his cousin's plantation to Ashley Hill along one of the better private roads he had seen in the state over his weeks of travel southward. Some five or six miles from the junction with the Ashley River Road, he and his companion had forded a creek at a crossing spot that had been made into a small way-station where horses could rest and drink before continuing the journey. Stone shelters had been built on either side for the comfort and convenience of riders and passengers.

A movement out of the corner of his eye caught his attention. His presence in the camp had finally been noticed. Two soldiers were coming his way.

He vaulted the fence, took hold of Arion's mane, and swung himself onto the horse's bare back. Gripping hard with his thighs, he dug his heels into Arion's sides. Arion responded instantly, breaking into a canter, and making a wide circle as August turned him to the right by pressing against his left side.

August could hear the soldiers' shouts, but they seemed to come from a great distance away. He urged Arion into a gallop and headed directly for the fence. He felt the connection between himself and his horse, mind to mind.

In a long, sweeping movement that felt like flying, they soared over the fence and galloped away to the west.

Chapter Nineteen

Nessa left Harry with some hasty words of comfort and exhortation—at least, she supposed she did. She wasn't sure what she'd said. Never before had she left the hospital in the middle of a shift, but she did so today. She had to speak with General Greene immediately.

But when she reached the place where the command center had stood, she found the living and dining marquees gone, with nothing but two oblongs of dead, bleached, flattened grass to show where they had once been. She hurried off to the document tent in search of Rory—and there he was, looking exhausted but triumphant, surrounded by neatly labeled crates.

"Where is General Greene?" she asked without preamble.

"Gone," Rory replied.

"To Charlestown?"

His eyes narrowed. "You're the second person to ask me those two questions in the past quarter of an hour. The other was August."

Nessa drew in a quick breath. "August? He came back to the camp?"

"Aye. He said he's decrypted the cipher."

Nessa clapped her hands together softly. "That's wonderful! What does it say?"

"He didn't tell me. There wasn't time. He was spotted by some soldiers, and—"

"They arrested him?"

"Nay, he didn't give them the chance. He leapt onto Arion's back, cleared the pasture fence, and galloped off without a strip of tack. 'Twas the finest piece of riding I've ever seen."

"Did he get away?"

"I think so. I heard some shots, but I don't believe they hit him. Some riders took off after him, but they'll be hard pressed to catch him. Arion is faster than any of the horses left in camp, and he had a head start."

Nessa stood silent a moment, hugging the knowledge to herself. August had decrypted the cipher at last. Perhaps it had stirred his memory. Even if it had not, it must have given him a clear course of action. God had guided his path, just as August had said he would.

"I've found out something as well," said Nessa. "From Harry Beach."

Rory blinked. "Harry Beach?" he repeated.

"Aye. He was one of the sentries on duty the night August first came into the camp. When Harry was questioned, he said that no one had passed—but he was lying. He was asleep, because he'd been drugged by Sergeant Boyd. Poor Harry. He was afraid to tell the truth."

Rory considered that. "So...he doesn't actually know whether anyone passed or not?"

"Nay. But he did wake up some hours later to see a big dark horse galloping past, without saddle or rider, leaving the camp."

"Arion," said Rory.

"Aye. Harry saw August riding him the day of the trip to Wappoo Cut and recognized him."

"'Twas as we supposed, then. Arion was spooked when August was attacked, and ran away."

A brief silence fell. Then Nessa asked, "So August decrypted the cipher, and came back to the camp to tell General Greene what it said?"

"Aye, and left again to follow him—but not to Charlestown. Major Elliot said the city wasn't safe for the general, that he was as good as dead if he went to Governor Rutledge's house. The general's going with him to Magnolia Grove instead. I told August so—and, Nessa, he remembered the road to Magnolia Grove."

Nessa pondered all this, turning it over in her mind, trying to arrange it in some sort of order. Had August traveled the Magnolia Grove road on his way to the camp? Did he now have reason to suspect that the changed plans regarding General Greene's accommodations were known to the conspirators, and that the general would be attacked on the new route? Could there be spies within Major Elliot's household?

Before she could make any sense of it, a party on horseback came their way—twelve armed men in the blue coats of the Continental Army, with four additional horses carrying baggage. The foremost man was around fifty years of age, wearing a cocked hat and gold epaulettes on his shoulders, each with a single silver star—the uniform of a brigadier general. He had a sharp, intelligent face with penetrating dark eyes and a long, beaky nose.

He rode directly to Nessa and Rory, his sweeping gaze taking in the empty ground where the command center had once stood. Without bothering with introductions, he asked, "Where is General Greene?"

"General Greene has left the camp," Rory replied.

"He is safe, then?" the visitor asked. "Unharmed?"

Nessa and Rory exchanged glances. "So far as I know," Rory said.

"And who are you?"

"My name is Rory Shaw. I am one of General Greene's clerks."

The man's eyebrows lifted. "Shaw. Aye, I've seen your name affixed to some of the documents the general has sent to me. You write a fair hand. I had no idea you were so young."

Rory bowed his head. "May I know your name, sir?"

It was a presumptuous question, but this was no time to stand on ceremony, and the visitor made no objection. "I am General George Weedon."

"From Fredericksburg?" Nessa asked.

Her surprise was plain in her voice. There hadn't been any major military engagements fought in Virginia for over a year, and most of the army there had mustered out. What business could have been pressing enough to impel General Weedon to travel some four or five hundred miles from his post to see General Greene in person?

"Aye," General Weedon replied. "We've been on the road for some weeks."

"Was General Greene expecting you?" Rory asked.

"He was not," said General Weedon. He stared at Rory a moment longer, then said, "As a matter of fact, I'm here on an unofficial errand. A few months ago—the nineteenth of September, it was—I sent a trusted aide to General Greene with some important and sensitive news which I thought it best not to put in writing. My aide ought to have arrived here within three or four weeks, and I expected to receive a response from the general by the end of October. When that did not happen, I began to fear that some mischance had befallen my messenger and that the general had not received my communication at all. So I set out myself on the sixteenth of November—and here I am."

A tingle of premonition ran up Nessa's spine. "Who was your courier?" she asked.

"His name is August Fairfax, former captain of artillery, First Virginia Regiment. Have you had any word of him? Quite apart from his errand, the importance of which I cannot stress enough, I value him highly, and his absence has caused me great anxiety."

Nessa couldn't answer. Her heart leaped within her, and she pressed her fingers to her lips. August Fairfax. Captain of artillery. Here at last was August's full name, free from the stain of doubt—the name of an honorable and trusted officer in the Continental Army.

Rory spoke up. "May I ask, General, if your errand concerned a certain conspiracy?"

"It did," Weedon replied. "Captain Fairfax was chosen for this errand not only because of his personal abilities, which are considerable, but because he has family in this area—particularly a first cousin, Major Andrew Elliot, to whom he is close."

"Major Elliot?" Nessa repeated. "Major Elliot is August's cousin?"

She remembered Major Elliot's face upon seeing the ring she'd made from August's button, tarnished from its baptism by fire. She remembered the poisonous words he had spoken to her, planting seeds of doubt about August's fidelity to the Patriot cause, casting him as a traitor, when all along...

General Weedon shot her a keen glance. "You do know him. Did he arrive safely, then? Is he well?"

"I would not say he arrived safely," said Rory. "But he did arrive. And he was well enough when I saw him last, not half an hour ago. He set off in pursuit of the general, who is traveling with Major Elliot to Magnolia Grove."

Nessa broke in. "General Weedon, I am afraid that Major Elliot is not at all to be trusted. And I believe that August knows this, and that he means to save the general from harm at Major Elliot's hands."

Rory stared at her in shocked silence, while General Weedon's mouth pressed into a thin line.

"Take me to him," the general said.

Chapter Twenty

August cleared the sentry point at a full gallop, ignoring the guard's shouted command to halt. It was a place he'd heard Nessa and Rory speak of before, the low spot between two batteries where a single sentry was posted. He recognized it from its description, and he also knew it from memory. A voice in his mind said, *Oh,* that *sentry point! Of course!* He remembered stopping there with his cousin's servant, who had accompanied him from Magnolia Grove—Scipio, that was the man's name. He remembered being admitted by the sentry—and the sentry was Sergeant Boyd! The short dark hair, the large nose, the dirty hunting shirt—how had August failed to recognize the dead body from behind the crates in the supply depot as the sentry who had let him into camp? The memory was there now, plain as day—like some lost item suddenly appearing in a spot where he was certain he'd already searched for it.

But Sergeant Boyd had surely not been one of the men to whom August had been shown later to see if any of them recognized him—which suggested that he was not the official sentry who had originally been assigned to guard that entry point that evening. Andrew must have gotten the official sentry out of the way somehow, and put Boyd in his place during the time when August was expected to enter the camp.

A shot rang out, and something brushed past his sleeve. He leaned low over Arion's neck and dug in his heels. Arion ran like the wind. As August rode, it occurred to him that he had technically just stolen a horse from the Commander of the Southern Department. He was a horse thief now. It was quite possible that, after all the perils he had survived, he would end up being hanged for stealing his own horse—always supposing he lived long enough to stand trial, which, considering the forlorn hope in which he was now concerned, was not especially likely.

He soon passed out of musket range, and the track joined a road, which was overhung on both sides by live oak trees that met overhead in an endless arch of thick green—the Ashley River Road. He had ridden a different part of it with Kościuszko's men, on their way to Wappoo Cut, and he now remembered traveling this same stretch in the opposite direction, two months earlier. He turned right without slackening his pace.

The memories were coming hard and fast now, one after another, in no particular order.

Laying a saddle on Arion's back for the very first time. Nudging Arion's lips open and slipping the bit between his teeth. The smell of leather and clean, healthy horse.

A cloud shadow passing over a field of grain.

A library with towering shelves reaching to a dizzyingly high ceiling, filled with polished round tables, oversized chairs, the big globe that he liked to spin in its sturdy frame. The scent of tobacco as he sat on his grandfather's knee, learning the Greek alphabet.

Running down a packed dirt sidewalk in Virginia, pushing a wooden crate in front of himself in some elaborate childhood game. The edge of the crate catching in a crack, sending him face-first onto the hard ground. The shock of pain in his chin, followed by the sound of his own wailing cry.

Round-bellied puppies tumbling about on sweet, crackling straw. His own childish belly laugh at the touch of their tickling noses.

The deafening blast of artillery fire slapping against his eardrums. Heavy ordnance arcing through the sky. One of his gunners falling to the earth with his leg blown off at the knee. August stepping up to take the wounded man's place. Elevating the gun to fire into the enemy's line. Touching the slow match to the priming powder. The choking stench of sulfur. His throat raw with smoke, his shouts swallowed by the roar of bursting shells.

Patsy, the old cook at the house where he grew up, feeding him gingerbread in the pantry. *Only one slice, Master August, or you'll spoil your dinner.*

His mother sobbing softly beside him, her head on his shoulder, his cravat stiff and scratchy, as his father's casket was lowered into the ground.

His first taste of whisky at the age of seventeen.

He had ridden only a few miles when he saw another road ahead, veering left from the one he was currently traveling. Struggling against the flood of memories, he forced himself to think. The new road followed a more westerly approach—and it led to Magnolia Grove. He remembered the dead oak tree in the corner of the Y. Without slackening his pace, he directed Arion onto the road to Magnolia Grove.

Holding to his present speed, August would soon overtake the coach. But Andrew would see and hear him coming and have time to prepare for him. What August needed was to get ahead of the coach, and lie in wait in some spot where he could take Andrew unawares—say, at a water-crossing.

He might leave the road, and skirt around it a little to the left. Once he reached the creek, he need only to turn right and follow it downstream to the rest stop that he remembered.

Almost as soon as he'd formed the thought, he saw a trail that broke off from the road on his left, broad enough for a man on horseback. It might be exactly what August needed—or it might lead him to disaster. The trail might not meet the creek at all. It might merely bend back around and rejoin the road. It could veer too far from the road, or meander too much, to do him any good.

He halted Arion a few yards from the trail. He wished he knew the country better—but he didn't, and right now the trail appeared to be his best option. If it showed signs of taking an erratic or unhelpful course, then he might cut cross-country, though that was risky in an unfamiliar land.

Arion was standing with his head slightly inclined to the left and his left ear turned, awaiting August's command. August sent up a quick prayer for guidance. Then he clicked his tongue, and turned Arion down the trail.

"WHAT DO YOU THINK YOU are doing?" Rory asked in the lofty, authoritarian, superior tone that always set Nessa's teeth on edge.

"Saddling a horse," she answered shortly, and made good on the answer by laying a worn saddle on the blanketed back of one of the healthier-looking beasts from the pasture. The horse was none too lively for all that, and Nessa was sorry to ask it to do anything, but at least she was probably a lighter weight than it was used to carrying.

She would hitch up her petticoats and ride astride, the way she had done when she was a little girl. It was a good thing her gown had been made at a time when full skirts were in fashion.

"I hope you don't think you're about to chase after August and Major Elliot," said Rory, sounding more insufferable than ever.

"Why shouldn't I?" she retorted as she threaded the cinch strap through the buckle and pulled it tight. "I've as much business going as you have."

"General Weedon's company needs me to show the way. You'll only slow them down."

"Nonsense. I've been riding since you were still wearing baby dresses. And if I do fall behind, the general needn't wait on me."

"But why should you go at all?"

"Because I'm in love with August!"

His eyes met hers over the horse's back. They were wide with shock. Brilliant scholar though he was, Rory could be remarkably dense about some things. With his unkempt mop of hair and a sprinkling of freckles across his nose, he suddenly looked very young.

"Oh," he said in a different tone. "Well...be careful. Don't do anything rash or foolish."

"You be careful too," she said.

"I will," he said. Reaching behind him, he pulled a pistol from the back of his belt, beneath his coat, and stowed it in his mount's saddle scabbard.

It was Nessa's turn to look surprised. Catching her eye again, Rory said, "I've been carrying it for a while now. I thought 'twas best, given the state of affairs. *Praemonitus, praemunitus.*"

The two of them said in unison, "Forewarned is forearmed," and grinned at each other.

THE MEMORIES KEPT COMING as August cantered down the trail.

Studying languages and Classics, philosophy and mathematics, at the College of William and Mary. Reading artillery manuals and engineering texts late into the night to prepare for the threatened war.

His first command. All his book-learning feeling as insubstantial as tissue paper against the hard realities of combat. Grizzled old Sergeant Haynes, a veteran of the late French War, who had taken him under his wing and taught him how to keep his head and lead his men.

The Battle of Long Island in 1776, when he was twenty-four years old. Smoke and noise and stench. More blood than he had ever seen in his life. He lost Sergeant Haynes there. He lost a lot of men over the years. Other men replaced them and were lost in their turn.

More battles. Trenton. Brandywine. Germantown.

A letter from his mother. His grandfather had been killed by Tory raiders under Major Henry Craig. The house at New Bern, with its library and pianoforte, had been burned to the ground.

Something was rising up in him, thick and choking like the smoke from black powder—the collective grief and rage of years, hitting him all at once with fresh force as if the losses had occurred only that day.

He pulled himself together and put the memories in a different part of his mind to deal with later. The war had taught him that.

The cloud cover was too heavy for August to judge direction by the sun, but based on tree growth and wind, the trail seemed to be taking him more or less due west. It did not meander, but went straight ahead, and struck the creek after only a couple of miles. Now all August had to do was follow it downstream to the ford.

The bank was firm and broad, with open stretches that allowed for a canter. After a mile or so, the creek made a tight curve to the right. August slowed to a walk. They rounded the bend—

And there it was, the way-station he remembered, with the stone shelter and bench, and the ford. The road stretched off to the east, back toward Ashley Hill.

More memories. The anxious ride from Richmond, taking the legislature and Governor Jefferson to safety. Jefferson's servants at Monticello, refusing to leave until all the household goods were saved, with the British only hours away.

The pitch and roll of a wooden deck beneath his feet—his father's schooner, the Margaret Ann, named for his mother. Every year the family made the trip, traveling from their home in the busy port city of Norfolk, Virginia to his Nash grandfather's estate in Craven County. The voyage from Norfolk to New Bern took about a week. They'd sail up the Neuse River to New Bern and then travel overland. His mother's sister had married a planter from South Carolina—Andrew's father. The two families met each summer at the sisters' childhood home and spent a month together. The cousins had a special bond—like brotherhood, but without the irritation born of overfamiliarity.

Andrew...Cousin Andrew...

Don't think of him as Cousin Andrew. Think of him as Major Elliot. An adversary. A traitor.

It wasn't until now that August fully appreciated how woefully short he was on strategy. His mind had been focused on reaching the ford ahead of the coach. He had done that, but what was he to do now, alone and unarmed, against Andrew—Major Elliot—and however many men he had with him? With all his heart August wished for those two revolvers of his, given to him by his grandfather on his twenty-first birthday, and later stolen and hidden away by Sergeant Boyd. A detachment of light infantry troops under his command would not come amiss either. He wished, too, that he'd told Rory where he was going, and why. But there hadn't been time. And what could Rory do to help him, really? And how was August going to convince General Greene of Andrew's—of Major Elliot's treachery? He had no proof other than the deciphered message in his pocket, and the general would have to take his word for it that the cipher said what August said it said, unless and until August was able to sit down with him and explain it all.

Perhaps he should have left the decrypted cipher with Rory as evidence of the plot. If today's encounter did not go his way, there would be no second chance for him to crawl out of a shallow grave. His cousin would make sure August was good and dead before putting him in the ground this time, and the papers in his pocket would never be seen again.

Saving General Greene was the main thing, but not the only thing. This conspiracy stretched as far as Virginia, Georgia, and North Carolina—perhaps farther. How many agents did it have, in how many cities? Until it was rooted out and destroyed, the threat to governors, legislators, and general officers would continue.

A sound of running water drew his attention back to the present. At this season the creek was mostly quiet and still, but he'd just reached a small waterfall. A stone trough had been built on the bank near the waterfall, with a pail hanging from a peg in the masonry for the convenience of travelers, who could fill the trough from the waterfall rather than making the horses drink directly from the creek. The whole arrangement was screened by brush so that it couldn't be seen from the rest stop, and a path led inland up a gentle slope to join the road.

Across the creek, August could see the other way-station where he and Scipio had stopped on their way to Ashley Hill. Scipio had been a quiet and courteous companion to August on the ride to the camp, and all along he'd been prepared to act on the instructions given to him in the note. *If he will not turn he must be ended.*

August dismounted and drew some water for Arion. He didn't have time to fill the trough, but let him drink from the bucket.

While Arion was noisily slurping, August took all the papers out of his pocket, along with the pencil stub. On the note Andrew had written him from Ashley Hill, he drew an oblong around the hidden message. On the salutation line, next to *Mortimer*, he wrote *August Fairfax*, and in the signature, beside *Hotspur*, he wrote *Andrew Elliot—my cousin*. He almost smiled at Andrew's chosen code names, characters from a Shakespearean play. Hotspur was a rebel trying to overthrow the rightful king; Mortimer was the well-meaning cousin whom he pulled into his plot. It was just the sort of allusion that Andrew would enjoy, and that August himself would have made in his place.

The solution to the cipher was already written on the back of the note. He laid it at the top of the sheaf of papers, rolled them together, and looked around for some means of securing them. He found a thin and fairly pliant vine and used it to tie the papers in a bundle, which he then tied to Arion's mane. He wished he had the time, and additional foolscap, to write some sort of explanation, and a saddlebag to stow the papers in, but this was the best he could do. If all went well, he himself would be available to make all the necessary explanations in person to General Greene. If it did not, he could only hope that Arion would somehow make his way to Patriots who, if they did not understand what the documents meant, would at least turn them over to the proper authorities—and that those authorities would not be part of the conspiracy.

It was a lot to hope for.

He wished again for a weapon—any weapon. He looked around and saw a sort of trash pit in a brushy area nearby. A wine bottle, broken at the bottom, lay near the top. He picked it up by the neck.

Arion drank half his bucket, then abruptly lifted his head, water dripping from his lips, and pricked his ears toward the road. A second later, August heard it too—the distant rumble of coach wheels.

He poured out the rest of the water and led Arion back the way they'd come, past the rest stop. He found a screen of wax myrtles and left Arion behind it, hoping the horse would not come sauntering out at an inopportune moment. Then he went back to the rest stop and hid himself behind a yaupon holly near the bench.

He hadn't long to wait. A coach came down the road, driven by a black man—Scipio. August had never met his cousin's steward until arriving at Magnolia Grove two months earlier. Nor had he seen Magnolia Grove, though of course he'd heard much about his cousin's estate over the years. It seemed a bitter irony that he'd been selected by Governor Harrison and General Weedon for this task in part because of his South Carolina cousin, a well-known Patriot whose loyalty was beyond question. He remembered the relief he'd felt upon finally reaching his cousin's home, and knowing that he could now place the tangled problem of the suspected conspiracy in Andrew's capable hands.

But Andrew hadn't been at home. He had gone back to the army and was working in the Quartermaster Department in the camp at Ashley Hill. It was Scipio who'd received August at the house, and fed and housed him, and given stable room to Arion. August told him only that he needed to consult his cousin on an urgent matter of national importance, and Scipio sent a messenger to Andrew at Ashley Hill. And Andrew sent a note in reply, summoning August to him at the camp, with Scipio as his guide. The hidden message to Scipio showed that Andrew had guessed at once the nature of August's errand.

The coach's curtains were drawn, hiding its passengers from view. Scipio halted the coach near the rest stop and applied the brakes. Then he stepped down from his seat, secured the reins, and opened the coach door.

From behind the yaupon holly, August watched as Scipio helped Andrew out of the coach. Even from this distance, the sight of his cousin was like a knife blade to the chest, reviving all that he'd felt earlier on discovering that he had been nearly done to death by one he looked on almost as a brother. Shock there was, and anger, but mostly a kind of acute mental anguish, a species of hurt feelings, that for a moment took all the fight out of him. Andrew had given the order for August to be killed, as casually as if he'd been instructing Scipio to butcher a hog.

August's heart pounded so hard that he could hear his own pulse, and his stomach heaved so violently that he was barely able to prevent it from emptying itself then and there. The cracked skull, the pain and disorientation, the weeks of not knowing his own history—all this had been the work of Andrew's hand.

Of Major Elliot's hand, he corrected himself, and then gave up the semantic struggle. He could not fool himself, or pretend he did not know. His cousin was a traitor, a murderer, and a kinslayer.

But August was not the only one Andrew had harmed, or planned to harm. There would be more killing, far more, if Andrew were not stopped—and August was the only one who could do it.

August waited for General Greene to follow Andrew out of the coach, but he did not, and Scipio shut the door behind Andrew. Was General Greene even there? Had Rory made a mistake? Had Andrew perhaps pulled off a double bluff, with the general really in Charlestown after all, or someplace else altogether?

Had Andrew already killed him?

August was almost as shocked now by his cousin's changed appearance as he had been two months earlier. August and Andrew were the same height, and had been the same build, but Andrew's once powerful body had wasted away.

Andrew exchanged some words with Scipio that August couldn't catch. Then Scipio unhitched the horses and led them down the gentle slope toward the trough, while Andrew walked to the bench and sat down.

The moment had come. This was the opportunity August needed, and it would not come again.

The murmur of the waterfall was enough to disguise his careful footsteps as he approached the bench where his cousin sat. A second later, August had his left arm around Andrew's neck and the bottle's jagged edges pointed at Andrew's right eye.

"Call out to your servant, and I will lay open your face and cut your throat," he said low in his cousin's ear.

Even as a child, Andrew had always possessed great presence of mind. It did not fail him now. Only a moment's shocked silence passed before his voice said coolly, "And what will that get you, cousin? A dead war hero and blood on your hands."

"Aye, you like to keep your own hands clean, don't you? You get others to do your filthy deeds for you. It was Scipio who crept up behind me and knocked me on the head while you talked treason to me, and Boyd who dug my grave. Did you get Scipio to kill Boyd and Ballard as well? I can see why you got rid of Boyd. He was a blunt tool to be used once and then thrown away. And Ballard—I suppose you wanted him out of the way so you could kill me."

Andrew turned his head just enough to show August his profile. "Boyd was always a liability. Even before I learned how badly he'd failed to dispose of you and your belongings, I knew he'd have to be put away. It didn't occur to me that he might be careless and greedy enough to keep your saddle and pistols for himself, but it should have. I ought to have had Scipio search his tent before leaving those incriminating Caesar ciphers in there for General Greene to find. As for Ballard, I didn't know that he'd been assigned to follow you until two days ago—or that you were alive at all, for that matter. I missed the whole uproar over the mysterious stranger with no memory, because I was not in the camp. I was lying ill at Magnolia Grove, half-dead from my old wound."

The corner of his mouth edged up in a cold smile. "It was Nessa Shaw who told me about you. Otherwise I might be in the dark yet. Do you know what that girl did? She took one of the buttons from your burned frock coat, wove it into a grass ring, and put it on her finger. You can imagine what a shock it gave me to see it. But I kept my head. A few friendly questions from the kindly Major Elliot, and the silly girl was telling me everything I needed to know about the object of her affections."

August sucked in a hissing breath and moved the bottle's jagged edge closer to Andrew's face. "Don't speak of her that way. You're not good enough for her to wipe her feet on." Then he thought of something else. "You tried to poison her against me, didn't you? I knew something was wrong when she came back from gathering her herbs that day."

"Well, I had to do something, and quickly. I couldn't count on your amnesia to continue forever. You might suddenly remember our last conversation, and the task you'd been given by General Weedon, and—well, everything. I had to discredit you in case your memory returned before I could put you out of the way permanently."

August's stomach churned again at hearing his own cousin speak so casually of such monstrous deeds. It was a nightmare more horrible than the one he'd had his first night in Rory's tent, because there could be no waking from it.

"Where is General Greene?" he asked. "Did you already kill him, and leave his body on the road?"

"He's in the coach, dosed with laudanum. Really, things couldn't have worked out better if I'd planned them this way all along. 'Twill make for a fine, plausible story, your waylaying our coach and killing the general before he could reach the safety of Magnolia Grove. I'd been planning to blame General Greene's assassination on Tory firebrands, but you make a much more convenient scapegoat—especially now that Corporal Ballard's death has been laid to your account."

"You're the one who's been feeding suspicion of a conspiracy all along, aren't you?" August asked. "It was all a misdirect. You caused General Greene and his officers to fixate on an imagined threat from the British, when all the British actually wanted was to get on their transports and go home. That left you free to set up your own foul Tory plot to kill the army's senior leadership and overthrow the government."

Andrew stiffened. "Don't waste your sympathy on the poor, maligned British. They are indeed keen to go home, but only after seven years of a civil war that's of their own making. They stirred up strife between neighbors and brothers, promising the Tories protection and reward as blood money for turning on their countrymen, only to leave them high and dry when the war became too expensive to carry on with. And don't you dare call me a Tory. This is *my* country. I never turned my coat and I never, *never* took an oath of loyalty to a British king."

"You took an oath of allegiance to the United States and the Continental Congress."

Andrew's voice sharpened. "The United States used up the best years of my young manhood, and then discarded me when I got my wound at Guilford Courthouse. By all rights, I should have been promoted to colonel long before then, but General Greene passed me over in favor of lesser men. Now he's being given thousands of acres of good land in the South as a reward for his service—and what do I get? Mountains of debt and a wound that will never heal."

"So that's all it is," August said, enlightened. "Jealousy and hurt pride. Listen to yourself! You sound like Benedict Arnold, nursing your sense of grievance into a justification for base treachery. Open your eyes, Andrew. You are not the only man to be wounded in this war. Others have bled and died, and lost family and friends, land and fortunes."

"You don't understand."

"I understand perfectly, cousin. You're neither a Tory nor a Patriot. You're on no one's side but your own."

"We could be on the same side, you and I," Andrew said. "You're all the family I have left, August. You could have an honored place in the new national order. The Articles of Confederation are worth less than the paper they're printed on. This country needs a strong centralized government with able men in control. I could give you the governorship of Virginia. You could marry Miss Shaw, if you want her, and make her a great lady."

August recoiled in disgust. "You spoke fair promises before, after you lured me to Ashley Hill. I remember now. They were nothing but empty words. You never would have shown your hand so freely if you hadn't already made up your mind to kill me if I refused."

Andrew gave a brief sigh. "You're right, cousin. You're a clever man—but not clever enough."

Some alarm bell of instinct went off in August's head, making him move aside. A white-hot stab of pain sliced through his side. He looked up to see Scipio raising his knife for a second strike.

Everything seemed to slow down. Several things happened in close succession, and August was able to see them as distinctly as if they were stretched out over an hour.

Andrew slid along the bench, out of Scipio's way, and pulled out a pocket pistol.

August slashed his broken bottle across Scipio's chest.

The coach door opened. General Greene lurched out, sluggish but determined, like an irate bear emerging from his den partway through his winter's hibernation, and lumbered toward Andrew.

Hoofbeats rumbled up the road, and a company of horsemen appeared. August recognized some of them. General Weedon. Rory.

Nessa?

Andrew and the general wrestled for control of the gun.

Scipio's white shirt turned red. His face contorted in rage as he lunged toward August with his blade lifted high.

A sound like a thunderclap went off, and then another.

Chapter Twenty-One

Nessa was riding at a full gallop, riding as she hadn't in years, not since she was a carefree, high-spirited girl in North Carolina with her skirts hitched up on the saddle and her hair streaming in the wind. She leaned forward, pushing against time, every atom in her body crying out, *Hurry! Hurry!*

Her mind whirled with thoughts as the woods streamed past her on either side. Major Elliot, a traitor—and August's cousin! There was a certain physical resemblance between them, now that she came to think of it, especially in the blue-grey eyes, and a gravity and dignity of manner common to them both. But she had never noted it before, perhaps because she had never actually seen the two of them together. She remembered how Major Elliot had questioned her that day after seeing the button ring on her hand. How cool and collected he had appeared, when he must have been inwardly reeling with shock that his cousin had survived the attempt on his life! And she'd stupidly answered all his questions, never suspecting a thing. It was through her that Major Elliot had learned that August was still alive. Her foolish prattling had given him the chance to plan his next move.

How far back did his treachery reach? That encrypted message, found on the man who'd been stopped and searched on the road to North Carolina—how many months ago was that? At least two months before August had come to Ashley Hill, and perhaps longer. She winced at the recollection of the suspicion she'd felt when she'd seen the copy of the message sticking out of August's boot. He'd been doing his utmost to uncover the conspiracy, even without the memory of his mission from General Weedon—doing it of his own volition, because that was the sort of man he was. And she'd doubted him! But of course she'd been primed to doubt him by Major Elliot. She'd let herself be manipulated. She had admired the major for his patriotism, and pitied him for his wound—

She gasped. Major Elliot's wound! She'd treated him for it the day after she'd found August. Scipio had said that the major had been over-exerting himself—and indeed he had, meeting with his cousin in the woods on the edge of camp, luring August to his death. Did he strike the blow himself? Probably not. He didn't have the strength. But he must have watched while it was done. Nessa imagined August and Major Elliot sitting on stones or tree stumps in the clearing, facing each other, intent on talk, their grey-blue eyes locked in a matching penetrating gaze, while someone, perhaps Scipio, stole up behind August and bludgeoned him on the head. She imagined the light going out of August's eyes as he pitched forward and collapsed without a cry—innocent and trusting to the end, never suspecting that his cousin could turn on him. She imagined him lying pale and still, making no groan or murmur while being stripped of waistcoat and breeches, down to an anonymous body in plain linen shirt and drawers, sunk deep in unconsciousness, in the darkness and confusion of an injured and disordered mind. He must have made no sound or movement, even when he was dragged over the rough ground, and dropped into a hole, and covered with dirt. He might have died there, and no one would ever have learned what became of August Fairfax. She would never have known him, never smoothed the golden-brown hair off his brow, never heard his voice singing or quoting Latin, never seen his face tense with concentration while he worked out some intricate intellectual problem, never felt his arms go around her in comfort, never rested her head against his shoulder.

She couldn't lose him now, just when his memory and good name had been restored. She loved him, unreservedly and irrevocably.

Up ahead, she could see the coach, parked near the creek, with one door hanging open. On the ground in front of a stone bench, General Greene was grappling with Major Elliot. Farther back, August, his shirt wet with blood, gripped what looked like a broken bottle in his hand. He was thrusting and parrying against Scipio, who was armed with a long knife.

She was not the first to reach the creek, or the second or third. Rory got there ahead of her, followed closely by a few of General Weedon's men.

Two gunshots rang out in quick succession, startling some crows, which rose up from the top of an oak tree, flapping their wings and crying out in their harsh voices. The loud reports sent a painful jolt through Nessa's chest, as if she were the one who'd been shot. She felt sick. What had happened? Had Major Elliot killed General Greene—or August? Was the man she loved bleeding his life out at this very moment? Was he already dead?

She pulled her horse's reins and sat low in the saddle. Almost before the beast had come to a complete stop, she had her feet out of the stirrups and was dropping to the ground. The next instant, she was running toward the place the shots had come from.

But she stopped when she saw Rory standing with his feet planted firmly apart and his arm outstretched, the pistol still smoking in his hand.

Beyond him, four bodies lay on the ground—two pairs, each a confused tangle of limbs, as if they'd been struggling or grappling together, and suddenly fallen motionless at the same moment.

The first to recover was General Greene, who was lying face down on top of...someone. The general's bulk stirred, and he got to his hands and knees. Beneath him was Major Elliot, flat on his back with his left arm outflung and his right hand resting at his sternum, still clutching a pocket revolver. A blossom of red spread over his shirtfront. His eyes were wide open and staring. His mouth worked as if he would speak, but no words came—only a sigh of breath, and then nothing.

Nessa turned her attention to the other pair. She saw a dark waistcoat and the back of a head covered with close-cropped black hair. It was at this man that Rory's pistol was aimed.

Slowly he shifted and rolled onto his back, revealing the face of Scipio, Major Elliot's servant—was pushed onto his back, rather. He flopped lifelessly and did not move again. A long knife was clutched in his fingers. There was blood along the edge.

August sat up, blinking dazedly. He was gripping a broken bottle in one hand. He held it up and looked at it a moment, as if not sure where it had come from, before dropping it.

Then he flinched and glanced down at his own side, which was wet with blood.

Nessa ran to him, kicked away Scipio's knife, and knelt beside August. "You're hurt," she said.

"Nessa!" he said. "What on earth are you doing here?"

"Never mind," she answered. "Let me see what he's done to you."

She found the gaping slash that Scipio's knife had cut through August's shirt. With shaking hands, she took hold of the edges and tore it farther open to expose the wound. It was a long cut, but not deep.

"Only a scratch," he said.

She took a shaky breath and let it out again. A wave of weakness washed over her, and her heart pounded. August laid his hands over hers and held them tight for a moment.

Then he pushed them gently away from himself and stood.

Nearby, General Weedon was helping General Greene to his feet. August joined them, taking the major general's other arm. Together, he and Weedon guided Greene toward the stone bench.

General Greene was staring at General Weedon with an expression of almost comical bewilderment. "George?" he said, slurring the word a little. "Is that you?"

Weedon gave a dry chuckle. "In the flesh, Nathanael," he said. "I came to pay you a visit, and to find out what had become of my young courier, here."

He jerked his head toward August, and General Greene swiveled his head around.

"Your courier? August?"

"That's right. I sent him to you on a most important and delicate mission."

Weedon glanced at August and said, "You've certainly been a long time about it, Captain."

"My apologies, sir," said August. "There were complications."

"So I surmise. Well, you managed to save the major general, at any rate, which counts as a success. I will expect your full report soon."

The two of them eased General Greene onto the bench. "How are you feeling, sir?" asked General Weedon.

"Very slow and stupid," said General Greene. "But all things considered, I suppose I should be thankful to be alive." Turning back to August, he said, "I am in your debt, sir. It appears I owe you my life."

"I did no more than my duty, sir," said August. "I'm only happy I got here in time. It was a near thing."

"A very near thing indeed," said General Greene.

August walked over to Rory, who had lowered his pistol but didn't appear to have moved otherwise. August laid a hand on his arm.

"Speaking of debts," August said, "I am in yours. You saved my life, Rory. Thank you."

Rory looked at August. His eyes were wide and glazed in his pale face, and for a moment Nessa thought he was about to be sick. Then he swallowed hard and returned his pistol to his belt.

Nessa went to her brother and put her arm around him. His body felt as straight and stiff as that of a tin soldier. Then some of the tension seemed to go out of him. He laid his own arm across her shoulders and hugged her close to his side.

GENERAL WEEDON'S MEN went quietly and efficiently to work. A search of Andrew's coach revealed no other occupants, but it did turn up a couple of blankets, which were used to cover the dead. When August saw one of the men attending to Major Elliot's horses, which were still standing patiently at the trough, he remembered Arion and went to fetch him from the brushy area where he'd been hidden.

August untied the bundle of papers from Arion's mane and brought it to the generals.

"I hid these in case I didn't—in case I wasn't available to explain in person," he said. "General Greene, I'm sure you remember the encrypted message found some months ago on a traveler heading to North Carolina. I've been trying to decipher it for several weeks now, and I finally succeeded. Here is the plaintext." He glanced at General Weedon. "The conspirators were planning to kill General Greene, and the governors of Georgia and the Carolinas, as well as some assemblymen whom they thought best to put out of the way. In the ensuing chaos, they meant to take over the governments of those states and break away from the Union. Apparently there are many conspirators highly placed in the South, ready to step into the offices to be vacated by assassinations. My cousin planned to take over as governor of South Carolina following the death of Governor Mathews."

General Greene stared down at the note in his hand. "Major Elliot was always warning me about British plots," he said. "'Twas nothing more than a screen for his own treachery."

"Aye," said August. "Any suspicious activities connected with the actual conspiracy could be attributed on the British, with the actual assassinations being blamed on radical Tory hotheads like David Fanning. Naturally no one would dream of suspecting the noble and gallant Major Elliot."

"'Twas a clever plan," said General Weedon. "In the panic and confusion that would surely follow mass assassinations, the new leaders would very likely have been given extraordinary powers. We might have ended up with as dictatorial a government as the one we've spent the past seven years fighting to escape."

"You're right," said General Greene. "And I'm afraid the threat is far from over. We must place extra security on the governors, assemblymen, and general officers in the Continental Army. Most importantly, we must untangle the rest of the plot. We cannot purge the conspiracy without knowing who the conspirators are."

He was speaking clearly enough, but with exaggerated care, like a man trying to keep his wits about him after having too much to drink.

"Aye," said August. "To that end, General Greene, I would like to go to Magnolia Grove at once and make a thorough search of my cousin's private papers. Major Elliot was my cousin, and I know his mind better than any man living. If I were given access to his papers, I hope and believe I could lay bare the rest of the conspiracy."

"You have a knife wound that needs tending," Nessa said.

August turned and gazed at her. She and Rory were standing together, holding tight to one another, looking lost and forlorn. There was something almost pleading in her expression, as if she couldn't bear to let August out of her sight again. Her red-brown hair had come loose and was spilling over her shoulders in deep waves. He wasn't entirely sure how she'd even gotten here, unless she'd kilted up her skirts and ridden alongside the men. Aye, she would be equal to that. His heart seemed to swell within him. The love of such a woman was a precious treasure—but he still had work to do before he could claim her for his own.

"I'll be all right," he said gently. "'Tis only a shallow cut. General Greene, we must act quickly. We don't know what plans have been made, or what events might even now be in motion. We cannot afford to lose another minute."

After a brief discussion, it was decided that August would remain here, conferring with the generals, while one of Weedon's men would escort Nessa and Rory back to camp and convey a message from General Greene to an infantry captain, ordering him to bring a detachment of soldiers to accompany August to Magnolia Grove. There was no way of knowing how many of Andrew's household servants might be involved in the plot, or how they would react to August's arrival. For his part, August doubted whether his cousin had confided in any but Scipio, but General Greene thought it best to take precautions.

Rory was to remain at camp only long enough to pack his own meager wardrobe, and August's, before joining August at Magnolia Grove. Whatever records and correspondence Andrew had kept pertaining to the conspiracy were certain to be encrypted, and August said he must have Rory's assistance in deciphering them. This was true, but not the whole truth. August recognized the glazed shock on Rory's face. Rory had seen violent death before, but today might be the first day he had personally killed. He needed an absorbing intellectual task and the company of a fellow soldier.

August walked Nessa to her horse. "Are you all right?" he asked her.

"I'm well enough," she replied, "only tired. I feel as if I could sleep for weeks. It seems as if we've been running a footrace, and every time we reach the finish line, someone moves it back."

"I know," said August. "But we must keep on, and do the work that's before us. I might have several weeks' worth of decrypting ahead of me, but I'll have help, and I'll be able to work freely, instead of trying to do frequency analysis on a Vigenère cipher while sitting in a live oak tree, scribbling on scraps of paper with a stub of pencil."

She gave him a tremulous smile. "And you have your memory back," she said.

"I do."

A silence fell. August had so much to tell her, and not enough time to do justice to any of it. But there was one thing he could and must say to her now.

He took her hand. "I have no wife," he said. "But I hope to change that before many weeks have passed."

Joy lit her face, and her fingers tightened in his. He wanted to kiss her, right here and now, before soldiers and her brother and generals and all. But he had to content himself with lifting her hand and pressing it briefly to his lips.

Chapter Twenty-Two

In his spotlessly clean, crisply pressed dress uniform, complete with sash, medals, and epaulettes of brilliant gold, General Greene was looking more magnificent, and more miserable, than Nessa had ever seen him. Glittering chandeliers hung overhead from the arched ceiling of the assembly room of Dillon's Hotel, and the polished floors gleamed with reflected light. Up in the gallery, the musicians were beginning to tune their instruments—two fiddles, a cello, a double bass, and an Irish pennywhistle. The air was redolent with the clean, honest scent of beeswax, as well as a rich, meaty aroma coming from the supper room.

The general sniffed. "Is that oyster stew I smell? I do hope so. I've been laboring over those staff appointments since before sunrise and haven't had a bite to eat all day."

Caty Greene gave her husband a mischievous smile. "Careful, my love," she said. "You might accidentally enjoy yourself."

Ever since the invitation to the Victory Ball had been extended to the general and his wife, and to whichever of the officers could be spared to attend, General Greene had been grumbling about the inconvenience of the timing. He still had much work to do in reorganizing the army, particularly in retiring some officers and shuffling others into staff positions—work that he did not enjoy any more than the affected officers did—and thought it rather hard to be forced to devote an entire evening to amusement.

Nessa knew all this, because she had been staying with the Greenes at Governor Rutledge's house. They seemed to have taken it for granted that she would remain with them until Rory had finished his work and could return home with her, and she had gratefully accepted their hospitality. After eight months spent living in a tent in a military camp, the large, gracious abode on Broad Street felt like paradise.

Now the general chuckled and shook his head. "Oh, Caty, Caty. I think I can hardly avoid enjoying myself, now that you are here. I'm afraid I shall have to resign myself to passing a pleasant evening with a beautiful and charming lady."

Nessa had little heart for such affectionate exchanges. It was now the second of January, and she hadn't heard from Rory or August in more than two weeks. She knew from General Greene that August had an entire staff of intelligence officers working under him now. He was busy, and productive, and happy—or so she supposed. That would surely explain why he had not sent her a single line of writing or word-of-mouth message since the day they'd parted from one another at the creek.

The recollection of that parting had sustained her at first. August had all but made her an offer of marriage. But that had been seventeen days ago. He'd had time to adjust to having his memory back, and was doing work he enjoyed among men who respected him. During their weeks together at Ashley Hill, likely she had taken on a disproportionate importance to him, simply because he'd had no one and nothing else. Now that his past was restored, perhaps she had dwindled in his affections. He might be remembering girls he had known in Virginia, and regretting the words he had said to her at the creek ford.

It seemed a strange chance that just when August had so much work to do, she herself had none. The General Hospital had been closed, with the remaining patients either moving into other accommodations or else returning home. Harry Beach had set off back to his mother, sadder and wiser, and with one fewer hand, than when he'd left. All Nessa had to do was act as a companion to Mrs. Greene, which was certainly no hardship. Caty Greene was such a comfortable person to be with—younger and livelier than her husband, and always cheerful. She had taken at least as much interest in Nessa's ball gown than she had in her own.

And the question of what Nessa would wear to the ball had not been easily answered. There wasn't much to be had in the way of dress goods in Charlestown at present, and even if there had been, Nessa would have felt uneasy about spending her work wages on a new gown appropriate only for gala occasions. Mrs. Greene had offered to make over one of her own old silk gowns for Nessa, but Nessa couldn't allow this. In the end, she had accepted the gift of a plain homespun gown from Mrs. Greene, and spent many happy afternoons and evenings ripping out old seams and sewing new ones to fit her own figure.

The result was surprisingly becoming. The homespun was dyed a rich shade of green that exactly suited Nessa's coloring. She had added a narrow ruffle to the scoop neck and draped the overskirt in the polonaise fashion. And now that the assembly room was beginning to fill, she saw that she was not the only young lady to be simply dressed. Cotton and linen appeared to be more common than silk this evening—fittingly enough, considering that they were celebrating the end of a long and wearying war.

The Greenes were called away to greet some town officials. Nessa wandered to a window in the front of the building, looking out over Meeting Street. The assembly room was on the second floor of Dillon's Hotel, and several high windows flanked a pair of French doors that led onto a deep veranda. The chandeliers' reflections on the windows made fairy lights that seemed to float in the air over the street below.

Someone stepped up beside her. "Good evening, sister."

It was Rory, looking sober and handsome and terribly tall in a frock coat she'd never seen. He had even combed his hair.

"Rory!" She took his hands in hers. "How good it is to see you! I didn't know if you would be able to come."

"Aye, we've been busy," he said. "But most of the work is done now. We've decrypted ever so many messages, and sent expresses to governors and military leaders throughout the South, informing them of who the principal conspirators are."

"I see," she said. Of course they had been busy, doing important work vital to the security of their country. Disabling a conspiracy didn't leave time for romantic fancies.

"I hope I may have the pleasure of dancing with you this evening," Rory said.

Nessa almost laughed. "Certainly you may. I think you could hardly avoid it if you tried. You may have the first dance, if you like."

"Nay," he said. "Not the first dance, I think."

He smiled at something or someone just beyond her shoulder.

Her heart skipped a beat. Slowly she turned and saw Caty Greene, eyes twinkling, with August standing beside her.

He was wearing a dark-green coat and a waistcoat of warm brown. His hair was the color of old gold in the candlelight, and his eyes were shining.

Mrs. Greene spoke. "Miss Shaw, allow me to present Captain August Fairfax, a single man of good character, formerly of the First Virginia Regiment. Captain Fairfax served with distinction in the war, and in recent months has mustered out of the service and returned to private life. He belongs to the Fairfax family of Norfolk, Virginia, and has ties to commercial and shipping interests. He greatly desires to make your acquaintance."

August's gaze was fixed on Nessa with an intensity that made the heat rise to her cheeks. She smiled, but her lips were trembling, and she feared that she might disgrace herself with tears.

She dropped a curtsey. "Captain Fairfax," she said. "How do you do?"

He bowed. "Miss Shaw. I am very happy to meet you. Will you do me the honor of dancing the Virginia Reel with me?"

The musicians were playing the opening bars of "Haste to the Wedding." August held out his gloved hand. Nessa laid her own hand in his, and together they walked to the dance floor. She felt as if she were floating on a cloud as they took their places opposite each other as top couple. Other couples lined up alongside of them as the musicians finished the introduction.

The men made their bows, and the women made their curtseys. Then August and Nessa stepped toward each other, took hold of hands, and led down the middle of the set, weaving between the side couples. After reaching the bottom of the set, they let go and worked their way back alone, weaving their way through the others again.

Once back at the head, they stood still for some time, facing one another, while each of the side couples in turn led down the middle of the set. Merely to look at August was all the joy Nessa could bear.

In a low, grave voice, August said, "I've missed you."

"I've missed you too," Nessa replied. Perhaps that was an unmaidenly admission, but she couldn't dissemble.

"I wanted to write to you."

"Why didn't you?"

"Because I wished to do things decently and in order. Our—courtship, if it may called that, has been most irregular. I wish to remedy that. I have taken the liberty of writing to your father—"

"My father!"

He looked alarmed. "Is that all right? I expressed no improper feeling, I assure you. I only told him of the great affection and esteem I have for you, and that I would be grateful to have the opportunity to prove myself worthy of your approbation."

Nessa was too stunned to answer. Then she realized that the last couple had returned to the foot of the line and it was time to swing partners. Her arm linked with August's, and they spun in a circle. She could feel him watching her, but she was too agitated to meet his gaze. After all they had been through together, and living in close, primitive quarters in an army camp, it was bewildering to hear him speak of courtship, earning her approbation, and writing to her father. She had seen him less than half-clothed. She had washed him, and put him to bed, and watched him sleep, and cut his hair, and seen him shave himself.

But the war was over now, and order was being restored to their world—a new and better order, but one that was being founded on the oldest and truest principles. The best things in life didn't change.

It was time for the grand right and left. The couples formed a circle, men and women facing one another. Nessa and August touched hands briefly, then traveled past each other in the circle, men and women going opposite directions, alternately clasping right and left hands. Nessa's body went on performing the dance without conscious effort on her part. She seemed to be carried along on a current of joy.

Then they were facing each other again, crossing arms and holding hands for the promenade.

"You wrote to my father?" Nessa asked.

They moved together in a serpentine pattern around the circle. "Aye," August replied. "And he has written back."

Nessa stopped dead, and someone bumped into her from behind. She made her apologies and hastened to catch up. By now she and August were starting to attract attention. She could feel the curious stares of the other dancers.

"He has written back?" she echoed. "How was there time?"

"I sent an express rider. I thought it best to act quickly, since this is a matter of some importance."

"And what did he say?" she asked faintly.

"That he will be happy to discuss the matter when we meet in person. He has invited me to his home. I am to go there once my business at Magnolia Grove is finished."

The room began to whirl. Suddenly August's arm was around her, bearing her up, half carrying her off the dance floor. Fresh air, bracingly cold, met her face and chest.

"Nessa! Nessa, are you all right?"

They were on the veranda at the front of the building, with the glittering French doors standing open. Nessa could still hear the music, but barely. She stood up straight, detached herself from August's embrace, and pulled herself together.

"Forgive me," she said. "I'm perfectly well. I just felt a little faint for a moment."

She was heartily ashamed of herself. She, Nessa Shaw, who had dressed musket ball wounds and assisted at surgeries, coming over faint because August had written to her father, and her father had invited him to visit! It was absurd—and yet her heart was racing still, and her breath was coming in quick gasps that made little clouds in the wintry air.

August gazed into her eyes. "Do you—do you *want* to marry me?" he asked.

She laughed shakily. "There is nothing I want more," she said.

He let out a sigh and smiled. "Oh, Nessa," he said. "I love you so."

"I love you too," she whispered.

He bent his head toward her and then stopped, as if unsure whether he ought properly to proceed. She slid her hand around the back of his neck and drew his lips to hers.

She could hear the music for the Virginia Reel as they kissed beneath the Charlestown sky.

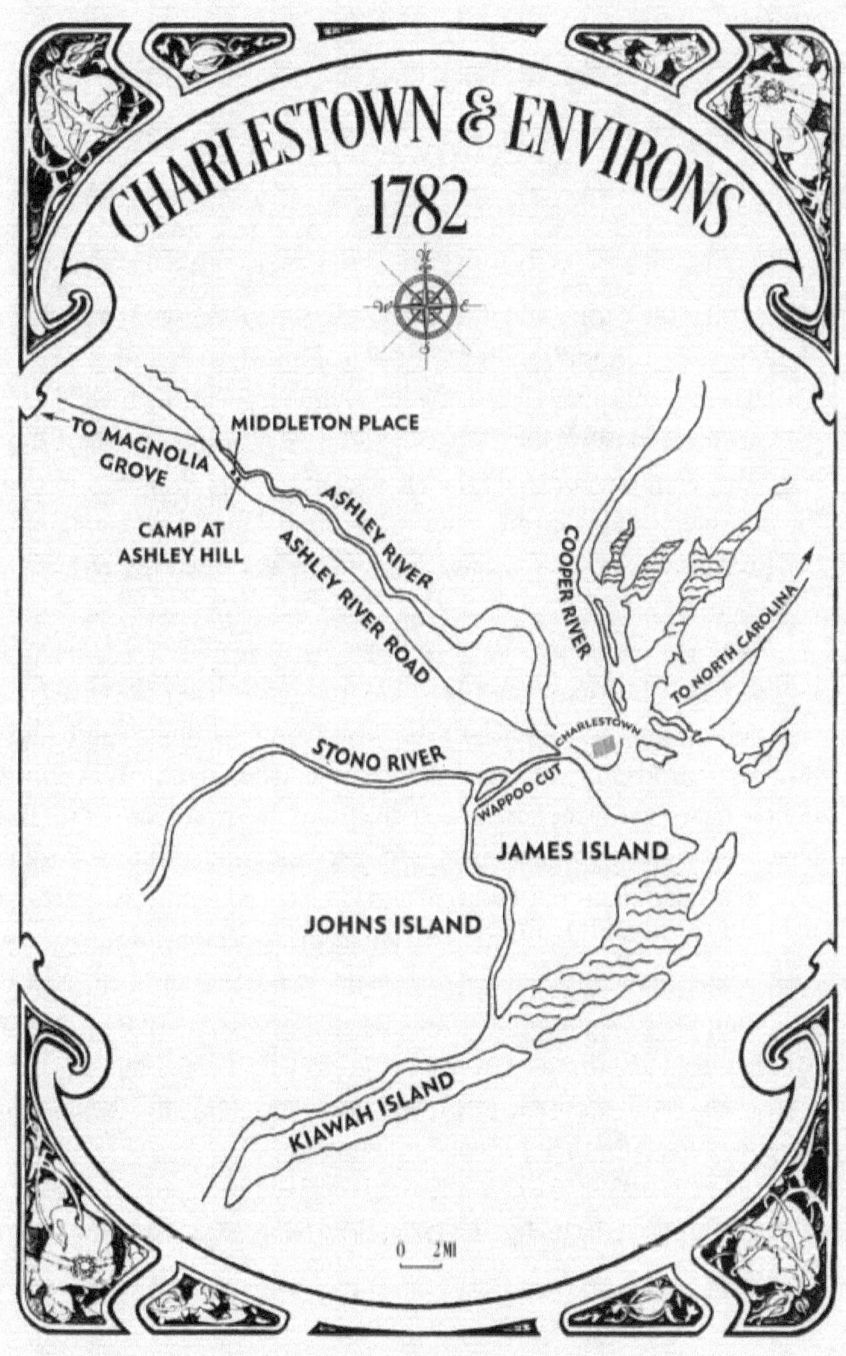
CHARLESTOWN & ENVIRONS
1782
TO MAGNOLIA GROVE
MIDDLETON PLACE
CAMP AT ASHLEY HILL
ASHLEY RIVER
ASHLEY RIVER ROAD
COOPER RIVER
TO NORTH CAROLINA
CHARLESTOWN
STONO RIVER
WAPPOO CUT
JAMES ISLAND
JOHNS ISLAND
KIAWAH ISLAND
0   2 MI

Acknowledgments

Unlike the earlier volumes in the Cape Fear Legacy series, this book departs considerably from the actual historical record in depicting a fictional Tory conspiracy late in the Revolutionary War. My friend J.D. Lewis read my ideas for ways the Patriots could have plausibly lost the war at this stage and, as always, offered valuable suggestions and insights. I'm thankful for his help, and for his dedication in making and maintaining his comprehensive website, carolana.com, which has aided my research again and again.

Many thanks are due to my critique partners—Cheryl Crouch, Mary Johnson, Janalyn Knight, and David Martin—for their help in the shaping and polishing of this book. Thanks also to my editor, Sharon Oitzman, for her friendship, encouragement, and painstaking work during a tighter-than-usual production schedule, and to my cover artist, Darleen Dixon, for crafting gorgeous images for use inside and outside this volume.

Jeff Neale, Curator of Research and Collections for the Middleton Place Foundation, answered my questions about the geography of the Ashley Hill area, where the Continental Army made its final camp in the South. He also volunteered some information taken from letters written by Arthur Middleton and Nathanael Greene. I'm grateful for his assistance.

As always, I thank family, particularly my husband, Greg, and my daughter Grace, for their patience and support.

Finally, thanks to the enthusiastic readers of the Cape Fear Legacy series who have enjoyed the books and taken the trouble to let me know, and to ask for more.

Historical Notes

The War in the South

The Southern Theatre of the American Revolutionary War has largely faded from the national memory. Mention of the war conjures up thoughts of Paul Revere's ride, Washington crossing the Delaware, the Siege of Boston, and the encampment at Valley Forge. Apart from the decisive American victory at Yorktown, most of the better-known battles—Lexington and Concord, Bunker Hill, Ticonderoga, Trenton, and Saratoga—took place in the northern states. But these were all early battles. By the second half of the war, the scene of action had effectively shifted to the South. This was due in large part to the British Army's "Southern Strategy," which was based on a belief that the southern states were hotbeds of Loyalism that would quickly and gladly submit to royal rule if given an opportunity. It's impossible to state definitively how many Tory military units were raised and armed by the British government in the South, but it was enough to turn the conflict into an increasingly savage civil war. South Carolina in particular was the scene of more military actions—ranging from pitched battles through minor skirmishes, raids, and other incidents—than any other state in the Union. Many of these were fought by Americans against other Americans, without any British presence at all.

The Continental Army's encampment at Ashley Hill lasted from July to December of 1782 and comprised somewhere between two and five thousand men. That's as many men and about as long a time as at Valley Forge, making Ashley Hill a major encampment. The precise boundaries and layout of the camp are unknown, but it was south of and adjacent to Middleton Place, home of Arthur Middleton, a signer of the Declaration of Independence.

The Southern Army's previous encampment had been at Bacon's Bridge, a swampy area where many soldiers had contracted malaria. The high bluff of Ashley Hill was considered a more healthful location, and probably was, although the change of scene could not cure the men already infected. At the time of the Revolutionary War, it was believed that malaria and other diseases were caused by noxious air, sometimes called miasma (the word *malaria* is an Italian derivation meaning "bad air"). The miasma theory dates all the way back to Hippocrates in the fourth century BC. Like many old theories, it contains a grain of truth; bad smells are often caused by unsanitary conditions or humid environments that provide breeding grounds for pathogens. It wasn't until 1880, nearly a century after the Ashley Hill encampment, that Charles Louis Alphonse Laveran learned that malaria is caused by a single-celled parasite. By the late 1890s, it had been demonstrated that mosquitoes were carriers of this pathogen—and of course mosquitoes thrive in swampy areas.

Mutinies

The attempted mutiny in the Southern Army, described by Rory Shaw to August Fairfax, was plotted in April of 1782 at the camp at Bacon's Bridge. Sergeant George Gosnell (or Gosnall, or Gornell, as he is named in various sources) was the ringleader. The conspirators planned to kidnap General Greene, but the scheme was discovered, and Gosnell was tried in a court martial and promptly executed by firing squad.

The roots of this incident reach back to an earlier mutiny that took place in January of 1781 among the Pennsylvania line, which was then stationed at Jockey Hollow near Morristown, Pennsylvania, and counted Sergeant Gosnell among its numbers. Here again, Gosnell was a ringleader. The mutineers' grievances included deplorable living conditions and lack of pay. Pennsylvania had always been comparatively stingy in compensating its soldiers; at the time of the mutiny, New Jersey was giving enlistment bounties of $1000, and Pennsylvania itself had begun paying relatively large bounties to new recruits, while soldiers already serving had received no pay beyond their initial bounty of $20 three years earlier. To their credit, the mutineers did not want to defect to the British, even after Sir Henry Clinton, then

Commander-in-Chief of the British Army in North America, made them an offer to give them their back pay if they'd switch sides.

The Jockey Hollow mutineers received a lot of public sympathy, and the Continental Congress, against the wishes of General Washington, met their demands. Unfortunately, their success inspired other mutinies, including one later that same month in Pompton, New Jersey. This time, General Washington sent an armed force of five hundred to quell the rebellion. Two of the three ringleaders were executed by a firing squad composed of twelve of their fellow mutineers.

After the Jockey Hollow mutiny, the Pennsylvania line was reduced and reorganized. Eight hundred men taken from the remaining six regiments, including Gosnell and other former mutineers, were sent south to join General Greene. They departed in May of 1781 and reached Bacon's Bridge late in March of 1782. Less than a month later, the Bacon's Bridge mutiny was in the works.

Undoubtedly, the uptick in mutinies in the Patriot Army was due in large part to fatigue among the troops and exacerbated by the inactivity and uncertainty of the latter days of the war. As late as March of 1782, Washington was dealing with a conspiracy among his officers in Newburgh, New York. Here again, lack of pay was a major factor. Washington ended up heading off this potential mutiny with a humble personal appeal. Another six months would pass before the Treaty of Paris was signed, ending the war, on 3 September 1782, and a couple of months more before the news reached American shores.

Camp Followers

Camp followers like Nessa Shaw played a major role in the war from the start. Most of them were women, usually family members of soldiers. They were not prostitutes, but legitimate workers filling vital support roles in nursing, cooking, sewing, and mending. Some camp followers were men, often former soldiers who were no longer fit for combat but could still provide services such as blacksmithing, metalworking, and construction.

Major General Nathanael Greene

Washington's most trusted general was born in 1742 to a prosperous Quaker family in Rhode Island. Greene's father, also called Nathanael, owned many businesses: a farm, a foundry, a sawmill, a gristmill, and a general store, as well as a sloop called the *Fortune*, whose unlawful seizure by the *H.M.S. Gaspee* in 1772 made British offenses against the colonists a personal matter to the future general. The elder Nathanael Greene didn't consider an extensive education necessary for his sons and put them to work at a young age in the various family businesses.

Young Nathanael suffered from asthma, and a childhood accident had left him with a permanent limp. In spite of his lack of formal education, he did his best to learn all he could through diligent reading. His interest in military matters and support for the American Revolution ultimately led to his expulsion from the pacifist Quaker community.

Greene took a prominent role in organizing a militia unit in his community, only to be told that his limp disqualified him from being an officer. Undeterred, he dutifully served in the ranks as an enlisted man for eight months before his standout abilities made it plain that limp or no limp, he was officer material. By age thirty-three, he'd been made the youngest general in the Continental Army. At that point, he had never seen battle, and most of his military knowledge came from books. He was the only general officer other than Washington to serve the entire eight years of the war, and the only one to begin as a private in the militia and end as a major general in the Continental Army.

General Greene was a natural leader: cheerful, hardworking, and devoted to the cause of liberty. He expressed himself well in the written word and was a wonderfully prolific letter-writer. During the Race to the Dan, while leading the Patriot Army across North Carolina to the Virginia border with the enemy in hot pursuit, he wrote a vast quantity of letters to coordinate movements and gather intelligence, and the letters he wrote and received while encamped at Ashley Hill provide valuable insight into the final months of the war. Some of his correspondence reveals his concerns about major cultural differences between the northern and southern states, and an almost prescient fear of future conflict between them. The Rhode Island Historical Society is to be commended for publishing his extensive personal and military wartime correspondence in a thirteen-volume series.

After the war, the state of Georgia awarded Nathanael Greene a 12,000-acre estate, Mulberry Grove, near Savannah. He died there of heat stroke at age forty-three, just three years after the end of the war in which he had served his country so faithfully.

Tadeusz Kościuszko and Agrippa Hull

One of the many European noblemen who voluntarily journeyed across the Atlantic to take up arms in the cause of American independence was Andrzej Tadeusz Bonaventura Kościuszko, born in 1746 to a family of small rural landowners in eastern Poland. As a member of the Polish Lithuanian gentry, Kościuszko was familiar with the lot of his country's serfs, whose lives were regulated by draconian laws that severely limited their freedom and mobility. The gentry's income came directly from their serfs' labor, and each nobleman was a law unto himself. In Kościuszko's day, a nobleman could buy, sell, or loan out his serfs. They owed him the bulk of their time and could not practice a trade without his permission.

Kościuszko's family, which owned only a single village, was near the lower end of the nobility spectrum, and the death of his father in 1758 made their financial situation even more precarious. His mother used her influence to gain his acceptance at age nineteen to Warsaw's new Royal Military Academy. Here he not only learned literature, languages, history, geography, law, mathematics, and military engineering, but also came under the influence of Oxford-trained Englishman John Lind, the school's superintendent, whose curriculum supported a philosophy that encouraged the students to reshape their country's government with the goal of eventually elevating their peasants into citizens. Kościuszko ultimately finished his military education in France, where he was exposed to the work of François Quesnay, Jean-Jacques Rousseau, Abbé Guillame Thomas Raynal, and other Enlightenment thinkers. Taken together, their writings explored the basis for a sound national prosperity, exposed the moral bankruptcy of slavery, and linked the plight of Polish serfs to that of American slaves. The developing struggle in North America between England and its colonies mirrored the conflict between Poland and the eastern European powers that were determined to carve it up and annex it. At some point in 1776, he made up his mind to cross the Atlantic and offer himself to the Continental Army, which desperately needed competent military engineers. By the middle of October, he'd been commissioned a colonel. In 1779, Private Agrippa Hull was assigned as Kościuszko's orderly.

Agrippa Hull is little known today outside of the Housatonic River Valley of western Massachusetts where he spent most of his life, but he was a remarkable figure. He was born in 1759 to Amos and Bathsheba Hull, black Americans who had managed to gain their freedom. Agrippa's parents were members of the local Congregational church during the ministry of Jonathan Edwards, and Agrippa was baptized there as an infant. Amos died in 1761, late in the French and Indian War. Five years later, Agrippa was sent to live with an aunt and uncle in the farming village of Stockbridge. Most of the village's population was American Indian, with white and free black families as an ethnic minority. The village's children played together without constraint, and one of Jonathan Edwards's sons was for a time more fluent in Mohawk and Mahican than in English. Indian landowners dominated the village's government when Agrippa arrived at age seven, but an influx of land speculators swindled them out of their property. By the time Agrippa enlisted in the army at eighteen, the Stockbridge Indians had lost their seats on the village's board of selectmen, along with most of their land.

Although Stockbridge was a relative backwater, it was not unaffected by the rising storm of the American Revolution. On 6 July 1774, the town hosted a county convention that condemned the Intolerable Acts and pledged a boycott of English imports. Ten months later, after the first shots of the war were fired at Lexington and Concord, Stockbridge's militia mobilized and headed east to join General Washington's Continental Army, arriving in time to join the Battle of Bunker's Hill.

Hull himself enlisted in 1777 and was soon assigned as an orderly to Colonel John Paterson, who had been promoted to brigadier general by the time Hull actually joined him at Ticonderoga on 1 May—just in time for the Saratoga Campaign, a British offensive designed to gain control of the Hudson Valley. In one of the more surprising upsets of the war, the Patriots gained the upper hand, and on 17 October, General John Burgoyne surrendered his entire army to General Horatio Gates. The Patriot victory at Saratoga was a seminal event in the Revolution. It raised the prestige of the Continental Army enough to persuade France to enter the conflict as an open ally. It made the reputation of General Gates, who was eventually promoted beyond his desserts, leading to the disastrous Patriot defeat at Camden three years later, in 1780. And it sowed seeds of resentment in General Benedict Arnold, who would betray his country to the enemy in that same year.

One of Hull's duties as Paterson's orderly was waiting on Paterson's table. Some months before the concluding battle of the Saratoga Campaign, Paterson supped with a group that included four subordinate officers and Kościuszko, newly arrived from Poland to fight in the American cause. Hull's wit, intelligence, and diligence made him a favorite with Patriot officers. Kościuszko in particular took a great liking to him, and in 1779, as a personal favor to Kościuszko, Paterson had Hull reassigned as Kościuszko's orderly.

After the theatre of war shifted to the South, Kościuszko, restless for action, sought and received an appointment as principal engineer of the Southern Army. Hull was the only orderly willing to accompany him on the southward journey. The two became excellent friends and served together for the remainder of the war. They arrived too late for the disastrous first Battle of Camden, but Kościuszko's engineering expertise was crucial to the Continental Army's success in the Race to the Dan, and he and Hull continued to serve under General Greene in the Charlestown area during the time when Nessa and Rory Shaw were at the Ashley Hill camp. In June of 1783, six months after the conclusion of August and Nessa's story, Hull and Kościuszko sailed out of Charlestown Harbor together in, along with General Greene's pregnant wife. They arrived in Philadelphia in time to witness the turmoil caused by yet another mutiny by the Pennsylvania Line. According to legend, Kościuszko begged Hull to return to Poland with him, but Hull refused. Hull mustered out in July of 1783, having become one of the longest-serving Patriot soldiers in the Revolutionary War. He returned to Stockbridge, where he married and lived to the age of eighty-nine as a beloved and valued member of the community.

Kościuszko returned to Poland, where he continued his distinguished military career by leading an insurrection against Russia in 1794. Today, he is venerated as a hero by his countrymen and by Polish Americans.

Spycraft and Cryptology in the American Revolution

Spycraft in the United States was still in its infancy during the American Revolutionary War, but it did play a part in the war effort on both sides. So did cryptology. General Washington and General Greene used a numeric cipher for sensitive information in their letters to one another, and General Clinton used a mask cipher like Andrew Elliot's in a letter written to General Burgoyne in 1777, during the Saratoga Campaign.

Truth and Fiction

There really was a Victory Ball held in Charlestown after the British evacuated the city. General Greene really did grumble about the time it took away from all the work he had to do, and he really did have his beloved wife with him by that time. The relationships between the Greenes and Nessa and Rory Shaw are of course fictional, but the Greenes did miss their own children, and the general's letters reveal his anxiety over the education of his own young son.

The letters General Greene wrote during the encampment at Ashley Hill show him to have been in a constant state of flux between expecting the British to leave Charlestown any day and fearing that they would try to find a way to reverse their losses in America. He suspected conspiracy within the camp—not unreasonably, considering all the actual mutinies that had already been planned or carried out. There is no evidence of a strictly Tory conspiracy in the South like the one in *Treason Trail*, but the idea is not as far-fetched as it might seem. The Tories had ventured much for the Crown and had been promised security and reward by their British allies. Now they were being abandoned. In the aftermath of the war, many of them suffered severe losses of property and livelihood, not to mention ties of family and friendship. It's easy to imagine how they could grow bitter over their desertion, and resolve to take back what they considered rightfully theirs.

Bibliography

Bakeless, John. *Turncoats, Traitors & Heroes*. Philadelphia: J.B. Lippincott Company, 1959.Borick, Carl P. *A Gallant Defense: The Siege of Charleston, 1780.*

Conrad, Dennis M., Roger N. Parks, and Martha J. King, eds. *The Papers of General Nathanael Greene*. Vol. 11. Chapel Hill: University of North Carolina Press, 2000.

Conrad, Dennis M., and Roger N. Parks, eds. Assisted by Elizabeth C. Stevens and Nathaniel N. Shipton. *The Papers of General Nathanael Greene*. Vol. 12. Chapel Hill: University of North Carolina Press, 2000.

Dunkerly, Robert M. *Redcoats on the Cape Fear: The Revolutionary War in Southeastern North Carolina*. Jefferson: McFarland & Company, Inc., 2012.

Hemphill, C. Dallett. *Bowing to Necessities: A History of Manners in America, 1620-1860*. New York: Oxford University Press, Inc., 1999.

Lee, Henry (Light Horse Harry). *The American Revolution in the South*. New York: Arno Press, Inc., 1969.

Lee, Henry, Jr. *The Campaign of 1781 in the Carolinas*. Philadelphia: Quadrangle Books, Inc., 1962.

Nash, Gary B., and Graham Russell Gao Hodges. *Friends of Liberty: Thomas Jefferson, Tadeusz Kosciuszko, and Agrippa Hull.*

New York: Basic Books, 2008.O'Donnell, Patrick K. *Washington's Immortals: The Untold Story of an Elite Regiment Who Changed the Course of the Revolution.* New York: Atlantic Monthly Press, 2016.

Still, William N., Jr. *North Carolina's Revolutionary War Navy.* Raleigh: North Carolina Department of Cultural Resources, Division of Archives and History, 1976.

Van Doren, Mark, ed. *Travels of William Bartram.* New York: Dover Publications, Inc., 1955.

Don't miss out!

Visit the website below and you can sign up to receive emails whenever Kit Hawthorne publishes a new book. There's no charge and no obligation.

https://books2read.com/r/B-A-WVWY-BKOVC

BOOKS 2 READ

Connecting independent readers to independent writers.

Also by Kit Hawthorne

Cape Fear Legacy
Savanna Storm
Carolina Crossing
Treason Trail

Watch for more at https://kithawthorne.com/.

About the Author

A lifelong resident of the American South, Kit Hawthorne makes her home on a Texas farm that has been in her husband's family for seven generations. She spent several years as a semiprofessional musician, singing, composing, and playing Irish pennywhistle in a Celtic folk band. All those ballads and boat songs awakened in her a love for a Scottish heritage that spans both sides of the Atlantic. She's an avid reader, especially of history, biography, mystery, theology, and romance, and enjoys logging her reads (and plotting her life) in her Bullet Journal. She also enjoys drawing, sewing, quilting, knitting, and restoring old furniture to beauty and usefulness.

Read more at https://kithawthorne.com/.